THE YEAR OF BAD MAPS

Sophie Radice

to Hugh

Love
Sophie xxx

APS BOOKS
Yorkshire

APS Books,
The Stables Field Lane,
Aberford,
West Yorkshire,
LS25 3AE

APS Books is a subsidiary of the APS Publications imprint
www.andrewsparke.com

Cover artwork by Sol Golden-Sato

First published worldwide by APS Books in 2026

In 2016 when the description of the Calais Refugee Camps takes place in this book, those seeking sanctuary in the UK were not taking the channel route to the UK as many had already crossed the Mediterranean and considered it too dangerous and were trying to enter the UK in the backs of lorries and cars.

THE YEAR OF BAD MAPS

Dedicated to my children Louis and Ella
who read this book again and again.

entrance
underpass
tents
main drag
(food distribution)
Syrian area
official mother
and baby unit
Afghan
area
ethiopian
church
eritrean
area

REGINA v MS KATE MANCINI & OTHERS
May 2018

The court had been told to rise as Judge Jeremy Hargreave entered the court. The bench was illuminated by copious downlighters while the rest of the court was dimly lit. The Judge sat down in a chair of blonde wood, a neo-gothic design with a ridiculously high back. Sitting facing him, but far away at the back of the court and encased in a box of thick yellowing glass, were Kate and her two co-defendants sitting in a trembling row. The jury were to Kate's left-hand side, with all three defendants' friends and family moved up to the gallery rather than being allowed to sit in the well of the court. Her lawyer had told her that the Judge felt they were too 'distracting'.

As soon as they had discovered his name from the court list Kate and her kids had googled the shit out of Judge Jeremy Hargreave. They were encouraged. He didn't seem to be particularly harsh in any of his cases – certainly as covered in local newspapers online. No case he had presided over had ever made national news. He had directed for leniency in a case that involved young Stroud mother shoplifting clothes. He had been married to a brewery heiress, who had died five years previously, leaving him with two teenage daughters and they had found an interview on a Hampshire radio station in which he had praised his wife and her contribution to charities, both as a board member and a founder. He was said to be intending to set up a charity in her name, which would help Hampshire state schools to expand their music departments because she had been a keen flutist who had attended the Royal College of Music. He looked younger than his sixty-two years, with a plump, smooth face and voice that was deep and attractive - not absurdly posh. They could not find the charity set up in his wife's memory.

"He seems human, at least. He's suffered a great loss, so it should mean he's more understanding of other people's plights, and he has two daughters, so he probably feels warmly towards women," her daughter Billie said.

“Come on, Judge Jeremy; be nice to my mum, please,” said Charlie into the laptop as he watched the video of the interview.

Judge Hargreaves sat down, and the court usher told the court that they could now follow suit. The Judge leant forward into his microphone and his gown slipped slightly off his shoulder as he did so. He said their names, struggling a little and when the clerk read the charges of *Assisting unlawful immigration to Member States, contrary to section 25(1) of the immigration act 1971*, he smiled a little.

“Can I firstly apologise to the jury for the quality of the map included in the bundle of documents. I don’t think you can really call it a map. It’s more like a doodle and a poor one at that.”

At that the Judge openly laughed.

Kate couldn’t help letting out a puff of irritated breath which made a slight mist on the glass wall in front of her. She had drawn that map in a couple of minutes for her lawyer Jitendra in January 2017 when she had been trying to explain the events of the day of her arrest. She hadn’t known it was going to be used in court a year and a half later as an essential part of both defence and prosecution evidence. At the time, when Jitendra had asked her to ‘jot down a bird’s eye view of the Calais camp’ it had made perfect sense to her as she had drawn in biro on the sheet of A4 paper Jitendra had pulled from the printer.

Ranim and Ebeid sat on either side of Kate, both women holding their hands up to their necks, clasping the edges of their hijabs to their throats, Ranim’s was a beautiful turquoise cloth embroidered with the tiniest of orange flowers, Ebeid’s a dull, coarse brown, almost sack-cloth material. Kate could see that both women’s lips were moving in silent prayer. They all knew that they were not allowed to speak to each other outside the courtroom and so had assiduously ignored each other and each other’s families and friends. They had not seen each other since their arrest, but when they had walked into the dock, they all instinctively reached out and held each other’s hands.

Ebeid squeezed Kate’s right hand tight enough for her grandmother’s wedding ring to press painfully hard against her little finger. Ranim’s hand was warm and dry against the nervous clamminess of her own. Kate would have liked to have carried on holding their hands for a bit longer, but the others let go suddenly as they were told to sit down. Kate thought that she could hear all their hearts thumping in unison but perhaps it was just her own. She felt like she wanted to cough or retch, or both. She was mortified when she burped loudly instead and felt the two women turn a little towards her. Her burp smelt of the toast and egg her children had encouraged her to eat in the beach hut that morning, and Kate wanted to apologise as she knew the women were fasting for Ramadan and had refused the white plastic cups of water the sweet court usher had tried to give them.

Detective Chief Inspector Ian Cookson sat right in front of the dividing glass, so Kate had plenty of time to despise the back of him - his small sloping shoulders, shiny bald head, and suit so oversized it looked like his mother had bought it for him to grow into some day. The man could barely contain his manic little giggles at any attempt at humour from the Judge or barristers and had perpetually flushed and excited pink skin on the back of his neck. He hung around the barristers during break time when they gathered to the side of court to discuss the proceedings like an unpopular boy at school allowed to hang out with the cool kids. He had met Kate and her colleagues when they had been arrested and driven over from France by Eurotunnel to Hythe station, each handcuffed in a separate four by four. He was the one who had pushed this case forward until it had reached Crown Court.

The judge had great difficulty with their names and particularly, it seemed with her surname. That first morning he had looked towards the court and said, "How on earth am I meant to pronounce this one? Where is it from? Is this a Syrian name? I don't think I can be expected to get this one right."

Kate found herself whispering, "It's Italian, mate." to the glass in front of her. Sometimes he mixed their names up in a foreign jumble, which always got an appreciative snigger from the Detective Inspector.

Despite his tragic bereavement and having daughters, it swiftly became clear that the judge had little sympathy with the three defendants in the dock. He seemed particularly irritated with Kate. He quickly took it upon himself to act as something like a second prosecution barrister, always asking further questions of the defence team from the bench. After Kate's barrister had read out her opening statement, the judge had given the jury a lie directive against her, explaining to them that the implausibility of something in her statement indicated to him that she may be unreliable and that everything she or her defence barrister was going to say could be untrue. "I find it very hard to believe that a woman would urinate in a public place and risk being seen by a large group of refugee men."

As terrified as Kate was about standing up in the witness box when it was her turn to be cross examined, she found that her anger made her almost look forward to explaining to the judge and jury that for a camp of nine thousand - mainly men - there was a bank of just ten portaloos. They had been advised by organisations that were permanently working in the Calais refugee camp not to use them as there had been rapes and sexual attacks on women who had been pushed into the cubicles. This was apart from the fact that they had not been emptied for months. Anyway, Kate never had had much of a problem about peeing outside, as her family and friends in the gallery all knew. Billie told her that one of Kate's neighbours, who had turned up out of the blue at court to support her, had recounted a story of Kate peeling off on the heath to pee behind a bush. "I think she likes pissing outside, doesn't she?" Susan had said.

Jitendra took her into a small side room in the courthouse to sum up how things had gone on the first day. The first thing she did was to take off her stiff, horsehair wig and violently itch her scalp with fanned out fingers. Kate and Jitendra had built up a good relationship over the last eighteen months. They had often sat in Morgan, James and Bennett's Camden office with the big poster of Angela Davies dominating the pokey basement room. Jitendra would act as the cruel prosecution barrister, even though she wasn't really allowed to tutor her through her cross-examination on the witness stand. She would sit with the two-hundred-page police bundle in front of her, tearing into her, going over every detail the prosecution might bring up, often concentrating on her 'I don't know' in the police interview. She seemed to enjoy it.

"Why didn't you just say that you did know that Ebeid had someone she was meeting there when the police asked you? You did know that didn't you? So why didn't you just say that?"

"Because they asked me if I knew that she had her son at the camp, and I only found out at the end of the day," Kate said.

"So, you did know by the time they interviewed you?"

"Yes." Kate had gone on to explain to Jitendra it was not as simple as that. On the confusing and stressful day of her arrest Ebeid wasn't the first person she was thinking about. She told Jitendra that she had been interviewed after nearly twenty hours in a cell on her own. That day in the camp all her energy had been put into trying to cope with the intense desperation all around them as the camp was dismantled. She had spectacularly failed to keep all the women safe, and above all, that had been her job and her mission. She was used to feeling that she was good at her work and could cope with most situations thrown at her, even before she went travelling on her own for a year. Hadn't she been the one who had persuaded them all to come after her boss Juliet, founder and CEO of the refugee charity she worked for, had become so keen for them to go to Calais on the day of demolition? The fact that a right-wing newspaper had agreed to come and cover the story was seen as something of a coup, for once not preaching to the converted. She had texted and phoned both interpreters many times until they had agreed.

So, in saying 'I don't know' when she was interviewed in Hythe Police station, she meant to express that she didn't know what had happened. Had she been lied to or manipulated? She didn't know. Or had Ebeid's son simply seized an opportunity created by the chaos of the day and her own stress and scattiness. She didn't know. Perhaps this had been the only opportunity he would have before he was finally removed from the camp, and it was flattened by the French police. This was his chance to try and come to the UK to join his family after six months of trying to jump in the space behind the cabs of lorries or to get into cars at the big French supermarkets British holiday makers went to so they could load up on booze and fags. How had he got in there? Kate didn't know. Did she wish that she had arrived back in London and opened her car boot at home, and he had jumped out and no doubt shocked the living daylights out of her, and run off and joined his family somewhere on the outskirts of London - oh yes she *did* know that she would have been fucking delighted, but of course she understood that there was to be not even a whiff of that in court. Not even the slightest whiff.

"If it hadn't been for that bloody 'I don't know' and the dick of a photographer making a statement against you, I doubt we would be in court today."

Jitendra had gone on. "The impatience of the good people of Maidstone with anyone trying to get into this country through the tunnels of Kent is palpable. This court often sees people who have been caught coming by jumping on trains, and now by lorry or car and sometimes even by boat. And you won't be the first nice middle-class person working for an NGO who has been caught with an illegal refugee in the boot of her car but the difference between you and them is that you are being tried with two Syrian women. The prosecution's angle is that you three have been plotting together for weeks and weeks. Your Italian surname is not helping you either. The jury are very Kentish and Anglo-Saxon, and a couple of them look like retired prison wardens, but at least more than half are women; although the woman who looks like a crackhead has already fallen asleep a couple of times. I'm not sure how much they like me either – being a brown woman, but anyway, I did warn you about that and you still wanted me to represent you."

Jitendra only ranted when she was nervous. It made Kate feel jittery too. She had never told Jitendra that no other lawyer wanted to touch her with a barge pole.

"Yes, I did want you to represent me Jitendra, and yes, you did warn me of all those things. I consider myself lucky and I'm grateful to you. You know that I don't like the term illegal refugees, though."

Jitendra's face pinched up. "Please don't say anything remotely like that on the stand please. It won't help you."

"Remotely like what?"

"Like telling someone off for using the wrong term for refugees and asylum seekers. It will not endear you to anyone. Especially not in Maidstone."

"OK."

"I have drilled into you many, many times that it is not enough to be innocent. You have to perform your innocence now with any latent acting skills you may have. The cliché that the court is a stage is a truism. Oh, and I have spoken to the two other women's barristers, and we've agreed that we will not mention certain aspects of each other's cases."

"What do you mean?" Kate asked.

"Well, we will not press home that Ranim didn't make it clear to you that Ebeid's son was in the camp before you left that day."

"Oh, yes."

"But only if she does not labour the point that you were standing outside the bus with the mother and the son and the photographer for a good five minutes before you went to the toilet."

"Right," Kate said.

"I mean, it could help our case if we highlight the possible guilt of others, but it could also backfire. This is a perfectly normal thing to do if there is more than one defendant."

"I understand."

"I am very unhappy about the judge questioning that you peed between the cars. I was not expecting that at all. I didn't think he would take against you in this way. I have to say that I thought he would see that you are a middle-class, well-meaning British woman and give some props for that, but he seems to want to pick you out for particular attention. He wants to make a big deal of your foreignness, with all that name mispronunciation stuff. I knew we should have gone with your married name. What was it again?" Jitendra said.

"Goodall"

"Oh God, Kate Goodall would have been so much better."

"But I'm divorced, Jitendra. And he was a violent, embezzling, man-child."

"Right." Jitendra didn't have time to sympathise with Kate about the horrors of her ex-husband.

"You really think he had taken against me?' Kate said.

"Well, his questioning of the truth of your story of peeing in the camp obviously doesn't help with your credibility."

"It's only the first day though, isn't it?" Kate said.

"Yes, yes of course. It's only day one," Jitendra continued. "I think you will present very well, and you have some great character references. Just make sure that you speak slowly but not too slowly and think before you speak. One word can make or break a case."

Jitendra sat up straight and gave her a tight smile. "It is very, very important to remain positive. Now go and get some fresh air on the beach with your kids."

That evening Kate and her two children walked along the shingled beach of Seasalter, the muddy estuary water close to the shore. The May light was dazzling in the golden hour before the sun went down, giving her children's skin an apricot glow.

"Jitendra should have made a big deal about the judge calling you a liar and stood up and said something to him. She should have defended you when he went on about the bad map. I'm not sure how good she is, Mum. You should have got someone else. Someone more assertive."

Billie looked at Charlie with narrowed eyes. "I think Jitendra knows what she's doing. She's won some massive cases. Like The Heathrow 20. I've read up about that case, and she did brilliantly in it."

Charlie ran backwards in front of them.

"OK, fair enough. Come on Mum. Run a bit. Get that court day out of your system. I think I'm starting to smell like the British Justice system." Charlie pulled the neck of his sweatshirt to his face. "Argghhhh, it stinks like the court."

He pulled the sweatshirt off and waved it about his head. Kate had changed out of the smart navy dress that she wore for court as soon as they got back to the beach hut, but when she smelt her hair, she too thought she could smell bleach, and the sickly fear smell of the court. It smelt rather like the prison cell in Hythe.

Her children pulled her along with them. "Come on Mum. Run, run. You move like a demented fawn, Mum. Why do you take such small steps? You can do better than that." Charlie shouted.

"At least I don't have such big feet that I slap them down like a clown, even when I run."

"Mum, don't be mean." Billie said, ever the watchful peacemaker.

"Well, I'd rather have big feet than tiny little hoofs, mum." Charlie said.

Kate laughed. "I've actually got quite big feet, love."

"You can't do Mum. Look at your tiny little hands. Oh my God, I'd never noticed. It must be so weird to be walking around with such weeny hands at the end of your arms."

"You're meant to be boosting my confidence so I can do well in the witness box. I've always been a bit self-conscious about my little claw hands and my massive head."

"Sorry, but I do think you could do with a run to clear your head."

Charlie took her in his big, hairy arms and tried to get her to move fast.

"I can't bloody run on these shingles. I'll just walk briskly. OK?"

Jenny's kindness and sweet and curious nature was reflected in the prettiness of everything in the small space, the paintings of boats, shelves of penguin books, shells and driftwood on the windowsills and rows of different sized wellies. It was so helpful that they could go back to Jenny's cosy beach hut each evening from Maidstone Court together and Kate had even managed to sleep last night in the bed she shared with Billie. Standing in the one room that made up most of the hut's floor space and looking out of the long glass doors facing out to the estuary, Kate thought that even though she had seen many sunsets on her travels, this was one of the most beautiful. Without saying anything Billie went out through the doors, down the path and through the low wooden gate. Kate could see her small, slim figure walk down to sand by the estuary shoreline and hold up her hands above her head. Kate knew that Billie was shouting into the water for things to go well over the next week, for her mother not to be sent to prison, for luck to be on their side. Fierce burnt orange light seemed to swirl around Billie's form and Kate felt her throat constricting with love and fear.

Her son came out to the patio and stopped next to his mother. He put his arm around Kate and squeezed her a bit too tightly around her ribs.

"We can do it Mum. It's going to be alright. We can do this. They can't destroy you. Even if you get sent down, they can't kill you. Us three can survive that together. Just take all the stuff you learnt when you travelled around on your own last year and apply it here."

"Oh, yes, I'll do that."

"Mind you, I sometimes think ..."

Charlie stopped holding her with one arm and let it drop to his side.

Kate turned and looked at him quizzically. It was unlike her son not to say what was on his mind.

"What?"

"Never mind." Charlie backed away from her.

"Come on. Tell me. I can take it."

"When you came back from travelling you were so full of the joys of life. It was ridiculous how happy you were. Like you were just too happy. It was quite hard to deal with, even for those that love you. It made people feel uncomfortable. I could tell you felt brave and completely invincible, didn't you?"

"Yes, I suppose I did. That's exactly how I felt. I've never felt anything like it. I'd met so many people and been in so many different situations that it made me feel as if I could cope with anything."

"I just knew something would happen to you to bring you down to earth. It was as if the universe couldn't let anyone be that happy. It also made you vulnerable, I think. People could see that you were reckless and a little crazy."

'You think I was hubristic?'

"I don't know what that means."

"Means I was a bit of a cocky arsehole with an overconfidence that probably had to be punished by the gods, brought down a peg or two."

Charlie looked at her and smiled.

"Yes, I suppose that is what I mean. We all knew it was a stupid idea to go that day. Your head was floating along in the clouds somewhere and so you thought everything was going to be fine. You thought that everyone was lovely because of all the lovely people you met when you were travelling. Your guard was down. It was as if something just had to happen to pull you back downwards crashing to earth, so that you could carry on living on this planet with the rest of us."

THE TET SUICIDES
January 2016

Lok got up especially early to put the lotion on his hair so that his wife would not see and mock him once again. He found that since he hit fifty, he had to apply the expensive colour dye every two weeks otherwise the telltale zip of grey in his parting would show. With his slimmish body and unlined face, he could get away with knocking a decade off his age for tourists who wanted him to take them around Hoi-Chi Minh City. They didn't want some old, grey-haired guy to be their guide. They didn't want a man whose calves, ankles and lower back ached and cramped from years and years of rickshaw driving for big-boned,Western tourists. Most days Lok's lungs hurt, and he sometimes got shooting pains right up his arse and through the very core of him as if someone was using some dark magic and sticking a big hot pin up inside him.

Sometimes Lok's soul was so beyond weary that he felt like a malevolent ghost had inhabited his body and eaten out all the crazy energy, wild optimism and laughter that used to be his *Unique Selling Point.* He felt close to turning his scooter right into the oncoming traffic and ending it all there and then. At least he could have a proper, dark-cloaked rest without any worries to peck at him throughout the day and night.

Lok knew that he had to pretend to have a sunny, jokey, friendly nature, and cut a speedy dash through the traffic - "Okey-Dokey, hold onto your hats my friends, let's go onto the pavement and hit a fat-arsed American! No, worries, it's not our day to die! There are no rules in Saigon, Baby. No worries. Take it easy. Lovely Jubbly!" - otherwise no one would get on the back of his small motorbike. And he had a serious and clever son studying architecture in Hanoi, a wife who worked hard as a waitress in The Hotel Continental restaurant and had a frozen shoulder, and a newish house outside Saigon bought with the bit of money his brother had given him when he took over their parent's famous restaurant, The Orange Lantern. No, the Fish wanted a happy, young, knowledgeable, and completely unjudgemental guy to make them laugh and show them the exotic delights of Saigon, whatever they imagined that might be.

He sat on the edge of the bath, Vaseline around his temples so that the dye would not stain his skin, the gunk burning his scalp a little, looking out of the small window to where the first light had begun to pour through from the small courtyard into the tiny pale green bathroom. Lok thought for the hundredth time that he must fix the tile that had fallen off inside the shower over a year ago and sat propped up above the sink, reminding his wife of his lack of DIY skills each time she came into the bathroom.

From the courtyard a gecko called out and he answered back. He managed to get that little tired groan right at the end of the second part of the call perfectly. His brilliantly gifted son Sa'ng used to try when he was a small kid, but he just couldn't capture that pathetic exhausted moan. Sa'ng had never been physically worn out so it wasn't surprising really. Lok thought that if there were ever such a thing as a gecko imitation competition, he would probably win it hands down. He let himself imagine a village competition of gecko calling that he would happen to chance upon - perhaps when he was taking a tourist on one of his longer tours into the countryside - and how he, a Saigon lad born and bred, would amaze and astound them all. He smiled to himself.

Lok tried a little bit of meditation with his hands on the bottom of his ribcage, feeling his lungs fill and empty, rise and fall, trying to regulate his breathing and draw some strength and peace into his body and at the same time not to inhale too much of the fumes from the evil smelling dye. His breathing exercise had just started to make Lok feel a little calmer when his wife, Da, burst in with tears streaming down her plump face. His heart sunk into his feet. In all the many years they had been married it seemed she never tired of making these terrible, emotional scenes. It wasn't a good sign for the year ahead that she was making these wailing sounds so close to Tet. She held his phone and waved it in the air in front of him.

"What is this? You monster! Is this what you amount to? At your age? Is this how you spend your time? With whores? Do you want me to phone our son and tell him what his father has been up to?"

She then screamed one of her mother's sayings into his face. "Close to Ink, then Black, nearby Light then Bright. If you spend your time with bad people in the shadows then you will soon be an Evil Man. When the time comes to dig up your bones and wash them for reburial there will be nothing there but ash."

She slapped him around his head with her left hand - where was her frozen left shoulder now? - while with her other hand showing him a picture of himself with Damian and Cory the randy young Irish fellows from the other night and four grinning bar girls. She threw his phone into the corner.

'Argghhhh. What is this brown shit on my hand! Is it shit? What the hell are you doing? What is this on my hand? It's stinging me." She went to wash her hands but just carried on sobbing, snot running down into her mouth. He wished she would at least blow her nose. It was horrible to see her like that.

"It's stained my hands. What are you doing you old freak? What are you putting on your hair? Why are you trying to look so young? Is it for these young girls? Do you have no dignity?"

He leapt to where she had flung the phone to check it was all right. It was. He tried to tell her that of course he had to take men on girlie tours. The pictures were from last week when he had taken the Irish lads on a tour of the bars and clubs of Saigon. He was paid something by the nightclub owners to bring in the punters and then a bit extra by the Fish if they were happy. He had made a decent amount of money last week and managed to pay the money lender something back. Of course, he never used prostitutes himself. How could he afford it? And he was so stressed that he didn't even know if his thingy would work anymore. He couldn't remember the last time he had managed a hard-on. It was just something he had to do, after taking tourists to the sites of Saigon or Hoi Chi Mien as the foreigners carefully called it. He tried to remain calm, telling her yet again that sometimes he just had to do what the customer wanted and that there were many western men wanting to pay to sample what he described to them as 'really feminine women full of Eastern Promise'.

She just wasn't listening, the words spewing out of her. "If I had known that you would run with whores when you were a fifty-three-year-old man I would never ever have married you. I would certainly never have had a son with you!"

"I'm fifty-two! You know I'm fifty-two! Do you want me to go back to being a rickshaw driver and kill myself with tiredness? The young guys don't ask the rickshaw drivers to drive them around the bars and clubs, now do they? But yes, they ask motorbike drivers. Do you understand?" he said.

Da wept some more. "You shame me. You bring shame on your son. You shame me in front of our new neighbours. They all look down their noses at me anyway. Now I won't even be able to go to the market. All those stuck-up women will be laughing at me behind their hands."

Da stamped her small, slippered feet. Lok felt like pushing his wife's face into the mirror. He imagined her actual look of shock and surprise and her reflected look of shock and surprise just before her face hit the smooth, shining surface.

"Da, listen to me. I am really struggling here. I mean really, really struggling. It's Tet soon and I must pay the moneylender back. Go and get some more money in and then you can start demanding who I take on the back of my bike and where I go."

If she got some more money in, he wouldn't even care how she did it. It was not the time to be prim for either of them. It was Tet in two weeks, and Hoi was going to be knocking at the door for the rest of the money for New Year. It was very bad luck to start the year with a moneylender on your back. He stood up, hands on hips and lent over her, a few important centimetres taller. She tried to hit him on the face again. He held her arms down by her side to stop them flaying against him.

"Let go immediately! You're hurting me. What are you doing? I'll scream to the neighbours if you don't stop. Ahh, my shoulder!" She grabbed her left shoulder with her right hand.

He put his face close to hers so that he could see the little lines that had started to form around her mouth. There was no other way to get her to shut up.

"You are going to listen to me now. I am trying my best. Do you understand? This goes beyond you being jealous or upset at me for taking stupid tourists on girlie tours. This is what I do. I have no choice. Now you are going to get out of the bathroom and let me wash this hair dye from my head before it burns all my hair off and then I'll have to go out and try and catch a Big Fish today. And you are going to have to stop with your disgusting noise before you ruin my day and ruin our luck for Tet. Do you understand? Get on with the Tet preparations, clean up and sort out some gifts for our ancestors and bring us some fucking luck!"

Da left the bathroom in silence but turned back to look at him with glittery hatred in her eyes.

He heard her talking at their altar of ancestors, complaining to her dead mother about him. "Mother, I am so sorry I didn't listen to you. You told me he was a bad one. Told me he was weak and would be a dreadful disappointment to me. Oh, Mother, tell me what to do. What to do, Oh Mother of mine? Please give me a sign."

He knew that she spoke deliberately loudly so that he would hear. He slammed the door as hard as he could and the gecko started up his call to Lok again. He wasn't in the mood anymore for a gecko call and response and told the gecko so. He immediately apologised for telling the poor creature to shut up. It wasn't the gecko's fault that Tet was looming, he had no money and a hysterical wife.

He had to go back into the house once he had stepped across the threshold because he had seen a woman on the street first thing. Business was bad if you saw a woman immediately after leaving your house. He closed the door upon himself again, waited for ten minutes and sat on the toilet so that he did not have to see Da, who was bad luck personified. He then went out again and thankfully saw a teenage boy on his fancy foreign pushbike. He drove into town, approached a young German couple outside the French Post-Office and they waved him away as if he was a fly that had just flown off a dog's shit and he cursed them under his breath for their horrible rudeness. He had three fishing rules but if he got desperate enough these rules could go up in smoke like paper offerings to his ancestors.

The Fish could not be too fat or too tall. His friend Phong had a fat American woman on the back of his bike a month ago and his bike had never been the same since.

A Fish could not be American unless he was desperate. Ancestors would not tolerate an American and would heap bad luck on him. They didn't like the French much either. He didn't need the Ancestors fucking with him so close to New Year.

The Fish could not be too scruffy or poor looking otherwise it would be him who would be paying for their Pho at lunchtime, like that French girl who said that she had been robbed in Hanoi.

He spotted her across the road like a heron from above into a river - his shining Fish. She was trying to hide the fact that she was attempting to read a map of the city and trying to work out where she was, turning her back on the road and pavement and facing the wall of a shop. She was having problems folding the map up properly and it pained him to see how she resorted to just pushing it into her rucksack folded all wrong. She was obviously a bit lost, looked new to the city and was middle-aged - a not too fat or tall woman. And she seemed to be totally on her own. There was no big protective man who had her back and if she was trying not to show that she was alone she was not doing a very good job of it. Lok also spotted that she was also not so nice-looking that some busy body would ring up his wife, but she was also not so ugly that the other motorbike men would laugh at him for his horrible looking catch. He had to reach her before another motorbike guy or tour guide toerag swooped down on her and poached her from under his nose. She was a decent catch, and he was going to get her. He quickly parked his bike so that he approached her on foot, rather than cruising her from his bike and perhaps frightening her off. He guessed from the slightly sloppy way she was dressed that she was British. You would never get a French woman walking around like that but then again, he would always choose a British woman over a French woman. British women were a good combination of quite tough and easily pleased.

"Hello, are you lost? Can I help you?"

He knew that his accent was very, very good for a Vietnamese person and he enjoyed the way English felt in his mouth. He would love to travel to the UK if he had the money or ever got the chance to go outside Vietnam. It was a dream of his.

"I think I'm alright thank you. I'm enjoying just walking around."

"Where are you thinking of visiting in our beautiful city?"

"Well, I was thinking of going to The War Remnants Museum?"

"The Atrocity Museum? Which way do you think it is, out of interest?"

""I think it is straight ahead. Yes, according to my map it is straight ahead."

"I think it must be a terrible map. I'm sorry to say that you are completely and utterly lost, Madame. Let me look at that map."

She gave it to him sheepishly.

"This is an awful map of the city. Where did you get it from?"

"From the taxi driver who brought me from the airport. He said he came from a family of mapmakers."

Lok couldn't help laughing.

"I haven't got my Vietnamese sim card yet, so I had to rely on an old-fashioned map," she said.

"He took you for a fool, I'm afraid. I won't even ask you how much he charged."

She raised her eyebrows at him. He didn't want to go too far in showing her up for a mug, otherwise she would feel humiliated and want to get away from him.

She pushed her messy hair out of her eyes. Lok noticed that there were some small dark stains on her red tunic dress and even a couple of little moth holes.

"Why don't I take you on my motorbike? It's a long way from here," he said.

"Oh, no. I think I'm fine to walk there."

"What else do you want to see in Saigon?'

"I was thinking of going to the market after the museum and then perhaps to look at the sunset with a drink from the Sheraton Tower."

"I know a better place to look at the sunset. A place where locals look at sunset. It is called Thu Thiem Bridge."

He had read her well. She started to concentrate properly on him when he said that it was a place where locals go. She was nearly reeled in. He mustn't fuck up on the final pull in. "You don't want to go to Sheraton. They don't let locals in there. You wouldn't want to go to a place like that, I think? That didn't let locals in?"

"Oh, no. Come to think of it. The person that recommended it to me was a bit like that."

"I'll take you on a day tour. Would you like to read my book of recommendations?"

He handed her his red hard-backed exercise book. She read the glowing comments from the Irish lads, the Australian boys, a Dutch couple and a British man. She started to read the French ones too.

"You understand French?"

"No, not really. I was trying to impress you." She smiled at him.

"You don't have to impress me. You are just fine, as you are. What is your name?"

'Kate. What's yours?"

"I'm Lok. Lokky by name, Lokky by nature."

She smiled. He knew what her next question would be. And it was.

"How much?"

He had worked out that she had only just arrived in Vietnam and would not yet find it easy to convert sterling into Dong. Still, he didn't want to put her off by asking too much. If he played it right, she might want him to take her around for more than one day. But if it was only for one day, he had to make it worth his while. He balanced it up and decided to say:

"Forty dollars for the day. I'll take you on a tour of the city."

"Dollars? Why are you charging me dollars?"

"That's how it works around here. And if you want me to take you to the Chu-Chi tunnels tomorrow I can drive you and get you past all the queues, so you don't have to wait. And then I'll take you to the

Mekong River, somewhere a bit special. A bit unusual for you, I think. A crazy island where a crazy man set up his own cult, built a rocket ship, eat only coconuts and surrounded himself with beautiful women. I think perhaps you don't like to go where everyone goes. I'm I right?"

"Let's see how it works today. It would be good if you could take me to the museum and then the market and then the sunset bridge. But I can only give you thirty dollars as it is already eleven o'clock. Is that OK?"

"Thirty-five and then I will look after you. Show you all the places that tourists will never go. You will come and eat with me and meet my friends. I'll make sure you have an interesting time in Saigon. Follow me to my trusty steed."

He was glad to see that she followed him and that she had obviously accepted the extra five dollars. He looked back at her and wondered what on earth she thought she was doing wandering around a city like Saigon on her own at the age she was, in a thin red dress, with wild hair and a slightly broken mini rucksack. He handed her a facemask.

"What's this?"

"All women wear these. It stops the pollution and germs getting in their delicate lungs and makes sure that the sun doesn't burn their skin and ruin their fair complexion."

"Do you wear one?"

"No."

"Why don't you wear one? It's you that needs to wear one. It is you who's driving around in this thick air, day in and day out."

He coughed as a reflex action. "No. I don't wear one." He coughed again and it caught him, and he spluttered and just about stopped himself launching into a real old coughing fit.

"Why not?"

"Because I would look like a lady-man if I did."

"That's ridiculous," she said.

"All the other motorbike guys would laugh at me."

"Well, I'm not going to wear one if you don't."

This lady Fish was quite annoying. She spoke to him as if she had known him for years, which he found a bit off-putting. He wanted to tell her that he had a wife at home, thank you very much, and that she was more than enough for him to deal with.

"OK. Do what you like. But you must wear a helmet. I will get arrested if you don't wear this helmet. It's a good one. It will be a good fit."

She put on the helmet but struggled to do up the clip on the side. He had to do it for her as if she was a big fuzzy-haired baby.

She got on the back of the bike. Before she did so he gave her his sports jacket.

"You put it on back to front, yes?"

"Yes. Why does everyone do that here?"

"It protects better against the wind. Keeps the clothes underneath fresher. There, you look like a real Vietnamese woman now."

She couldn't have looked less like a Vietnamese woman, big thing that she was, with his jacket the wrong way around and a bit tight for her. He couldn't help looking down and noticing that her bare calves were at least twice the size of his. What did they feed these British women? His poor motorbike.

When they set off, she did that thing of putting one of her arms behind her with the other free and balancing and holding on with her thighs. He felt that she was showing off that she had ridden on the back of a motorbike before and trying a bit too hard to appear relaxed and nonchalant. They joined the throng of a thousand scooters, motorbikes and cars moving along the boulevard. He felt her body tense up behind him as he approached the roundabout.

"Don't worry!" he shouted. "I know what I'm doing. I'm a good driver. A very good driver. Put your arms on my shoulders please. That way our bodies will balance well with each other."

She put her hands on his shoulders. Her touch was confident. She did not seem at all intimidated at touching a man's body. He could feel her small breasts against his back at first, but she then moved a little to create a bit of distance between them. He knew that she wouldn't be able to help resting those little titties on his back at some point in the day, however much she tried. She gasped a few times as they stopped and started and made their way through the traffic. When he mounted the pavement and weaved in and out of the pedestrians, he enjoyed hearing her cry out.

"Don't worry this is how I do it. Take a fat American tourist out at the same time. Ha, ha, ha."

She didn't laugh. He reached out as he drove and ripped off a flower from a pretty Ochna itegerrima bush being sold outside a Tet shop. He handed it to her, twisting his arm backwards whilst driving off the pavement and onto the road to join the throng of traffic.

"You still there? Not fallen off the back. Got both eyes closed by any chance? A flower for you. For Tet. Vietnamese New Year. Happy New Year!"

"Oh thank you."

She took her arm off his shoulder to take the flower he was holding back to her. She pushed it into one of the little holes on the side of her helmet. They stopped outside the Museum of Atrocities.

"I'll meet you outside here in an hour."

"Oh, you're not coming in?"

No, of course not. Think for a minute you fucking idiot lady. He knew what the US Army did. He did not need to be told in a museum. He was alive then. He had lived through it. Why were these tourists so ignorant? A young boy living with his mother, father, and brother. His parents worked hard running a restaurant in District 1 that was popular with foreigners and locals alike. The food was good and fresh, and his parents created a famously warm and welcoming atmosphere. His father was the kind of man that everyone wanted to be friends with because he drew you in, with his wide shoulders, handsome face and loud, infectious laugh. In the war Lok remembered only too well the dark curfewed streets, a drunk GI throwing a bottle of beer at him and his brother as they made their way to school and of course the bombings of the Tet offensive. A house four doors down had been completely flattered. His parents forbade him and his brother to go outside but, in the confusion of the hours immediately afterwards, with their parents getting essentials and checking up on the restaurant and friends and family, they had managed to sneak out and peek at the smouldering ruin. They walked down the side of the house and through the dust and smoke they saw a huge beam under which their grumpy neighbour Cien was lying. It was strange how peaceful he looked even though that thing was on top of his chest, his arms pinned down and a thick layer of white dust on his face and hair. His brother started to cry loudly, and Lok punched him on the shoulder to get him to shut up. From then on, his parents kept their heads down, whispering even at home, narrowly avoiding being sent out to the new farming zones, keeping their famous restaurant going but without the relaxed warmth, serving the communist elite and their families now, his brother taking over when their parents reached their seventies.

Could the British woman really think that he wanted to walk through all those pictures with all those sweating fucking tourists either looking too shocked or not shocked enough.

"No. I'll just wait here."

Lok went to join a couple of other motorbike men waiting for their tourists.

"Nice one you got there, Lok. A bit old, so a bit richer, no?"

"You better hang around here or one of us will take her."

"What's her story? Why's she alone? What's wrong with her? Why has she got no man at her age? Does she smell?"

"They all smell a bit, don't they? These Western women. These Lady Fish smell a bit fishy?"

"With absolutely huge vaginas."

They all laughed loudly at the thought of the tourist women's massive vaginas. Two big, fat Australian looking women looked at them laughing as they came out of the museum and it made them laugh so much that they had tears dripping down their faces. Ca had to hold onto the wall to steady himself and Lok had to blow his nose on his special handkerchief, made from the heavy linen napkins from his parent's restaurant.

When she came out, with a cup of Phuc Long Coffee looking suitably sombre, he walked right up to her. Just in case she had any thoughts of jumping on another man's bike or had forgotten what he looked like, which did sometimes happen.

"Did you learn anything?"

"Yes."

"Why did the American Army come into the war?"

"Because they wanted to beat China and Russia who backed the North," she said.

"Correct. And they wanted to stop the spread of Communism. It had nothing to do with helping the South. They set up the Southern government. OK? Do you understand?"

She nodded.

"By the way how much did you pay for that coffee?"

Lok looked down disapprovingly at the paper cup she held in her hand.

"Fifteen Dong."

"What! I will take you somewhere where the coffee is cheap and good, and the company is even better. Promise me you won't buy anything in the tourist places again. Lok will save you money and give you food and drink that tastes good. You hungry?"

His stomach was aching with hunger. He hoped that she would say yes.

"Yes. I'm quite hungry."

He could tell that she wanted to talk about the things she had seen there. She wanted to go on about the terrible legacy of scorched earth. About the birth defects in babies being born today due to the poisoned land and the moving letter sent to President Obama by a mother whose two children were born without limbs recently due to Agent Orange poisoning. She wanted to talk about the picture of Kim Phuc and the terrified children. But he did not want to talk about any of it with her. He did not want to talk about it at all. It would make his day, that started off so badly, but had now improved, tip back into the anxious dark, stomach-churning feelings again.

"Hey, I'll take you somewhere in District 10. Somewhere that no tourist ever goes. The most delicious Mi vit Tiem man or woman has ever tasted. Let's go! Quick, quick. On the bike."

"What is Mi Vit Tiem?"

"It's duck soup. You will love it."

The other guys laughed and made facetious remarks as they drove off.

"Hey, Lok, your bike is tipping backwards with the weight of your fat girlfriend."

"What's that fishy smell?"

"Careful Lok, your tiny fishing rod will get lost inside her tunnel sized cunt!"

Kate leant forward. "What are they saying? I think they said something bad about me. Why are they laughing so much?"

"They said what a lovely lady. You're lucky to have such a lovely lady on the back of your bike."

"Mmmm. I don't think that's what they were saying. I think they were saying something very rude about me." She laughed.

Lok thought she was all right. She was not as stupid as she looked. Lok drove to District 10, shouting out sights of interest to her on the way. He noticed how a couple of other bike drivers in the throng would turn to look at them and wave at her. He thought that she must be smiling a lot with her helmet's visor up and catching people's eyes so that even a couple of the bad-tempered commuters seemed to like her. He drove her down a small alley off Su Van Hanh Street. His friends Kieu, Lam, Cao, and Cam were sitting on the small red plastic chairs eating and drinking just as they always were.

"Here Kate, come and meet my friends."

Kate laughed as she had to squeeze her big bottom into the chairs. They all laughed along with her.

Kieu leant over to her, his big bulbous, alcoholic's nose nearly touching hers. "Have some gecko wine, Baby. You look like you need it."

Kate looked to Lok to translate.

"He asked if you wanted to taste his gecko wine."

Kate nodded and they filled a small glass for her. She took a big swig. They laughed when she coughed a bit and said "Good" and nodded and smiled.

"It keeps you healthy and strong." Lok said.

Kate looked at Kieu with his greasy pallor and the maze of broken veins in his cheeks. She smiled, turned her face to Lok and rolled her eyes a little bit so that only he could see. It was true that Kieu did not look the picture of health.

"Hey, is she alone?" said Cam, who in Lok's opinion was more man than woman. Cam sat in her tight jeans and her skinny legs wide open and could drink as much as they could, perhaps even more. What came out of her mouth could shock even Kieu by its filthiness. Lok told Cam to speak English because he knew that she could speak it almost as well as he could. She had wealthy parents who once were high up in the communist party and she had travelled to Cambodia, Singapore and even to Hong Kong. She went to an international school when no one had even heard of international schools.

"How long have you been travelling for?"

"Just a day. This is the first country I've been to."

"You alone?"

"Yes."

Cam told her female friend what Kate had said. This friend wasn't like Cam. She was pretty in a nice green dress with slim legs and laughed at all the jokes they made. But she was as impressed by Kate as Cam was.

"I wish I could travel. I would love to be on my own too. I'm never on my own. I always have to care for people. The idea of just being free and not having to answer to anyone. For a woman it is a dream come true. Women never get any time on their own."

Cam explained to Kate what her friend had said. Lok was glad that Cam had taken over the translation duties for now.

"My children have grown up. I have worked and looked after them. And my mother may need my care soon but for now she is well. I saw a chance and I grabbed it. I rented out my flat and asked my work to let me have a year's unpaid leave. Now or never, I thought. I have not been very adventurous in my life."

Cam translated this to her friend.

"And your husband?"

“I don’t have a husband. I did have a husband. I got rid of him six years ago now. I loved having children, but I didn’t like being married to him that much. He was an angry man who shouted all the time.”

Cam translated what Kate had said.

'I'll marry you if you like?’ Kieu lent towards her. “You would take me back to England and set me up in a palace there. Your voice is like the Queen of England, darling. I think it is kind of sexy. I think you are kind of sexy.”

“I’m not translating that. Why would she marry an ugly old drunk with a nose like a burst pear?” said Cam. ‘It doesn’t look like she has to marry anyone. That’s the whole point. She’s got her children. She’s got nothing to prove anymore.”

“Maybe she will get lonely. Maybe she doesn’t want to be a sad old woman with no one to hold her tight at night.”

Cam looked at her. “She doesn’t look particularly lonely to me. I’ll ask her.” Cam turned to Kate. “Do you ever get lonely Kate?”

Kate thought about the question. “Well, I’ve never been travelling alone. I think I have done some stupid things because of fear of loneliness. I’ve only been alone for a day, so ask me in six months.”

“And you are not alone. You are with me!” Lok couldn’t help saying before she got too pleased with herself for being so bravely alone.

All of his friends decided to get on their motor bikes and scooters and come with them to the market, where they brought a whole lot of fruits for Kate to taste and then onto the bridge to watch the sunset. Lok pointed out to Kate the huge pink luxury apartment blocks by the river that had been abandoned due to the many ghosts that had been seen there. It was once an esteemed and luxurious residence reserved for military generals and high commanding officers, but had turned dilapidated and rancid with grimy, smashed windows. Not even foreigners would dare to live there now. Lok told Kate that people didn’t even want to drive past there because of the tremendous number of ghosts that lived there, including an American soldier who walked hand in hand with a small local girl. The trouble is that even pulling it down wouldn't stop the ghosts. They would inhabit the next building and the next so that there was no point doing anything much.

All of them stood in a row on the bridge looking out onto the river as the sun went down, spreading its pink and orange light across the dancing water. Everyone smoked enthusiastically except Lok and Kate. Lok nudged Kate and couldn't help pointing out that she was the only Westerner there, amongst the locals enjoying the sunset.

"I told you I would show you a place that only locals go."

Across the water they could see the next bridge down. There were blue police lights and a crowd of people lit up by the row of orange overhead bridge lights.

"What's happened?' Kate said.

Cam told her before he could get in with a nicer story. "The Tet suicides have started. It's the pressure to pay off all your debt before the New Year, so that you don't bring bad luck into the next year. It gets to some people. There have been three people fished out from the river in the last week. Too late. All three drowned. They just couldn't bear the stress and strain of it."

Lok scowled at Cam from behind Kate's head.

"What's the matter with you?" she said in Vietnamese.

"I want her to find Saigon a happy place. I want to guide her for two or three or even four days. I don't want you to depress her on her first day and make her feel this is a bad place where people kill themselves all the time."

"She's a grown woman. She knows that life is full of light and dark. I think she wants to see everything. Anyway, you told her about the ghost apartments."

When Lok got back home that night after dropping Kate off, his wife had left a note on the sitting room table. *I'm staying with my sisters. You can clean for Tet. I'm not cleaning for a man that runs with whores.*

He tried to phone her, but he gave up after six attempts, maybe seven.

The next day Lok picked Kate up from her *CoZybed* room in District 8. She was staying at the house of a Communist Party photographer and her grown-up son. Yesterday Kate had laughed with

Lok about how the woman had insisted on taking pictures of her standing stiffly like a communist official in different spots in her house as soon as she arrived. Kate had imitated the way the photographer had made her stand with her arms stiffly by her side, her face unsmiling, her neck long, her gaze looking away from the camera lens and proudly towards the distance and the great future of Vietnam.

The photographer woman answered the door to Lok with a disapproving face. "Where did she find you? If only she had waited and asked me, I would have recommended an official tour guide."

Lok didn't dare respond in the way he wanted, which was to tell her where to shove her official tour guide. If she decided to tell one of her party friends about him, life could become very difficult for him indeed. He had to make do with being overly polite which was almost as satisfying. This was a trick he had learnt from his mother when she was serving rude Communist Big Wigs in their restaurant.

"If you could just tell her I'm waiting for her, I would be most grateful. Thanks so much for your help in advance."

Her eyes narrowed. She knew exactly what he was doing. She paused before she answered him. "Yes, I will. Where will you be waiting for her?"

"I will be waiting directly opposite your exquisitely beautiful house."

"Not directly opposite. Directly opposite is my official parking space. So obviously you can't go there."

These Communist hanger-on types were the worst. He wondered who she had to fuck to get the job as an official photographer. By the look of her it would have been some years ago.

"Well, not directly opposite then but somewhere as close to the opposite as I can find without causing any inconvenience. I presume your car is in your official parking space so I would not be able to stand there."

"I do not have a car. But it is still my official parking space."

Lok didn't answer her but let her words just hang in the air in the hope that she would see the absurdity of what she had just said. But her expression remained the same. A pinched smile with her eyebrows raised.

Kate came out of the house. She was in a stripy clingy skirt and a black T-shirt. Oh dear.

"Kate. You will be crawling through the tunnels, as I think I explained, and it is not so nice in a skirt. If there is a man behind, he will be looking up your skirt. Do you have some trousers? Loose trousers?"

"Oh, yes. Sorry."

"Let me hold your bag and you go upstairs and change."

She gave the bag to him without even thinking. Thankfully the photographer woman had gone in the house, so he just stayed near the doorstep. He worried for Kate when she went to the North of Vietnam. They were much more dishonest there. He must remember to warn her.

Kate came out of the house again in a pair of badly fitting trousers. Well, she had really made sure that absolutely no one would be looking at her arse in the tunnels. You couldn't even make out where her arse stopped, and the backs of her knees started in those unattractive men's trousers. She got on the bike, and he had to help with the catch of the helmet once again. He wondered if perhaps she liked him helping her to do it.

When they had come off the motorway on the way to the tunnels Lok took Kate through the countryside, past children and buffalo in paddy fields, past temples and graveyards with sandy-coloured monuments to ancestors, the searing sunlight only broken by the staccato shade of trees which lined both sides of the narrow roads. He could hear Kate making sounds of delight at the beauty and newness of what she saw so he resisted telling her that this countryside had been decimated by American bombs and Agent Orange pesticides which still contaminated the soil. He would tell her later. For now, he would let her enjoy the delightful rural scenes.

When they got to the tunnel site, he nodded to one of the security guards at the entrance and he nodded back and motioned for him and

Kate to walk past the queues and go to a kiosk, which appeared to be closed.

"I've not seen you for some time, Lok. I thought perhaps you had retired from the hustle."

"I'll never be able to retire from the hustle. Never."

"Me neither, my friend. It is our fate. We will work until we drop."

Lok didn't consider a job lurking around the tunnels as anything as stressful as being a motorbike guide, but he didn't say so.

His friend only charged Kate local price to get in. Lok made sure to tell her that he had secured her this favour.

They walked around the site and Lok proudly showed Kate the reconstructed mantraps with sharpened bamboo sticking out of holes in the ground overlaid with branches– punji traps that would lacerate and slowly kill the Americans that were unlucky enough to fall in. He told her about the trip wires that would unleash snakes and scorpions on the heads of soldiers who had fallen in the holes. Kate's response was muted. There was the sound of gunfire all around them.

"What is that?" Kate asked.

"There is a firing range for tourists to fire guns used in the war."

"What? Why would anyone want to do that after seeing this?" Kate said.

"I don't know, but anyway, can you see how smart the Vietnamese are? We defeated a Superpower because we are so clever and quick. They bombed us from above and so we had to crawl deep and make a city under the earth."

Before she went into the tunnels Lok made sure, she knew that the tunnels had been widened so that big Westerners like her could crawl through them. They had to be sure that the American soldiers could not get into them. He did not want her to be fooled like the other tourists.

Lok stood talking to the old man who had set up a stall near the tunnel entrance selling sandals made from old tyres just like the Viet Cong used to wear. Lok promised him that he would bring the tourist he was guiding to buy a pair of the old man's ugly shoes, but when the other tourists came out of crawling in the tunnels Kate was not there.

She had obviously insisted on being taken further down. Sometimes if the guides thought that the tourist could stand it, they took them into the tunnels down below and into one of the rooms that had been made for bedrooms or hospitals. Lok felt quite proud of Kate that she could do this and congratulated her on her toughness when she finally crawled out, attempting to pat the red dusk from her trousers.

She smiled. "While I was down there, I thought I might as well see more."

Lok took Kate to the shoemaker. The shoemaker had been joined by his teenage granddaughter sitting on a small red plastic chair and squinting up at them. Together they managed to get Kate to take off her Nike trainers and try on a pair of tyre sandals. The old man pulled out a full-length mirror from behind the stall so Kate could see what she looked like. Kate was so happy that she had been the only tourist to be taken to the second level of tunnels, that she bought the sandals and put her American shoes in her rucksack. Lok kept quiet about the American Nike factory, less than ten miles away from where they were now.

Lok and Kate watched an informational film together just near the exit.

"It was very difficult for the US Army to infiltrate. The Viet Cong had hospitals, schools, theatres, kitchens and villages underground. There were a hundred and twenty miles of tunnels, and some went forty feet deep. The US Army tried to bomb the whole area around the Chu Chi tunnels and many Vietnamese died defending it. It was a great honour to be *A Great American Killer.* Here are some of our *Greatest American Killers.* the film voice-over informed them as they showed black and white portraits of young Vietnamese men and women.

Kate seemed to wince at the words *Great American Killer.*

"Those Americans and Australians were so young. They didn't know what they were fighting for. They were working class boys for the most part."

"Don't expect me to feel pity for the Americans. I'll save my pity for those who died just under where we stand. Driven underground like rats in a hole. I have friends that were born there, whose eyesight was ruined by being without light for so long. You expect me to feel pity?"

"OK, I'm sorry."

"I don't think you know enough to say anything. You only just arrived in Vietnam yesterday, so how can you even have an opinion?"

"Quite right. I'm sorry Lok." She touched his arm.

Lok snapped himself out of the anger that had risen in him like a fiery snake. He wanted to lash out at her but knew that to do so would be extremely foolish, particularly when he needed the Tet money. Instead, he laughed a little too loudly, took off his cap which was hurting his head and wiped his brow with his hand. He saw that some of his hair dye had stained the inside of his white cap. He quickly put it back on.

Lok knew he was tired when they set off on the drive home. With the absence of Da in his bed and worries about money and Tet and his son's future and the money lender who had a reputation for turning nasty, he had found it difficult to sleep. He kept thinking about the Tet River suicides and he had terrible half dreams about haunted buildings, river-monsters, big ugly fish, and floating, bloated bodies. On the busy Highway back to Hoi Chi Mien, he was in the fast lane in the slip stream of a lorry when he heard Kate's loud voice right into his ear and her hand hit him hard on the shoulder with her fist.

"Lok, Lok! Wake up. Come on Lok! What are you doing?"

Lok pulled himself back into consciousness just as he was about to run into the back of a slowing down lorry.

"Lok! Pull over. For God's sake! You nearly killed us." Kate was really screaming into his ear now. He got into the middle lane and then the slow lane and pulled over at a roadside café that had dozens of little stripy red and white hammocks. Kate got off the bike and angrily pulled off her helmet. She seemed to have no problems with the fastener this time. She shouted at him again. "Lok, you were asleep on the motorway, in the fucking fast line of a motorway you proudly announced was one of the most dangerous in the world. You know that I have two children. They depend on me. They need me. You must take care of me Lok! I don't want to be killed on the motorway so far away from my home! Not on my second day. Come on! I may be just a tourist to you, but I am still a person."

Lok felt the anger he had felt towards her when she commented on the informational film rise again. "So why don't you travel on the coaches like other tourists of your age? If your kids depend on you so much, then why are you travelling on your own? It is very irresponsible of you, I think. Why aren't you travelling with a man? What's wrong with you that you don't have a man? You attract danger I think." He shouted back.

"Oh, so it's my fault that you went to sleep and nearly hit a lorry? and when you say, 'your age' can I ask how old you are Lok?"

"I'm forty-two."

"No, you're fucking not. How old are you really? Tell me the truth."

"Look, I'm sorry. Don't tell anyone. If anyone finds out I fell asleep with you on the back, I won't ever get any work. I'm fifty-two, but please don't tell anyone. I'm so fucking tired of my life. I'm so fucking tired. It's so fucking shit."

Her face changed and softened. She put her hand on his forearm. He was mortified to find that her sudden sympathy made him shake and tremble and feel very close to weeping. He stopped himself speaking because he was terrified that the tears that had been kept inside him for so long would spill out and never stop and that he would just melt here by the roadside, and his wife would never know what had happened to him.

"Look Lok. Let's both lie in the little hammocks and have a rest. We're the same age and not as young as we used to be. Then, when you are properly rested, I'll buy you some coffee and something to eat and you can drink some cold water and we can talk. You look like you need some sleep, mate."

Lok nodded at the café owner and they both went and lay down in two hammocks opposite each other. For a few minutes Lok felt uncomfortable and restless, but when he craned his neck out of his hammock, he saw that she was already asleep in the hammock opposite him with her sturdy brown legs sticking out. Something about seeing her so peaceful and unselfconscious made his body relax into itself and he soon found himself drifting off too.

He woke up with Kate leaning over him smiling with a glass of freshly squeezed cane sugar juice.

"The owner said this was better than water. Did you have a good sleep, Lok?"

"How long have I been asleep?"

"Oh, an hour and a half," she said.

"Oh no, that's too long."

"No, it's just fine. You obviously needed it. She smiled down at him."

He sipped his refreshing drink and as soon as he had finished, she asked him to order coffee.

"Now tell me what's up? What's going on?"

His first instinct was to tell her that everything was ok, that he was Happy-Go-Lokky wasn't he? But looking at her, he saw that she was interested in him. She wasn't just faking it. She wanted to know something about him. And so, he told her. He told her about the loan shark and Tet, about his wife and their argument and the girlie tours, about his brilliant son who seemed to be studying for all eternity and that Da had left and that she wasn't answering his call and even though he found her terrible sometimes he missed her, and he missed her body in bed. He told her about his aches and pains and his palpitating heart and even the shooting pains up his arse - she told him that she sometimes got that too. He even told her a little bit about growing up during the war and his parent's restaurant and his brother who behaved like a bit of a shit over the sale of the restaurant.

"You're right about me too. Maybe I should be acting my age. I should have done all this when I was young, but I wasn't brave enough then. Of course I should be travelling in coaches, but I would much rather be on the back of your motorbike and hanging out with your weird alcoholic friends in alleyways. If I can trust you not to kill me that is. Can I?"

"Of course, you can. I'm the best motorbike driver in Saigon! I'm better now that I've been to sleep." He took a gulp of the coffee. "Do you know Kate? I would love to travel too. I know there is a big world that I would love to see. But I have so much to do and no fucking money. I fear that I will never get the chance, even to leave Vietnam. It's not happening Kate, it's just not happening. You can travel for me and be my travelling twin, though it will also annoy me that it is not me and Da travelling. I want you to take pictures on your phone and send them to me by WhatsApp. All the time. Do you understand?"

"Of course I'll do that. Now why don't you try and call your wife?"

"I've been trying, and she's not picking up."

"Do you want me to phone her? I've got a Vietnamese sim now, so it won't look like some strange foreign number?"

"OK,"

He read out his wife's number.

Da answered her number immediately. Kate handed it to him.

"Hello Da. I've missed you. I wish you would come home."

Da sounded mistrustful of him.

"Please come home Da. I don't know what else to say."

"OK. But only because I'm sick of staying with my sisters. She's being all smug about her boring, chubby husband and it's annoying me."

Lok smiled at Kate with a thumbs up. "Come home now Da. Please." He gave Kate back her phone. "It's OK if I take us home now? I would like you to meet my wife. I think she would like you."

"Shouldn't you just go home and sort things out?"

"It would be good for my wife to meet you. See that you are a respectable woman. And I think you are a lucky woman."

"You just said that I attract danger," Kate said laughing.

"I was upset. No, you will bring us luck for Tet if you step through our threshold. I'll get Da to cook you a real Vietnamese home meal. There are not many tourists who get to experience that."

Kate nodded enthusiastically. "OK, I'd like that."

Kate put the helmet back on her head, did up the catch and smiled.

To:Charlie.Mancini@gmail.com,
BillieGreenMancini@gmail.com

Subject line: First few days

Dear Charlie and Billie,
Thanks so much for the notes you wrote and hid in the beautiful notebook you bought me. I don't think I am the kind of person to make notes as I go along - I have already seen some travellers sitting in cafes in Saigon with their moleskin notepads writing down their observations - but I will try and see if I can take myself seriously enough to jot something down. I was so happy to find your words of encouragement when I flicked through it, though. It made me cry. You are both so lovely to me and don't think I don't know that. Some kids would be embarrassed of their late middle-aged mother suddenly deciding that she would take off for a year and basically copy her own children on their year off, just because she didn't have the balls to go any further than Florence when she was 18. I didn't even have to explain to you both why I needed to go away and see other places. Thanks so much too for rationalising my packing and I am hoping I will learn to love my green rucksack. We are not getting on well at the moment. I wish I had bought one that unzipped both ends and wasn't bright green. When I picked it up from the carousel at the airport, I wasn't that happy to see it. It was almost as if I wanted it to be left at Gatwick which is what I was told for half an hour until it was miraculously found from a pile in the corner.
I'm already irritating myself. I'm indecisive and have made my tidy CoZyBed room in a Communist Photographer's house look like a total tip. My clothes already look crumpled and scruffy. What will I look like when I come home in a year?
I bought some Vietcong sandals made from old car tyres and left my Nike trainers outside my CoZyBed House. I regretted this as soon as I realised how uncomfortable and unattractive they are. But too late, my trainers were already gone. Warning to self. Don't get too carried away.
I've already had a few adventures, and I am only on my second day. This is such a busy, mad and stressful city and thankfully I have lucked out with my motorbike guide Lok who has introduced me to his bunch of drinking pals and is taking me to some less touristy spots. Yesterday evening I went to his house to meet his wife, and she cooked the most delicious, fresh, fish noodle dish I have ever tasted with mint and what I think is Vietnamese

Basil. I went to the Atrocity Museum, and the Chi-Chi tunnels where Vietnamese families were forced to live underground for years. Both were harrowing in the extreme. I wanted to ask Lok about his life - He is about the same age as me so would have been a small boy during the Vietnam war - but he made it clear that he didn't want to speak of it. At first I had the feeling that I am just a big walking dollar-bill and then I forgot to be insulted by it and got used to it. Do you two know the feeling? You are both so much more well-travelled than me.

I have sent this on my hostess' laptop, and she is frowning at me now as I am in their kitchen/sitting room and not really welcome.

I love you both like mad. I hope Granny wasn't too annoying on the journey back from the airport. She would never admit it, but she was very scared about me going. You never stop worrying about your offspring, however old they are. She seems to have lost her edit button as she gets older doesn't she? I think that her younger self would be very shocked at her older self.

Love

Mum XXXXXX

PHOTOGRAPHER ON THE STAND
May 2018

Almost as soon as the photographer got into the witness box on the second morning, he started to reveal what Kate considered to be both his vanity and his insecurity. The prosecution took him through his movements that day and fed him what he had said in his statement. Jitendra was the first barrister to cross-examine him from the defence team. Kate sat up straight and strained to hear every word he said from behind the glass dock.

"Can you describe your job, please, Mr Harper?"

"I am a photographer for *The Daily World*."

"What kind of photography?"

"I photograph a range of subjects. I take portraits sometimes, but I have also photographed war and conflict. I have been to Syria, which is perhaps why my paper wanted me to go to Calais that day. There are many Syrians in Calais, and I can even speak a little Arabic."

Really? Thought Kate. There was no mention of him 'speaking a little Arabic' on the day of their arrest.

"That day in the refugee camp was a very long time ago, wasn't it? Almost a year and a half?" Jitendra said.

"Yes."

"Do you think you have a good recall of the events that day?"

"Yes. I think so."

"That's good. Now I'm going to give you a map. It is a map made by my client of the route you all used during that day. I apologise for the childlike quality, but I hope you can make out the landmarks of the camp," said Jitendra.

The photographer studied her map. "I'm finding this map very hard to follow."

Jitendra smiled at him. "Well, I think we all are but as it's the only map we could find of the Calais camp, we are all going to have to do our best. So, if you wouldn't mind taking a more careful look."

He reluctantly looked down at Kate's handiwork and Jitendra proceeded with her questioning.

"Mr Harper, how did you feel that morning when you met the group who were going into the camp at the petrol station?"

"What do you mean?"

"What sort of mood were you in?"

"I was a bit frustrated. I wasn't keen on taking my own vehicle having heard from other photographers about problems with cars being broken into. I had been told that I was to go in the car with the NGO women but was suddenly told that there was no room. I felt that there was an element of unfriendliness towards me from the group and in particular the English woman when I met them in the courtyard of the petrol station. She seemed to not want me to be there. She was quite rude to be honest."

"What did she say to you that made you think that she didn't want you to be there?"

"She told me that she didn't think that the women they were interviewing would want to be photographed and that it might affect the interviews of me even being there."

"Why do you think she thought you being there might affect the interviews?"

"Because I'm a man, I suppose."

"You understand that the English woman as you call her, was not only to guide you and your colleague around the camp, to arrange meetings with women who would tell their stories but to protect the women she knew there, many of whom did not want to be identified."

"Yes. As I said, I have been to several places where we rely on fixers and guides, so I do understand, yes."

"So, you understand that it is a complex role? That Kate Mancini was in effect your guide or your fixer that day and had multiple responsibilities."

Kate wondered what all the guides she had met when she was away would think if they saw what had happened to her so soon after returning home. She had failed in her guiding that day in the camp. She had failed to show people places and things they didn't know without putting them in danger. That is surely the first rule of the guide. To put the safety of those you are guiding first. Hadn't she been so outraged when Lok hadn't done that in Vietnam? When he dozed off while driving his motorbike on 'the most dangerous motorway in the world'.

"Yes. But even so, the English woman, sorry what's her name?"

"Kate Mancini."

He laughed. "Sorry, maybe she isn't English. Maybe I shouldn't describe her as an English woman."

"Why do you say that Mr Harper?"

"I mean, her name doesn't sound particularly English, does it?"

Kate saw some of the jury shift in their seats.

"Many English people have names that originate from other countries, Mr Harper."

Don't get into it Jitendra, thought Kate. *You told me not to get into any stuff like this. Valentine Harper is a nasty little twat, but don't give him the satisfaction of seeing you getting riled.*

Jitendra pulled herself back. "Back to the day in question. What was it about Kate Mancini that made you feel that she didn't want you there?"

"She seemed to be unwilling even to discuss the possibility of taking photos and this was frustrating and irritating considering that I was putting myself, my equipment and my new car at considerable risk. I also thought that she was lucky to get a publication like ours to come to the demolition of a refugee camp."

"Lucky. Why should she have considered herself lucky to have you there Mr Harper?"

"Because we don't usually cover stories about the plight of refugees. Our readers are not that interested in the plight of refugees. In fact, I would say that many of them are hostile to refugees. It was incredible to me that the English woman got one of our editors to want to do the story."

"So, you think that Kate Mancini should have been more grateful to you for coming?"

"Yes. I suppose I do think she should have been more grateful, and I certainly think she could have been more polite."

"OK. Can you look at the map, and we will go through what you did when you went into the camp? I know you have gone through it with my learned friend."

The photographer agreed that they had visited the Kids' Café with and then gone to the Mother and Baby bus, to the Syrian caravan area, to the official mother and baby home-office area, to the Kid's Café again and then back finally to the Mother and Baby bus. The photographer traced his finger on Kate's much maligned map.

"Were you all together?"

"No, the smaller Syrian woman left us at some point, and I think both the taller Syrian woman and the young black woman left us from the Kids Café."

"So, it was just you and your fellow journalist and who else?"

"The English woman."

"Do you mean Kate Mancini?"

"Yes."

"When you say the taller Syrian woman, you mean Ranim Dawoud?" She turned around and pointed to where Ranim was sitting, next to Kate.

"Yes."

"And when you say the young black woman, you mean Faven Kassa, who is not at court."

"If that was the name of the young black woman, then yes."

"Do you have your statement in front of you?"

"Yes."

"In your statement you say that both the tall Syrian woman, Ranim Dawoud and the young black woman Faven Kassa were with you until you went to the Blue Mother and Baby Bus, but you have just stated that they left you at the Kid's Café which was before going to the Blue Bus."

The photographer frowned. He took a while to speak. Kate saw his pointed Adams apple bob up and down as he swallowed nervously.

"I'm not sure then. Perhaps it was that way round. Look, I'm only the photographer. I just follow on trying to get photographs if I am allowed. I wasn't responsible for anything except my equipment and to be honest I was very nervous about that. I felt that no one was looking out for me, and this was a new place for me."

Kate felt herself rolling her eyes.

"Can you remind me? Did you say that you could remember everything when I began to question you? That you didn't have a problem with the events having taken place so long ago."

"Yes, but perhaps I can't. I'm not sure that I do remember where everyone was and at what time. It's a big ask."

"I understand Mr Harper. Let's go back to your statement." Jitendra picked up a sheet of paper from the bundle. Her hand was steady. "Here you say that the two Syrian women, the boy and the English woman, walked away together from the Blue Mother and Baby bus right at the end. But wasn't your colleague Priya Anand conducting a last interview with a Syrian woman?"

"Yes. I think that last interview was with a Syrian woman."

"Can you tell me again what you thought you saw?' Jitendra leant forward.

"Did I say that? Hang on, can I read my statement?" He read leaning hard against the front of the witness box with his head bowed. "Well, if I said that in my statement then that is what I thought I saw. I was interviewed only a week after it all happened."

Kate heard Ranim whisper something under her breath.

"Are you aware that the other interpreter – the young, black woman, Faven Kassa is Eritrean?"

"Yes."

"So can I ask you why she would have been the interpreter for a Syrian woman in that last interview?'

"I don't know."

"I'm sorry, could you say that again, to the court?"

"I don't know," he said a little louder. The photographer swayed a little in the witness stand.

"I am just trying to understand what happened that day, Mr Harper. An important part of the case is that you have said that you saw the taller Syrian woman Ranim, the English woman Kate, and the smaller Syrian woman and a young man, all walk away together at the end of the day while you waited for the interview to finish. At the same time, you are saying that the last interview was with a Syrian woman and yet you say the Eritrean interpreter went into the bus to interpret that interview and the Syrian interpreter stood outside with you. How is that possible Mr Harper?"

The Judge interrupted. "The Eritrean woman, Miss Kasa, was not charged with the women. And she did not want to act as a defence witness. Is that right?"

"Yes, Your Honour. Both those observations are correct."

It seemed to Kate as if the Judge was deliberately interrupting when the photographer had shown the unreliability of his statement.

"Your Honour, could I proceed?" said Jitendra.

"Yes, you may proceed."

"I'm sorry. Mr Harper, could you answer the question please?"

"I'm sorry, could you repeat the question."

"Did you or did you not say in your statement that it was the Eritrean woman who went into the bus and that the Syrian interpreter stood outside with you?"

"Yes, I did, but I can see that doesn't seem likely."

"And yet it is what is in your statement. I ask Mr Harper again. Do you think you have a good recall of who was where and at what time?"

"Er, No. It seems I don't. I think I made a mistake."

"Could you repeat that?"

"I think I made a mistake."

"So, if the Syrian interpreter was on the bus, how could you have seen her walking away with Kate, the small Syrian woman and her son?"

"As I said, I may have been mistaken."

'Thank you, Mr Harper, that is all."

Jitendra sat down.

CALAIS CAMP
October 2016

Kate opened the driver's car window and shouted to Priya and the photographer, who wound down the window of his shiny black four-wheel drive.

"Look for a place further up," Kate said, pointing to the top of the verge underneath the flyover where about thirty cars were parked. She had worked with Priya before, but she had only just met the photographer at their rendezvous point in a petrol station just beyond the French Eurostar tunnel. She had told Priya that it would be pointless to send a male photographer as the women they knew in the camp would not want a man around and it might make her interviews impossible. She advised *The Daily World* that they should use stock photographs of the camp because even if it was a female photographer, it was highly unlikely that anyone would want to be photographed in such an acutely sensitive situation. The women were always shy of the camera but on the day of the start of dismantling of the camp they would be feeling particularly edgy and vulnerable. He certainly would not be able to come in the car with them through the Eurotunnel, as Priya had at first asked, as Kate's colleagues would be uncomfortable to have to sit on the journey with a man they didn't know, and anyway there wasn't room.

Four days ago, Ranim had phoned her and asked if someone she knew from Syria could come to Calais with them to distribute clothes and food in the Syrian quarter as a humanitarian mission. The Syrian community in London was very concerned about the breakdown of the camp, and her friend was very worried as she had friends there. Ranim was a highly respected interpreter and ran her own Syrian community organisation. If she asked for something, then Kate's organisation tended to listen. Kate was weary of complications and that there would be more women to pick up in London on the way and drop off on the journey home. She was also concerned about their group being too large. Kate had phoned Juliet, the founder and director of the refugee organisation and asked her if she thought it was all right that another Syrian woman came and distributed food and clothes to the large Syrian community there and her boss had said yes.

The photographer was tall, with sandy hair, a thin mouth, small rodent eyes and a beard, which looked like it had been stuck on to his unusually smooth pink and oddly chubby cheeks. His beard reminded Kate of those magnetic file beard makers over a cartoon face that she used to get in her Christmas stocking. Kate and Priya got out of the car first and he greeted them on the forecourt of the petrol station while the other women stared up at him from their seats in the car.

"Hi, I'm Valentine Harper."

He shook her hand. She expected a firm handshake and got a rather clammy, half limp one.

"As I've covered conflict, the paper thought it would be appropriate for me to come to the Jungle today."

Kate suddenly felt even more tired than she had before. She couldn't wait for this day to be over, and it hadn't even really started.

"The people in the camp don't really like the term 'Jungle'. It's seen as dehumanising, and I can understand that. It implies that they're animals." Kate said.

"Well, you know that we work for *The Daily World*, so I think it's unlikely that we'll get our editors to agree to not calling it 'The Jungle'. Maybe you're just going to have to accept that if you ask a paper like The World to a place like this, there are certain things that you might have to put up with in order to get your story in."

Kate didn't care that her sigh was loud enough for everyone to hear. That's all they needed on the day of demolition. An arsehole of a photographer to drag around after them.

"OK, well as I said to Priya from the off, I really don't think that the women will talk if you are part of the group. That's why I made such a big thing about wanting a woman photographer to be sent or even stock images to be used. I made that clear, and my interpreters agree with me. The women here are understandably very nervous of strange men. My organisation has taken a year to build up relationships with the women here so that they trust us to speak to us."

"I hope you are at least going to let me try to photograph these women. Otherwise, what's the point in me coming?" He had vivid pink flushes on his cheeks now.

"You're not going to get any women to speak if you come into their tents or their caravans. I would rather cancel the interviews now than to frighten or upset the women who've agreed to speak with us. They're anxious enough about what's going to happen to them."

"OK, then tell me about the women you have set up interviews with?" Priya asked, trying to break into the argument that was brewing between them.

"One is an Afghan woman who came here pregnant having been raped as part of her passage payment in Libya."

"OK," Valentine said, seemingly unimpressed.

"Rape is very often part of the deal if women are expected to get across Libya."

"OK," Valentine said again.

"Another Syrian woman says that her family is in Britain and that she wants to be reunited with them. She is here with her husband and two children. She's pregnant and says that she fears she will lose her baby because of the terrible conditions here and the stress of not knowing where they'll be moving. There is a team of British midwives who come here a couple of times a week, but she says she hasn't seen one yet. She is very worried about being moved by the French authorities and that she will be detained and separated from her family."

"Right, OK," he said.

Was he doing that repetition of a flat, unimpressed OK to deliberately wind her up?

"Who else are we speaking to?" Priya said.

"Faven has a friend here who travelled on a boat in the Mediterranean with her two small children after travelling through the Sahara. She became separated from her husband who she thinks may be still alive, but in Malta. She's had bad experiences in the camps."

"What kind of bad experiences?" Priya asked.

"She says that she was attacked by a group of men when she went to get some water to wash. She says that they beat her and sexually assaulted her."

Valentine was lucky that this time he just nodded.

Kate had only recently got back to work from her months of travelling. Her son had said that she should try and tone down her smiles and laughter; that it could get quite annoying. Her daughter had asked her to only tell one story every two days from her travels and Kate had agreed. Many of her friends glazed over when she brought up things that had happened to her and she understood. Her boss was concerned by the length of time it had taken her to get back into the swing of things and Kate saw this trip to the Calais camps as a chance to show that she was concentrating on the task at hand and was back in full campaigning-activist mode.

Priya had written several stories for the Women's Page about Yarl's Wood detention centre and managed to get them onto the online edition of *The Daily World.* Kate and her director discussed how important it was that Kate would always judge the risks and make sure that everyone stuck together. Kate said that if things seemed too dangerous, she would gather everyone up and go back over the Channel. That she would constantly assess the situation.

"Are those women Syrian?" Valentine nodded his head towards Kate's colleagues in the car.

'Two are Syrian and one is from Eritrea."

"I was in Syria. I know about these people."

These people, those people. Kate thought it was never a good sign if someone used *these* or *those* before the word *people.* Distancing words.

She told herself to try and keep things cordial with Valentine otherwise the day would be even more difficult. It was her job to get good interviews, protect the women being interviewed and to keep everyone safe.

"We will ask the women we're meeting if they're prepared to be photographed by you, but as they're in such a vulnerable position, I think it is highly unlikely."

Valentine nodded and Kate thought she saw him raise his eyes to Priya.

"I suggest that we all use the toilets here. There is nowhere to go to the toilet in the camp. You have to go between cars. So sorry to sound Mummyish but I think it's a good idea if we all go now."

Kate had been appalled that her period now erratic in her perimenopause had started the day before and she had just about remembered to throw a few tampons into her rucksack that morning. She went with Ranim, Ebeid, Faven and Priya, to the female toilets. The photographer stood where he was with his arms folded, looking pissed off.

Faven realised when they entered the service station shop that she had left her purse in the car. "I need some chocolate before I enter the camp. I must have some energy if I am to do this properly."

Kate gave her the car key.

"I don't have a fob. You have to open it at the driver's door. Sorry" Faven came back into the shop as Kate was coming out.

"I don't think I needed these. The car seemed to be unlocked."

"Really? I'm sure I locked it."

"I don't think so," Faven said.

"Bloody hell. What an idiot I am."

Priya told Kate that she would go in Valentine's car for the five-minute drive to the camp because he was nervous about losing them and didn't have Kate's number. "I think he needs a bit of hand holding." Priya said.

"Even though he was in Syria?" Kate said,

Priya laughed.

"Priya, I did say that it was pointless bringing a photographer and that it might even hinder what we're trying to do."

"I know. But what can I do? The newspaper insisted upon it. I didn't know he was a bit of a dick. I've never met him before."

THE UMBRELLA FACTORY
February 2016

Su-Su was glad that the plane was not coming into Heho until the late morning and that Kyaw Soe, the boatman, would not pick her up until ten. Her mother had suggested that she should come to the school to help her for the early morning as there were a couple of badly behaved children who sorely tried the patience of the schoolmistresses, but Su-Su told her that she had to prepare for the British women and to look up something on her phone.

Her Mother looked at her quizzically. She knew that there was very little that Su-Su didn't know about Lake Inle and its surrounds. What could possibly be so special about these British women that Su-Su needed to suddenly increase her knowledge?

Last night Su-Su had come home very tired from taking a large group of Australians around the sites and so hadn't seen on her phone that she had received an email from Johnny Fowler, the head of the high end travel company, Bullscome and Fowler - *Tailormade travel with genuinely local guides to insure an authentic, once in a lifetime experience* - that for the most part employed her. Not only was this the first time she had received an email from one of the partners, but the subject title made her heart feel like it was going to jump right out of her rib cage. *Fancy a trip to Japan?*

Dear Su-Su,

Bullscome and Fowler will be participating in a travel conference in Tokyo this coming September and would be delighted if you would be able to attend as our Myanmar representative. Our clients have consistently told us how your Inle Lake tour was the highlight of their trip to Myanmar, particularly your understanding and discussions about lotus weaving and your tour of the Inle Weavers Co-operative. As you know, the Japanese are particularly interested in lotus weaving and I wondered if you would be prepared to give a short speech - 20 minutes max with PowerPoint - on lotus weaving on Inle Lake, on day two and three of the conference - we would only expect you to prepare one talk but to speak twice -. I don't need to tell you that the Japanese fashion industry is increasingly using pure lotus woven material as well as the mix of silk and lotus, so not only would it be promoting Inle Lake as a destination for Japanese tourists but the cloth of the weavers of Inle. I feel that it would be interesting to you not only to meet James (Bullscome) and I but also other Bullscome and Fowler Guides from all over the world. This is obviously an all-expenses paid trip, but it would be great if you could let us know if this is something that interests you and if you would be available for the dates of September 5th to the 10th. I look forward to hearing from you.

All the Best

Johnny

Su-Su's mother had looked up when she had made her initial cry of delight. She couldn't help it. Her mother had carried on watching her closely while she read the email.

"What is it?"

"Bullscombe and Fowler want me to travel to Japan in September to speak about Lake Inle for a conference in Tokyo of travel guides. For a five-day trip. They would pay for everything it seems."

Her mother's eyes went hard, and glittery cold and her mouth pulled into a downwards grimace just for a second when she said "Travel to Japan," before she started to congratulate her. Su-Su saw it and her mother knew she had seen it, because she looked down as she spoke in a rush.

"Oh well done, my clever little girl. Your Father would have been so proud of his precious daughter. You will get to travel like the rich tourists that come to you. Do you have time to prepare?"

"Well, it's not until September, Mother."

"I've heard that Japan is a strange place. You know how my father felt about the Japanese. I have heard that people from Japan do not like people from our country. They look down on us. They see us as servants."

"They want me to give a small talk about lotus weaving and yes, there is plenty of time."

"There will be much to organise. We are really going to have to start preparing, particularly if you are going to give a talk to a large audience.

We will need to find you a decent suitcase, and will you need new clothes? You may have to attend various important functions. Do you have the outfits so that you can feel proud of yourself and of your country when you are there?"

She would try not to let her mother's anxiety spoil this for her, but already a little knot of worry had formed in the pit of her stomach. She knew that she was a very good guide and as she was passionate about the exquisite beauty of the cloth made on the lake. She was also confident that she would do her best to convey her love and respect for the women that wove lotus and silk and their product. But she already felt worried about leaving her mother alone, even for five days. Her mother worked so hard at the small lake school and Su-Su had massaged her feet just before they went to sleep every evening since her father died.

"I don't know how big the audience will be and I don't think there will really be that much to do. I don't need any more clothes. I'll take some western clothes and some traditional clothes. After all, it's only for five days. They will do all the organising of where I will stay and what I'll have to do there. At least I think they will do all the organising. Yes, I'm sure it will be that way."

She saw that her mother was close to tears but was pinching her mouth so as not to let any of her sadness or anger come out. Su-Su knew that her mother would be harder on her pupils today because of her upset and anxious mood. Su-Su couldn't wait for her mother to be on her way, to hear her steps going down their rickety wooden stairs to their small jetty and hear the oars' initial rattle until they engaged with the metal oarlocks, and the sound of the oars' slow rhythm as they dipped into the water.

Only then she was able to break the news to her friends about the fantastic offer. She understood that this opportunity would make her mother feel a mixture of emotions. After all, her mother had not been able to travel under the junta, although they had visited Thailand together last year for a week touring the great Temples of Bangkok, an experience she wasn't sure her mother had enjoyed as much as she had expected, and which Su-Su knew would have been so more fun with friends of her own age. Su-Su hoped that her mother's maternal pride would soon overtake any feelings of sadness, and although it was difficult to admit that her mother felt jealousy towards her and regret about the limitations of her own life, Su-Su recognised those emotions as her mother's knee jerk response, and it saddened her. Why couldn't her mother just be happy for her? She felt that if she ever had a daughter, she would never be jealous of her triumphs. Su-Su felt a pang of guilt and with it a nub of less familiar resentment and irritation. Her mother and her grandparents had sacrificed a great deal to pay for Su-Su's guiding studies and her licence, but she was also greedy for new experiences and had a secret desire to live somewhere other than her beloved Lake Inle, even if just for a few months.

Su-Su looked out of the window and across the lake. In the near distance she could already see her mother rowing with her stiff little movements and her square back in her black school mistresses' long-sleeved tunic. She watched until her mother reached the red house belonging to U Than Maung, a two floored stilted house like theirs, but somewhat grander with its deep red walls and mahogany veranda that was swept on a twice daily basis by a servant. Two cormorants sat on the U Than Maung porch as if they were waiting for her mother. Perhaps they were. Her mother had been rowing at this time for the last thirty years, only taking time off to visit her own parents in the countryside of the Shan region, when her father was in hospital and on the Thailand trip with Su-Su.

Su-Su saw her turn her boat to the right so she could row down the canal of water which had the schoolhouse at the far end of it.

Only when she could no longer see her mother did Su-Su set up a small Facebook message group entitled *Guess what? I'm off to Japan!* Yin who worked at one of the many mobile phone companies that had moved into Yangon to try and capitalise on what she never failed to tell them was the "Fastest growing smart phone market in the world", Myo who was at university in Mandalay studying IT, and Thant who was working as a beauty therapist in one of the big hotels in Bagan. Thant answered her immediately.

"You must need someone to carry your suitcases? Oh, let me come with you?"

"And me!" Yin responded.

"But seriously, it could not have happened to a better person. Your sweetness has got its reward. We love you!" wrote Myo.

"I keep thinking about the last time we were all together in Bagan, hiking, eating, singing on the karaoke and laughing. Let's organise a trip after Japan so Su-Su can tell us all about it and about her Japanese boyfriend," said Thant.

"What Japanese boyfriend? Is someone not telling me something?" said Yin,

"The boyfriend she will have by the time she returns. Keep up," said Thant.

'Oh, that boyfriend?' answered Yin.

And they sent a barrage of laughing and loving emojis back and forth at each other for a while.

Su-Su carried on messaging her friends, veering off for a bit and all of them joining in with a bit of teasing about Yin's well-known crush on a Spanish Save The Children worker who lived in her apartment in Yangon.

"Be very careful," messaged Thant, 'You know what those NGO people are like. They are crazy. They will say anything to make you fall in love with them because they want to have a little taste of the local fruit and then they just go back to Europe without even a backwards glance." –

Su-Su realised that she would need to respond to the email quickly so that they should know that she very much wanted to come and wouldn't give it to anyone else. She said goodbye to the Facebook group with a few more jokes and happy emojis.

It took her an hour just to write a paragraph of email to Johnny. She felt it was so important that she got exactly the right tone, friendly but not over-familiar, interested but not childishly over eager, confident about the speech but still able to ask for guidance. She wanted to be sure that her English was correct but not too stiff and formal, so that he wouldn't know that she had pondered and argued with herself about every single word.

Dear Johnny
Thank you so very much for asking me to come to Tokyo to represent Bullscome and Fowler. It would certainly be an honour, and something I am very much looking forward to. I will visit Japan for the first time. I am sure it will match up to my expectations! It gives me much joy that your clients like to hear what I have to say about the lotus weaving and the women of the loom. I will also be happy to prepare a speech about lotus weaving. It is something very close to my heart. Could you tell me how many people will be in the audience? This may seem a strange thing to ask you, but it would help me to know. Will there be many other representatives from Bullscombe and Fowler? I will be extremely interested to meet you all.
Again, thank you for thinking of me.

My Very Best Wishes,
Su-Su

She heard the engine of the boat approaching and quickly applied the yellow Thanaka to her face to protect herself from the sun. As she was meeting the two British women for the first time, she applied the mustard-coloured paste to her cheeks and carefully made a pretty leaf pattern on each cheek. She climbed down the wooden stairs and noticed that her heart beat faster when she caught sight of the familiar form of Kyaw Soe.

She had been at school with Kyaw Soe and had known him since he was a boy, pinching and flicking her, pushing her in the water from the school boat, and putting frogs in her lunch box. She knew he did this because he liked her so much. Now she felt that his sternness towards her was because he had strong feelings for her still. He was the smartest boy in the class, and she was the smartest girl. It always surprised her that he had stayed in the village – working as a traditional builder and a boatman. When she was young, she used to think that he would rule the world because he always seemed to know more than anyone else.

"You look like the sun shone on your face when you woke up this morning."

"Oh, have I applied too much Thanaka to my face?"

"Ha, ha. No, you just look happy, Su-Su."

She sat close to him because she knew that once he started up the boat engine again, they would have to shout in order to hear. The side of her longyi nearly touched his bare, brown, square knee. She looked at him closely and saw that the sun and wind of the lake had beaten deep lines into his beautiful face. She admired the fullness of his lips, the unusual wideness of his jaw and the intelligent and questioning brightness in his eyes.

"I am happy. I have been asked to go to Japan for a visit."

He too did not look entirely pleased for her either. This disappointed her even more than her mother's anxious, envious reaction.

"Why are you going there?"

"It's for that British travel company I work for."

"To get even more tourists to come here? Oh, just what we need."

"No. Well, maybe."

"Japanese tourists?"

"I suppose."

Her "I suppose" was drowned out as he started up the engine.

She knew from the way that Kyaw Soe's head was turned away from her, looking out towards thc lake that he was thinking about the way the lake had turned from blue to red brown since their country had opened and they had built so many hotels around the lake. About how quickly the hyacinths grew and suffocated the holy lotus and the fisherman started posing for the tourists, standing on one leg with dead fish in their boats, asking for money. Yet here they both were, going to meet two British women, to take them around the lake for the next few days. Su-Su wanted to reach out and touch his back, to start at the top and go right down his spine with her finger. She wondered what his skin would feel like if she touched him like that. Instead, when it was time for her to get off the boat into the shore, she was deliberately prissy and dainty, holding onto her skirts as she walked down the long narrow boat, and then as she was about to disembark, she started deliberately rocking and swaying, so the boat started to move wildly with her.

"Hey, stop! Careful, you're going to fall in! What are you doing?" She made him laugh though.

"See you later!" and she gathered her skirt and ran off and over the grassy bank to where the driver waited.

Su-Su looked out for an elderly woman and her middle-aged daughter coming off the small plane and into the airport. She knew it was Georgina and Kate as soon as she saw them. An older woman with beautiful long white hair in a snowy plait and a stick, wearing an elegant dove grey linen tunic with matching wide-leg trousers. The younger woman had coarse brown hair and was wearing a traditional longyi and blouse. Su-Su could see even from where she was that she had not tied the longyi properly and it was back to front. She was not elegant like her mother, with big walking strides and turned-out feet. Su-Su saw the younger woman try to help the older woman by holding onto her arm and the older woman bat her daughter's helping hand away angrily. Su-Su saw the younger woman look up towards her. She held up her Bullscombe and Fowler sign on which she had written 'Georgina and Kate' in black marker pen. The younger woman, who must be Kate, said something to her mother and she also looked up. Kate waved and smiled, and her mother simply stared ahead.

"Oh hello. You must be Su-Su."

"And you must be Kate and Georgina."

The mother looked at her. Su-Su noticed that she had the most piercing blue eyes she had ever seen. The fierce life that radiated out of them made her lose her train of thought for a moment.

"My mother would like the toilet, rather urgently. Do you know where they are? We couldn't find any in the airport." Kate said.

"I am perfectly capable of asking for the loo myself thank you very much. You'll get used to this Su-Su. My daughter treats me as if I'm a half-wit. I'll give you a heads up. I'm very far from a half-wit."

Su-Su wasn't sure what that meant. Su-Su pointed to where the toilets were just behind them, in the airport forecourt.

"And I certainly don't need you coming to the toilet with me Kate, if you were thinking of doing so, thank you very much."

Kate laughed. "Alright, Mum."

The mother didn't laugh but hobbled off, muttering under her breath.

"Sorry about that. She can seem a bit stern at times, but the fact is she's eighty-three and doesn't like that she doesn't have the energy she used to as a young woman. She also says whatever is on her mind these days, so I apologise in advance if she's rude."

"She doesn't look eighty-three. She looks strong. Her eyes are very beautiful."

"She was a famous TV actress once. She was known as *The Girl with the Corn Flower Eyes*. Getting older is particularly hard for her because she was considered so good-looking."

Su-Su was flattered and a bit irritated that Kate spoke to her as if she was a woman from her own country. She also couldn't help noticing that Kate had perfectly ordinary light greeny-brown eyes. She wondered if it was difficult for her that her mother had the kind of eyes that would make a boatman fall into the water with admiration.

"My mother wanted to see Myanmar before it gets spoiled by tourism. She felt that she had waited too long since Ang Sang Su said that foreigners should come here. You see she was in Rangoon, I mean Yangon, as a small girl. She wanted to come back before it was too late. We went to the street where her parents used to rent a house, but there were so many new buildings there that she couldn't fit together her memories with what she was seeing. She got cross about that too."

"Yangon has changed so much in the last few years. So much foreign investment you see. Sometimes even I don't recognise the streets I know."

"Where are you from Su-Su?"

"I am from Lake Inle, where we are going. My father's family are from the tribe Intha, the lake tribe. My mother is Akha from the Highlands. It was hard for her to come and live in the middle of a lake, but she has been running the school there for many years."

Georgina walked slowly next to them as they went to the car park while Kate repeated what Su-Su had told her about herself.

Georgina listened carefully. "She's a sweet thing, isn't she? That yellow paste is unflattering to any skin except very dark black colouring. It can make a person look decidedly sallow. Don't you think? We should give her some of our sunblock."

Kate said, "Remember what I said about not saying personal remarks out loud. Try and keep them inside and then tell me later when we are alone if you really have to."

Georgina made a grunting sound.

Su-Su looked straight ahead as if she hadn't heard. This might be a very difficult couple of days. She was used to showing older people around the sites of the lake, but she wasn't used to them being so opinionated, so relaxed and intimate in the way they spoke to her even though they had just met her. She held the door of the people carrier open for Georgina and Kate and helped the older woman to get in. Su-Su noticed that the old woman accepted help from her, rather than from her daughter.

As they drove off Su-Su turned her body round from the front seat to speak to the mother and daughter. She told them that once they arrived at the lake, they would take a boat to their hotel on the other side of the lake. On the way she told them that she wanted to take them to the umbrella factory and then Indein Village of the ruined stupas.

"Oh no. I don't want to go to a factory. That doesn't sound interesting at all," the old woman said. "I'll go to see those temple things, but a factory sounds boring. We have umbrellas in our country, you see."

Su-Su had never had anyone say that to her before. Her clients usually found the idea of an umbrella factory interesting.

"It is not boring, but it is up to you. It's your holiday."

Kate smiled at her. "Perhaps we had just better go to the ruined stupas. I think that Mum might be a bit tired."

"Does she take sugar?" the mother said. Su-Su didn't understand that at all and Kate didn't seem to want to explain what her mother meant. Su-Su thought that Kate didn't want to go to the umbrella factory either and did not make any effort to persuade her mother to do so. No one had ever singled out the tour of the umbrella factory in their feedback to B & F though, had they? Perhaps everyone found it boring. It made her feel ill at ease. Su-Su liked to be excellent at her job.

To reach the ancient towers the women had to walk through an elegant white-stone covered walkway where women sold longyis and textiles, drums, plastic reclining Buddhas and tiny wooden stupas in crammed stalls. Kate's eye was caught by striped cloth with bright red, orange and blue stripes. Su-Su knew Qui the stallholder very well by now, considering she came here with tourists at least twice a week. Not so many people stopped here so Su-Su understood that it was important that she made a sale. Even so, Su-Su had to intervene when she heard Qui quoting a price that was three times the price she normally asked.

"Please, my first sale of the day. It will bring me luck if you are my first sale. Very important first sale," Qui said to Kate.

Su-Su butted in. "Don't overcharge my clients so much. It looks bad on me and then I won't want to bring them here. I will get to the temples through the other entrance. Please tone it down a bit."

"This one looks foolish. She wouldn't know a bit of cheap Thai cloth from Burmese silk."

Kate put the strip of cloth back with a polite smile. "It's very pretty but it's made of man-made cloth."

Su- Su immediately felt sorry for Qui who she knew was on her own with three young children. Her husband had gone to work in Thailand a couple of years ago and she had lost track of him.

"It's cloth that the women wrap round their heads. I'll show you how to put it on. The colours would look good on you I think."

Using the clips and pins from her own hair she gathered Kate's lion's mane into a ponytail and then twisted it to try and pin the ponytail to her head. She managed to get it to stay in some sort of shape and then wrapped the cloth around it and tied and tucked it. She then took her to the standing mirror owned by the stallholder.

Kate looked good in the head wrap. It made her look like a woman to be taken seriously. A woman with confidence and dignity.

"The Westerners usually look stupid in the head wrap, but this one looks nice. It does her a favour getting all that hair out of the way."

"I'll take it. I like it," Kate said.

She handed Qui the money.

"Show her how to tie a longyi as well. She looks like a fool walking about with it tied the wrong way. She looks like she is walking backwards, and such a big bottom. How long has she been wearing it like that for? People must have been laughing at her for days."

"Could I possibly show you how to tie a longyi? You haven't quite done it right. Would you mind if I undid it and did it up again?" Su-Su said.

Su-Su stood right in front of Kate so that no one would see her underwear, undid the skirt and did it up again.

Georgina stood and waited for them, leaning on her stick.

"All the women here looked so delicate and elegant. I fear Kate won't quite manage that. The way she eats Su-Su, you wouldn't believe it. It's as if it's her last supper every night."

"Come on Mum, you're being a bit mean. I want to buy some textiles from here."

The old woman was being mean, Su-Su thought.

"Do what you want. You always do. Su-Su, did she tell you that she is off halfway round the world on her own? Finding herself or losing herself is more like. Never mind about her children, her dog and her poor old Mum."

"I'll be back before you know it. And you have Billie living with you and you're enjoying that aren't you?"

"Yes, of course I am. Billie is a wonderful girl."

"Anyway, I take after you. You were a great traveller yourself once. much braver than me. Su-Su, my Mum, was a communist when she was young. She travelled to Potsdam in the former Eastern Europe every summer, didn't you Mum? It was a very unusual thing to do."

Su-Su wondered if she was expected to respond, then decided that she wasn't. She realised that they were performing, not for her particularly, but more for each other. She wondered what they were like when they were alone together.

Georgina's face lit up. "I'm not a member of the Communist Party anymore but I would very much call myself a Socialist."

"Mum, you're quoting Angela Davis."

"Oh, am I?"

"Yes. You know you are."

Georgina smiled again. She turned away from her daughter.

"Look Su-Su. You seem like a highly intelligent young woman. I would love to know what you really think of Aung San Suu Kyi. I've been reading *Freedom from Fear* and it seems to me that they have cobbled together some of her essays and I'm not sure you get a sense of who she is. Quite a cold fish. To be honest it's a pretty boring book, don't you think? And what about her treatment of the Rohingya Muslims in Rakhine? I mean we're just starting to hear about it in the UK. You would expect more of her somehow, wouldn't you? I mean it's something like ethnic cleansing, isn't it?"

Many of Bullscombe and Fowler's clients had *Freedom from Fear* in their bags. Some of them wanted to talk about it to her. None of them had ever criticised Aung San Suu Kyi in quite such a harsh way although a couple had spoken briefly about the Rohingya. She thought of the poster of The Lady in the bedroom she shared with her mother and how she liked to look at her calm and beautiful face each morning as she woke up.

"She inspires me in my life. It is hard to have opportunities as a woman here. My mother has worked hard as a schoolteacher all her life for very little reward. I am lucky that I will be able to see Japan in nine months and hopefully I will travel further. The feeling of being able to see the world and the world being able to see us is a new privilege and I believe that without The Lady it just would not have happened."

Georgina and Kate listened carefully.

When Su-Su had finished Georgina put her arm around her.

"I think we may have lucked out in having you as our guide. I like you, my darling. You've got some balls on you."

"Some balls?"

"Oh Mum."

Su-Su looked into Georgina's electric eyes and despite feeling a little irritated by the old woman, she couldn't help being deeply flattered by the attention from her too.

"I'll be going to Japan at some point on my trip. Let's keep in touch on Facebook and perhaps we can meet there," Kate said.

Su-Su thought that would be very exciting. To meet Kate after she had travelled to all these countries. She would be interested to hear of her adventures.

Georgina held onto her arm as they walked around the site of over a thousand-pointed towers, some golden and hitting the afternoon light, while some were run-down with tiny red bricks tumbling out from their insides onto the earth. Su-Su was glad that the old woman felt able to accept her help over the uneven ground. As they approached one of the broken-down stupas, three small children jumped out at them, screaming and laughing, making Georgina gasp and stumble, so that Su-Su had to steady her. They held out their small hands and started to chant.

"Maps for you- money please, money please, please money, money for map."

"My goodness, what beautiful, heavenly children. Do they live here?" said Georgina.

"Mum. Of course, they don't live here."

"Well, they live close by," Su-Su said, wondering why Kate had snapped at her mother over that. She pointed to some blue tarpaulin lean-tos close to the temple site.

"They spend all their day here waiting for tourists to sell their handmade maps and jumping out at them. I would tell you not to give them money directly because it only encourages their parents to send them out to beg each day, in these dirty clothes. But I set up a fund for them so that the tourists I bring here can contribute to their educational fund. Sadly, even though I paid for them to go to the local school for a month each in advance, they did not turn up except for the first few days. I should have come and made sure that they went but it is a bit far from my home to come and chaperone them each day. So, I would say that if you want to make sure, they do get food in their belly, you could give them some of your change today but buy a map. I will have to think of another way to significantly improve these children's lives so that their parents will stop relying on them to beg."

"Well, they are not strictly begging if they are selling us maps." Georgina said.

"Well, the maps are not real maps. They are not informative. They are just childish drawings," said Su-Su.

"Well, they sound jolly interesting and as real as any other map." Georgina said. "I mean, who can define what a map is? I mean, as long as it guides you in some way. As long as it symbolically describes something in relation to something else."

"Yes. I suppose you're right, Mum. Like those Pluto press maps you used to have on the wall."

"Oh, they were marvellous maps. Su-Su, you'd have loved them. They had maps that showed social injustice and inequality rather than just land, cities, roads and bodies of water. I wondered where those maps have got to. Did I throw them out?"

"Oh, I'm not sure Mum. Maybe when we did the big clear-out," Kate said.

"Oh, the big clear-out," Georgina said.

The children waited, staring at the two women talking animatedly to each other. The taller of the three jutted out her hand, close to Georgina's chest.

"Oh, goodness. Sorry children. I got carried away there."

The two women emptied their pockets of change and gave it to the children. The children gave them a scrappy hand-drawn map of the stupa site. Georgina studied the piece of paper. The kids had drawn a few spikey towers and what looked like Su-Su walking through them, in a longyi and with her hair up in a bun right on top of her head.

"Is that meant to be you Su-Su?"

Su-Su looked. "Well. I do come here most days," she said.

"Now isn't that adorably sweet? I'm going to treasure this. Much better than a boring old official map. What a talented lot," Georgina said and smiled without showing her teeth.

The children still followed them around, encouraged by Georgina's cooing over the little map, until Su-Su shooed them off and they laughed, the smallest of the boys making a raspberry fart sound at them.

Georgina made a fart sound back. This in turn rendered the children completely hysterical and Su-Su and the two tourist women walked around the site for the rest of their time there with a back and forth of rude sounds echoing around the ancient and holy stupas.

The two women were gratifyingly quiet when they saw the vast stretch of water of the lake. It was as far as the eye could see.

"My goodness," said the old woman.

Out of respect to her, Kyaw Soe the boatman, was polite to the British women. Su-Su saw Georgina's eyes sparkled when she saw how handsome Kyaw Soe was when he helped her into the narrow boat and into the low wooden seat. Georgina started to smile and looked back and forth from Su-Su to Kyaw Soe. Su-Su wished she would stop.

Kyaw-Soe carefully put a water-proof blanket over Georgina and asked Su-Su to explain that it was to protect her from the spray of the boat and that he didn't want her beautiful outfit to get wet. She pulled her long snow-white plait out from behind her in the low seat and brought it over the side of her shoulder and looked up at Kyaw Soe with the wide-eyed expression of a teenage girl. Su-Su asked Kyaw-Soe to go to the hotel via her own village.

"Mum, Mum look at that!" Kate pointed out to her mother the sight of a small black pig in a bamboo cage at the back of one of Su-Su's neighbour's houses.

"So, you live in one of these stilted houses, Su-Su? They're beautiful," Kate asked.

"I think my mother and I live in one of the most beautiful houses in the village. Kyaw Soe's father helped build it and Kyaw Soe helps maintain it."

"Who is Kyaw Soe?" said Kate.

"He is the boatman. He's a good friend of mine."

'I bloody bet he is." Said Georgina. "He's gorgeous. And I know a thing or two about gorgeous men. I've known a few in my time."

"Mum, please give it a rest," said Kate sternly.

Su-Su was thankful that Kyaw-Soe did not understand any English. The boat went past the schoolhouse and the British women smiled with delight as Su-Su called out to her mother and all the school children went to the window and waved and shouted out to Su-Su. Su-Su's Mother smiled from behind them and Su-Su felt a rush of love at the sight of the face she knew best in the world. "That's my mother."

"Hello Su-Su's Mother," shouted Georgina and waved her stick.

They passed a larger stilted building where there were ten or so tourist boats.

"That is the cheroot makers. Would you like to visit the cheroot makers?"

Georgina wrinkled up her face as if there had been a bad smell.

"I think Mum might need to get to the hotel now. I think the journey has made her very tired."

"Well, yes. I think I might be a little exhausted."

"Oh, that is a shame because we are just close by the Women's Co-operative that makes the lotus and silk cloth. I think you will find it very interesting."

Kate turned in her low wooden seat to look at her mother. "Oh Mum, I would love to see the weavers. Are you too tired? We can go right back to the hotel and visit tomorrow if you would like."

"Oh, come on then, let's see it. I'm interested in any kind of Women's Co-cooperative."

As Su-Su came off the boat a dozen of the weaving women stopped working on their looms and came to greet her and hug her. In a few days' time she would make a visit on her own to the weavers and tell them about the trip to Japan and ask them what they thought she should include in her speech, what cloth samples she should take and what images they thought were best. She wanted to reassure them that she would emphasise the spiritual significance of this, the most sacred of cloths. She wondered if a few of the older women would need to be asked permission to take photos of them at work. She hoped that they would deem her worthy of representing them.

Su-Su stood by Kate and Georgina as they watched the women painstakingly extract the individual fibres from the lotus stem with a knife and hand roll them together with water. She told them the story of Daw Sa U who first noticed the thin fibres that trailed from the stem of a pink lotus flower she had picked to offer to the temple. She was inspired to create a thread from the fibres and from those she wove the first lotus robe which she offered to a venerable Buddhist monk from Golden Peacock Hill. She continued to create lotus robes throughout her life, including small robes for the Buddha Statues at Hpaung Daw U Pagoda, the most sacred shrine on the lake.

Su-Su then walked them through the room of busy, clacking handlooms and on to the dye rooms where both strips of cloth and individual threads were being carefully dipped in brightly coloured vats. Su-Su showed them the deep coloured dyes made from jackfruit, bark, seeds and lotus leaves. Rows upon rows of brightly coloured cloth were being hung to dry from the wooden beams.

Su-Su found a lotus and silk scarf of a similar striking blue as Georgina's eyes and held it up to her face. The British women marvelled at the gossamer softness of the cloth.

"They call the pure lotus cloth the most expensive cloth in the world because it is so labour intensive. The smallest neck scarf requires about four thousand lotus stems and a large scarf requires about forty thousand thin fibres. That is what makes it so light."

Georgina picked up a bright pink and grey striped scarf and wrapped it round her daughter's neck.

"Oh, my love. That looks so beautiful on you. Just lovely. And feel how wonderful it feels on your skin." The older woman tenderly stroked her daughter's cheek with the cloth.

Kate smiled into her mother's face.

"Oh, Katey, I'd love to get that for you, darling. Is it so expensive Su-Su?"

The silk and lotus mix are not as expensive."

"Oh, but Mum, I want to buy you that blue one. It looks so lovely."

"Only if you let me buy that pink and grey one for you. I like the thought of it being with you on the rest of your travels and keeping you safe and you can use it to brighten up some of your outfits should you get asked anywhere smart."

The next day when Kyaw-Soe went to pick her up, the last of the morning mist was rising from the water and the yellow-tailed bee catchers were diving and dipping around the boat.

"I want to congratulate you on your forthcoming trip."

And then he turned on the engine before she could think what to say and instead, she turned a little away from him and admired the morning beauty of their lake. When she looked back at Kyaw-Soe he was looking out at the horizon too. He reached out with his free hand, whilst the other was guiding the motor, and took her hand. She was surprised when he pulled her much smaller hand towards him so that she was forced to stand up in the boat, the hard wooden seat pushing into the back of her thighs. It seemed entirely natural when he pulled her towards him and still guiding the boat, lent into her and kissed her with his soft lips, gently opening her mouth with his tongue.

Hey Lok, how are you? You were right about Hanoi. I didn't like nearly as much as Hoi-Chi Mien but then again, I didn't find a guide nearly as fun as you and couldn't find food nearly as delicious as your wife's so that may have affected how I felt about the city. It was also incredibly cold, everyone said that they couldn't remember it being so cold and people started street fires and all the tourists huddled around them. Myanmar is beautiful. I think you would like it. Flying into the city of Yangon from Hanoi you see so many golden stupas it is almost blinding when the evening sun hits them. My mother and I walked around the main Shwedagon Pagoda, and I saw two monks who were so handsome that British and American girls were queuing up to talk to them. This is a picture of the beautiful lake we are staying on, with the fishermen who stand on boats. I have found it quite difficult to be with my mother and am looking forward to going to India next. It's so big, I think I will stay a while. Our guide on the lake is a young woman called Su-Su and she has been so patient with us. I will keep whatsapping you from different places. Love to Da.

CALAIS CAMP
October 2016

Ranim's friend got her big bags out of the boot. Priya and Valentine walked down the sandy verge to meet them. There were dozens of men from the camps riding past on bikes, going back and forth from under the flyover, some of them stopping, balancing on their bikes and looking intently at them and at the cars.

Kate turned to the group. It already felt much more edgy than usual and they were on the outskirts of the camp. Kate tried to push down a deep sense of unease.

"So where are we going? Which contact has agreed to speak first?"

Faven told them that her contact had agreed to meet them at the mother and baby double decker bus.

"Right, I want us all to stick together. When you enter the camp from this side the French police might ask to see our passports. Sometimes they do, sometimes they don't. Has everyone got their passports or leave to remain cards?

Kate felt hers in the inner pocket of her jacket. Kate walked out in front with Priya as they went under the bridge, trying to avoid the puddles of murky water. Valentine started to take photos of the graffiti there. Kate noticed over the love hearts and flowers, and messages of hope painted no doubt, by the many British volunteers, there were big blood red letters saying *Fuck Off Journalists! Don't make money from our pain.* There were dozens of black armoured police vehicles parked randomly on the sandy wasteland, but the French police waved them through without interest. The group started to pick through the first wave of small, battered camping tents, where men sat on upturned buckets. A young British man was playing guitar and singing Cat Steven's Moonshadow to no one in particular. Ramin lifted her skirt to avoid the dark streams and patches of pink and white tissue paper next to clumps of matted seagrass. Katherine knew from her last visit that this was the least safe area, occupied by single men, who were a distance away from their national groupings of caravans and tents.

Priya turned to her and said, "I'm sorry if it seems a facile thing to say and please don't repeat this to anyone but it feels like the end of a hardcore, young music festival like Reading or something. All these broken tents and the smell of piss and shit and people aimlessly stumbling about."

"Yes, it is a facile comment," Kate said. "But I do know what you mean. Perhaps it would be a good way to describe it to your readers as long as you do it in the right way."

Kate turned back to Ranim and saw that she was walking with Faven rather than her friend. Still walking Kate shouted back at her,

"Where's your friend?"

"Oh. She's waiting by the car so she can have some help with the bags. Someone will carry them to the Syrian area. She has a bad back. It would not be possible for her to do it alone." Kate felt irritated. She was responsible for the safety of the interpreters and the journalists, so she felt it was a bit much to expect her to have to keep track of Ranim's silent friend as well.

On the journey the friend had smiled sweetly and distributed some delicious Syrian pistachio biscuits from a large Tupperware dish and then pulled her hijab over her head to get some sleep. Priya, Ranim and Kate had chatted together while Faven had her headphones on.

"Hey Kate, your year off sounds amazing. Travelling on your own like that. I'd love to be brave enough," Priya said.

Kate saw Ranim had turned her head and pointedly looked out of the window from the passenger seat. Ranim had been forced to leave her beloved country of Syria and travel through a great many countries and continents for her and her children's survival. Kate understood that she would not want to hear about Kate's sabbatical, particularly not today.

"Let's meet for a coffee to have a talk about it," Kate said.

Ranim then picked up from the awkward pause in the conversation to tell them proudly about her daughter who had just started her physics degree at Oxford. "I felt my heart would explode when my husband and I took her to Oxford University, two weeks ago. I have fought Assad for women's education and then to see my girl at Oxford. It is a very great thing for me." Ranim wept again, this time for joy. She used the corner of her hijab to wipe her tears. Kate squeezed her arm.

"I'm amazed I managed to get them to agree to let me cover this." Priya said.

"It does seem rather incredible. Thanks for making this happen." Kate said. Priya smiled and nodded to both her and Ranim in the front.

Kate realised that she had forgotten Ranim's friend's name. She asked Faven and Priya if they had caught it.

'No, sorry." Priya said. Faven shook her head. Kate shouted back at Ranim, "Can your friend please join us after she's dropped the bags off? I'd rather we all moved together today. We don't know what's going to happen or what it's going to be like today. I'm responsible for everyone here and I would rather know exactly where everyone is."

"Well, I'll try and get hold of her to get her to meet us, but I think she is very OK in the Syrian area. She has been here three or four times before. She knows her way around."

"Please. I want her with us."

French police and men in orange visibility jackets had already started to dismantle some of the makeshift food distribution constructions with big blunt hammers, ostentatiously smashing and then pulling and ripping away small planks of wood and tarpaulins. On a steep row of sand dunes behind the food distribution area men had climbed and gathered, waving flags made from rags bound together, flying kites made from sticks and plastic bags and shouting down at the police. Valentine looked warily at the rag-tail army of men and pulled his equipment closer to his body.

Most of the shacks that had not yet been set upon had large notices on them saying *Pour La Demolition.* Outside the Kids Café a group of teenagers loitered around. They stood in front of the group and started to talk very fast asking for help.

"Please, you must sponsor us to come to the UK. Please, my parents are in the UK."

"Please, money for food. We are hungry."
"Please, you must help me find my family."
"Kind women, please take us with you in your car."
Kate could see from their eyes that they were high. She didn't think that Ranim had noticed this. Ranim started to talk to the Syrian teenagers and then told the rest of the group what they had said.

"They are confused and frightened. They have been told to register with the French government officials here and get on buses to go to holding centres. They think that they should try and register as unaccompanied minors with the British Authorities, but most of them don't think they could not get away with that. There are such long queues to do both things that they are just waiting around here until they have more information, from someone about the best thing to do. Then they will start queuing, but they are not sure where they should queue. If the French pick them up, they are not sure where they will be taken."

Valentine suddenly swung his camera round to the teenagers and started to take photos of them. One of them spat towards him; another told him to fuck off with a perfect English accent, and the rest quickly turned their backs on him.

"Please Valentine. You cannot take photos without permission. The situation here is very inflammatory. Can't you feel it?" Kate said.

Valentine laughed a little to himself. "I've been in much more inflammatory situations than this."

"So, you keep saying."

"I'm sorry, what did you just say to me?"

Kate pretended she hadn't heard him and walked away in front of the group.

When they arrived at the Mother and Baby bus, the Eritrean mother they were going to interview was nowhere to be seen. Faven looked at her phone.

"She says she is sorry, but she had to attend an emergency UK home office meeting at the official mother and baby unit. Shall I go there and see what's happening?" Faven said.

Kate's director had told her about the UK Border Agency mother and baby meeting which she in turn had been informed about by an NGO on the ground at Calais. Her boss had thought that it might be useful to find out what was going on.

"Last time you were here, they let you in there didn't they? That's what Juliet said anyway." Kate said to Faven.

"Yes, the French guards let me in without any questions. They just presumed that I was part of the camp."

Priya looked at her phone.

"I really think we have to get on with the interviews. I certainly don't want to be here later than four. It feels quite menacing already." Kate turned to Ranim. "Right, let's go to the Syrian family area."

Faven started to walk off without saying anything, so Kate ran after her and took her arm. "Please Faven I was given strict instructions by Juliet to keep everyone together."

"I counted in the car. This is about the tenth time I have been here. It's OK. If you want me to try and get this interview, I think I should go. We haven't got that much time. The journalist woman has already said that she wants to leave in a couple of hours."

"Well, for God's sake keep your phone on. How much charge have you got?"

"Enough charge."

"Go straight to the official mother and baby unit please. Don't go to the Eritrean section."

"OK." Faven gave her a sulky look.

"Do you promise?"

"I promise."

Kate knew that Faven had a crush on a boy her age who had been in the Eritrean section for at least six months. Ranim had told her.

"It's much more dangerous today than it has ever been. Please keep in constant contact. After we have spoken to the Syrian women, we will come to you at the UK Border Agency mother and baby place. Go straight there and wait for us to come to you. Don't come out of there and wander around and try to find us please."

Before she went into one of the Syrian caravans, Ranim turned to the photographer and said firmly, "Please don't come anywhere near. Step away and move back. Priya, you can come in but please remove your shoes."

Kate had been to visit this family when she came a month before, sitting in the small but immaculate Eighties caravan that had been donated by a British church group. The mother had described how on the boats in the Mediterranean they had written things on their bodies with the ballpoint pens they had passed around because they were so sure that they were going to die in the sea and wanted people to know who they were. "I wrote on my child's arm. *My name is Bana I am 11. I died trying to escape from war. Please bury me with my family. My mother's name is Ghassan Awwad.*" Then the woman had written her own name and that of her children and husband on her own arm.

Kate and Valentine stood awkwardly together. Valentine absent-mindedly took shots of the battered caravans. "So how many people do you think are here?" he asked Kate.

"About eight or nine thousand, I think."

"All trying to get to Britain by jumping on lorries and breaking into cars? It used to be trains, didn't it?"

Kate didn't like the way he spoke about it. She didn't like the way he spoke about anything. "Yes, and then those big fences were built to make it very hard to jump on the trains. People come here and ask for money and put people into the back of lorries.People are now being forced to come in dingeys across the channel."

"Do you know people who have come over to the UK from here?"

"Of course, I do. I work for a refugee organisation."

"I suppose you think they should all be allowed into Britain. Open borders sort of thing."

She looked at this tall, rangy man with his hands in his pockets and his glib way of speaking and wondered if she had ever disliked someone as much.

"I'm not sure what I think, but I do think that Britain should look to itself and its own history. Britain cannot involve itself in a war in Syria and then be surprised when Syrians try to come to Britain. The ones that come here are the ones that can afford to pay passage across the deserts and on the seas. They come to try and escape imprisonment, oppression and the death of their families to a country which has always sold itself as the absolute bastion of civilised democracy and justice. So why are you surprised that people try to come to the UK?"

Valentine swept his hand across the skyline.

"And all these other people? All these men lurking around and sleeping in tents. Are they all from wars that Britain participated in?"

"Many of these people have links to Britain because of Britain's colonialism and involvement in wars or in border decisions. Many of these people have close relatives in the UK or communities they are connected to in the UK. They want to be with them, just like you would want to be with your family and friends if there was a crisis in the UK that meant that you couldn't work there or were at risk."

"What about all the Eritreans here? Can they really say that Eritrea was so affected by Britain?"

'Well, didn't Britain make all sorts of problems by stripping it of assets when it took over after defeating Italy. I think it made a bad border between Ethiopia and Eritrea, or was it Sudan?"

Shit. Kate couldn't exactly remember the details of the British involvement in Eritrea and slightly stumbled on her words. She often felt she let herself down with the details of things, forgetting the exact history and facts she needed in arguments with people like Valentine. She wished she had mugged up on all the different nationalities in the Calais camp before she came. Valentine smiled to himself.

"It's just that there seems to be so many of them. Too many for us to take in," Valentine said.

"Well, Britain doesn't take that many refugees. Last year we took far less than Germany, Hungary, Sweden and France."

Valentine raised his eyebrows.

"You do realise that you can't claim asylum unless you are physically present in the UK? It's not possible to apply from outside? That's why people are forced to risk so much."

Valentine shrugged his shoulders. The women came out of the caravan.

Priya didn't look happy.

"Look, I don't want to be here longer than I have to. The woman I have just interviewed had a very sad story about travelling overland with her kids and being pregnant, but we need something a bit more… I don't know, a bit more shocking if you know what I mean? For *Daily World* readers. If we are going to get them interested."

Ranim looked at Kate with widened eyes. Kate blinked heavily back at her. Today was turning out to be more difficult than she had imagined.

THE BOGUS CROCODILE
March 2015

Somehow the local newspaper photographer had caught the most heightened moment of his mother's anguish. Her mouth was open mid-howl, hair wild around her shoulders, her arms thrown upwards and her red and gold sari slipping from her shoulders. She was trying to throw her small body between the two yellow bulldozers, the thugs with sledgehammers and her beloved home and little clothes shop. This is where Vinod's mother sat at the front each day with her sewing machine making the dresses, baggy trousers and skirts the foreign girls loved so much. If the photograph had not featured Vinny's own mother and he and his brother and father trying desperately to hold her back, he would have said it was an excellent photo, of unusually good composition, worthy of *Time* magazine or *National Geographic* rather than the local Hespot newspaper.

It was only a month ago that the corrupt local government had sent their heavies to come and smash up his family home and shop on what they called 'The Other Side of The River' of Hampi. They were given just twenty-four hours to remove their possessions and their stock. Then they came with the two bulldozers and flattened the place as well as the 'Hidden' guesthouse further along the bank owned by Mitti, the German. When Vinny screamed at them to stop, shouted that they owned the land on which the house was built and so they had no right, no right at all, they pushed him aside and said that he had no licence for the clothes shop and so there were orders to put a stop to the family's activities once and for all.

"What?" cried Vinny. "Stop our family activities? Is that what you want? To not just stop us making a living but to stop us living? To kill us." His mother fell on her knees and begged for mercy.

The men did not listen to him telling them that they had applied for a merchant's licence at the same time each year but that this year it had been refused.

Vinny was convinced that the refusal had been a mistake and so he had gone to the government offices with an envelope stuffed full of twenty thousand rupees and waited for seven hours to be granted permission to go into the office of the local government officer who dealt with trade in Karnataka.

A plump man, with a long-pointed nose and a thin moustache that looked like he had drawn it on with kohl that morning, was sitting behind a cluttered desk and barely looked up as Vinny sat down opposite him. Instead, he continued to peer at the large, square, old-fashioned computer on his desk, hitting the keys in a random and overly loud manner. Behind him was a tatty map of Karnataka. Vinny couldn't help noticing that his white shirt had the biggest sweat circles below the armpits that Vinny had ever seen. They were ridiculous. Vinny was absolutely disgusted to see his hairy nipples through the wet, see-through cloth. One of the nipples seemed to have a double head on it. How was it possible that this disgusting pig of a man had authority over his family's future?

Vinny pushed the envelope towards him and asked about the merchant's licence. The man laughed when he opened the envelope.

"You know how much your land is worth now? Hampi is one of the most popular tourist sites in the whole of India these days. And that's saying something. Do you think you can hold onto your little home and your little shop with an envelope of money? How terribly, terribly naive you are."

Vinny looked at him and thought that he would be content to spend the rest of his life in prison just to pick up the heavy bronze statue of Lord Hanuman on the desk and smash him hard and repeatedly in his face. "That land has been in my family for many generations. We have always had a shop next to our home. You can't just decide not to give us our merchant's licence."

The man suddenly looked angry. Vinod could see that he was one of those noughts to one hundred angry guys. One minute his face was calm and the next minute, his eyes were popping out, and white balls of spit were flying from his mouth. He looked like Vinny's old

Headmaster, Mr Singh, who would fly into rages for no apparent reason, slapping the heads of passing boys just for looking at him.

The man threw the envelope back over his desk at Vinny. "Who are you to tell me what I can and can't do? You're just one of those Hampi playboys. Look at you in your denims hanging down and showing your behind and all that. The things that I hear go on in Hampi with Western women are immoral, against the whole principle of Hinduism and against what makes India the truly great nation it is."

More balls of frothy spittle flew out of his mouth and landed on the pile of papers in front of him.

"I hear that these women allow you to do all things to them. Anal sex and everything. They will suck your penis if you ask. Is that what you ask of them? Do you stick your penis up women's arses and into their mouths?"

The man was obviously a raging pervert. A bloated, ugly wanker. Literally.

"I am the son of a family that has always worked hard, and who has never avoided the law, or not paid tax."

"Isn't your mother a Vaishyas and your father a Rajanya? That's what it says on your papers. That makes you a half caste, doesn't it?"

Vinny wondered if it was written on his family files. When he had graduated from high school, they had put his mother's caste on top of his graduation papers, to prohibit him from applying for certain jobs. His father's family had still not accepted his mother, despite her bringing up two boys and working hard all her life. Vinny had barely met his father's family in the North, and he didn't really care to. How could anyone not love his beautiful, kind and funny mother? He hoped one day to meet someone with as much love in her heart as she had.

Vinny picked up the envelope and got up and left because he didn't trust himself in the same room as this arsehole. He found that he had bitten the inside of his cheeks so hard to stop himself from doing or saying anything that would jeopardise the family and he had the strong, metallic taste of blood in his mouth.

"Oh, by the way. That map behind you of Karnataka. You've got the temples of Hampi the wrong way round. The Virupaksha temple is where the Shree Vijaya Vitthala temple should be and vice-versa."

"Oh, don't be stupid. Of course it's not wrong. As if I am going to listen to the likes of you."

"It's not me sitting in front of a map that's got the most important temples in the region mixed up. If I were you, I would get it checked out. That's an incorrect map."

Vinny wept as he and his brother and three or four of his close friends tried to clear the site of rubble and put it in big bags to take down and empty in the reservoir. He felt as if he had not protected his mother, and that he had failed as an older brother and as a son to his father. While his father tried to get his mother to have some Chai and to stop crying and clawing her own face, the boys cleared the spot where the house and shop once stood. He was careful to take photos of the debris so there was evidence of the terrible act of injustice and violence to his family. There were lumps with purple plaster on one side from the bedroom he had lived in with Fiona, his Australian girlfriend. Photos of him with his friends that had been pinned on his walls were now lying on the ground ripped and covered in dust. He picked out a photo of himself as a young child, his eyes and eyebrows carefully outlined in kohl, a bindi painted on his forehead, dressed for some reason in some mini dictator's khaki uniform, along with fake felt medals across his chest. A tiny despot. What was his mother thinking? Why was dressing your child like a military dictator even a thing? He would have to ask her another time. Fiona had decided on the bright purple colour and at that point he would do pretty much anything she wanted. It was hard to believe that the room in which he had spent so much time making fast and furious and slow and sensuous love to Fiona had been so quickly and maliciously destroyed. He blamed Fiona for his bad luck. She had kicked it off by leaving him for an (apparently) famous French climber.

When Jay first arrived with three huge canvas bags in an auto that was leaning over with the weight of them Vinny didn't know what they were.

"These are for you, Bro."

"What are they? Elephant condoms?" Jay smiled.

"Tents, man. These are huge army tents. I got them from my cousin in Hospet who supplies them. I thought that you could still continue to trade and if they come and try and knock it down it doesn't really matter."

"That's genius Jay," said Vinny,

"That's right, man. I'm a bit of a genius."

"How much do I owe you?"

"Oh nothing. Just don't go for any of the girls I go for this season. Not even if they have perfect tits, a big round arse and long, long, hair. Promise?"

"I promise Bro," Vinny laughed.

"You know they always prefer you. So, don't even look at them, OK?"

"OK, I promise, Bro. What else can I say?" Vinny put his arm around Jay's neck and pulled him towards him for a tight embrace and much slapping of backs.

They spent the whole afternoon putting up the tents and going to his uncles and getting the clothes racks and putting his mother's beautifully made garments back on display with a big sign over the front with his mother's name – *Aditi*. When they showed their mother the tent she cried even more and could not speak and just touched the faces of her sons, while she pushed the corner of her sari into her mouth to stop herself sobbing. His father led her away and said that he did not feel she was able to start making and selling her clothes so soon. Give her a few days and make sure that he had a chance to at least get her to eat some dahl and rice and build her strength up from the shock.

Vinny and his brother and friends decided that the way they could cheer her up was to make some sales with existing stock so that at least she would feel that there was hope of recovery. The boys sat down on little chairs by the roadside and smoked beedis - all except Vinny - and admired their work.

A big crowd of sexy Israeli girls came walking down the road.

"Come on girls. Looking is free. Come and have a look at these beautiful clothes made by Vinny's mother. These are hot clothes and you are hot girls. It's a match made in paradise."

Jay high fived Vinod when the girls started giggling and came over the dust road and into the tent shop.

"Hey, this shop is great. I like it. It feels like Bedouin tent. It's really cool," said one of the girls. She had pale long legs, red hair and a bright green tunic.

"I think this dress would look perfect on you." Jay held a long turquoise dress with red flowers up to a small girl with brown skin and blonde curly hair. She laughed shyly and put the dress on over her T-shirts and shorts. Vinny held the long mirror up to her.

"I think you look beautiful," he said and flashed what he knew to be a dazzling smile - he was often complimented on the perfectness of his teeth, and he would inwardly thank his mother once again for brushing them with charcoal when he was a child.

Jay interrupted. "Hey, man, are you breaking your promise already?"

The three Israeli girls bought a dress, a top and four pairs of baggy trousers between them and Jay arranged to take them to the reservoir later that afternoon. For the first time in the ten days since the demolition Vinny felt the dark cloud that had gathered around his mind and heart lift a little and the sick feeling ease from his stomach.

As the girls left with their bags full of his mother's handiwork and started walking down the track to the river crossing, Sindura drove past. There was an older woman on the back of his motorbike. Vinny noticed that she was holding him round the waist and not by the shoulders. Sin stopped his bike. The woman got off. She was wearing an orange dress with leggings. She had on a black scarf, which she had wrapped around her head and shoulders.

Sin looked at the tent and sauntered in. "It was bad luck what happened to your house." Sin could not help smiling a little when he said this.

"Those bastards are trying to get us to move out. They want to build fancy hotels on our land. These tents are good. The German should use tents in his hostel instead of rebuilding the huts. He's going to rebuild with bamboo, but maybe this is even better."

Vinny and Sin had long been rivals. Sin was the best-looking boy in Hampi, but Vinny felt that he was more of a gentleman and besides Vinny didn't smoke weed or drink and that sometimes gave him the edge. When Sin was stoned, he behaved like an idiot around the foreign girls, over the top sexually and swaggeringly arrogant, sometimes grabbing the girls and making them angry. Vinny prided himself on always keeping his wits about him. If you came on too strong you never knew what later accusation you might face.

Sin had once put his hand down on the floor cushion and squeezed Fiona's arse as she sat down. Fiona told Vinny and he had immediately left Fiona in their purple bedroom and confronted Sin when he was sitting gambling with his friends at the Lotus Oasis bar. Sin had laughed at him and told him that Fiona would leave him soon, anyway. That he was a fool to give his heart to her. That all foreign girls leave and go back home and that it was only the stupidest Indian boy that would fall in love with the foreign girls.

When Fiona did leave him, Sin went out of his way to tell him that he thought it was good for him that this had happened, and that it would toughen him up for the world. Vinny felt like he was walking around with a gaping wound where his heart should be.

Raj spoke to Sin in Hindi. "Are you fucking a Granny now Sin? We saw the way she was holding you on the bike."

"No. As you know I get the first pick of girls. I might be able to get some money out of this one though. You know how desperate these old women are. And I've seen pictures of her daughter. She is gorgeous. I might ask her to get her to come out to Hampi."

"Yes, and these older women have loads of money to splash around."

"And this one has no husband. She's divorced."

"Great. How old is she?" said Raj.

"Fifty-two."

"She looks OK for that age. My mother is a year younger than her."

"Well, these Western women have easier lives than Indian women. They don't have to carry heavy things, and they do exercise classes to keep themselves in shape and very little else. And Western women this age will do absolutely anything for a young cock."

"Young Indian cock," Raj laughed.

The woman was looking at some tops made by his mother. She looked up at Raj and Sin and frowned.

"She doesn't understand Hindi, does she?"

"No, of course not."

She walked past them still looking a little angry and then crossed the road and stood in the full sun on the other side of the bike, rather than on the shady side near them.

"Oh no, look, Mummy's cross with you," said Raj. "Careful, your British Passport might get warped in the sun,' Jay said.

'Where's she staying?' Vinny asked.

"Well, she was staying in my brother's guest house. I've just taken her for a day round the temples," said Sin.

"What's a woman of that age doing staying on this side of the river in the first place?"

"I think she's a bit crazy to be honest. She's travelling around on her own all over the place. She's got a son our age and a daughter a bit younger. I wouldn't let my mother go around the world on her own. It's wrong if you ask me. She's asking for trouble."

"Where's she from?"

"UK. London."

"Oh, British girls are all a bit mad. And London girls are even madder."

"Mad about sex, you mean?" They all laughed.

The woman shouted out. "Sin, would you mind taking me back to the hostel?"

"Naughty, naughty. She's bought you for the day. You've got to get on with servicing her."

"You never know. I might do just that."

Sin swaggered over to her, flicking his long, black, shiny hair.

Vinny saw her again the following evening sitting on her own on Sunset Rock. Sin was sitting in the middle of a group of Spanish girls. He was doing his special party trick. Vinny had seen him do it many times before. He would manage to control the girls' fingers and made them 'play guitar' by tapping the sensitive part of their arm on their elbow crease. Many of the Hampi playboys had a touch trick that meant that they could lay their hands on western girls and hopefully turn them on a little in doing so. Vinny was highly skilled at body massage and a couple of times he had done little more than give a truly excellent shoulder massage and a Western girl had agreed to go to bed with him.

He sat himself down next to the older woman. "Do you mind if I join you?"

She looked at him a little warily. "Alright."

"Have you seen the sunset from here?"

"No, this is the first time."

"What more could you want out of life? Beautiful view of the golden boulders and temples of Hampi, me by your side and great music." And he laughed the naughty loud laugh that all the Western girls seemed to find so charming and funny. It didn't work on her.

"I don't like this music at all. It's awful. I know all these Israelis have just come out of the army and want to be stoned out of their minds to forget the horrors they've inflicted on Gaza and play the drums but the 'Theme from Mash' and 'Hotel California'. I mean, really?"

"What kind of music do you like?"

"Good music. Not this music. I want to hear Indian music."

Vinny couldn't help laughing. "Ha ha, we have to hear the same crap night after night and have to pretend we like it, and you're complaining about one night?"

"Why do you have to pretend?"

"Well, because we have to keep the Israelis happy. Most of the tourists who come to the other side of the river are Israeli."

She turned to him and they looked at the sunset together. She didn't take photos like everyone else.

"What's your name?"

"Kate."

"Kate, let's go and get something to eat at my uncle's place."

"I am really hungry."

"What do you like to eat?"

"I'm a bit obsessed with Palak Paneer at the moment."

Vinny smiled at her and gave her his hand so that she could climb down the rock.

"My uncle is great at Palak Paneer."

"I love it when the spinach sauce is really bright green. Not dark army green. Do you know what I mean?"

"Yes, I know exactly what you mean. You want it fresh and tangy, in contrast to the creamy paneer."

When Kate got off the back of his motorbike, he allowed his hand to rest on the small of her back. She did not appear to mind, or perhaps she didn't notice.

"Didn't I see you in the shop made from canvas?"

"Yes, that is my family shop."

"The clothes you sell are beautiful. Really nice. Really different from everywhere else in Hampi and so beautifully made."

"That's my mother. She's fantastic at designing as well as making the clothes. She's talented."

She ordered her Palak. She smiled and thanked Vinny's uncle. Vinny's uncle looked slightly warily back and forth between them but thankfully didn't make any comment.

Kate went on. "Sin said that your family house and shop were demolished by the authorities recently." Something about Sin telling her upset him. It made him feel as if people were talking about him.

"Yes, three weeks ago, they came and smashed it down."

He took the newspaper photograph of his wailing mother being held back by the men of the family out of his wallet. He unfolded it and gave it to her. She studied it carefully.

"That must feel terrible, Vinny. I suppose it's corruption. Some big shot has got his eye on your land?"

"Yes, yes. It's some fucking Government backed arseholes. A few years ago, they came and smashed down all the shops and houses in the Bazaar on the other side of the river, because they wanted to protect the religious sites. I can understand that more. But to come to this side of the river and start attacking us. I think my mother has had a nervous breakdown. She still cannot sleep, cannot eat. She cries all the time. She has no home. Those tents are good to serve as a temporary shop, but we cannot live there. She stays here, in this guesthouse, but she does not like it, even though her brother and his wife are being very kind. I'm thinking that I must open another guesthouse and restaurant somewhere like Kodaikanal. Find somewhere where they will not smash it down. I have a friend who wants me to go into business with him up there. He says that there are not enough guesthouses and so many Israelis go there. I need to expand so that we don't have all our concerns in Hampi."

"Kodaikanal? In Tamil Nadu? I was hoping to get there at some point on my trip."

He looked at her eating her Palak. He had just ordered dahl and rice. He couldn't help noticing how greedily and quickly she stuffed the chapatti in her mouth with the bright green sauce on it. It wasn't very ladylike. Was she hinting that they should go together? It would be good for him to do a recce to Kodi to see if the place was really the goldmine his friend had said. Perhaps this woman would pay for his train and bus fare and for hotel rooms. He thought that perhaps sex with her wouldn't be too bad. Older women knew things that younger women don't. Maybe he would take his karma sutra cards with him. She probably didn't get much sex in the UK because of her age. She would be grateful. He felt himself get semi-hard and shifted in his seat. Western women didn't give a shit about caste. In fact, they just didn't understand it and even if they did, they would probably not give a shit about it. She looked at him moving about in his seat for a moment and then cleaned the plate with the last of the chapatti.

"When were you thinking of going to Kodi?" he said,

"After this. After Hampi. I think you get a train to Bangalore and then a bus. I've been looking it up. I would love to see the mountains there."

"Have you ever taken a train in India before?"

"No, not yet."

"Maybe it would be good if we went together. I think Western women can find travelling by train difficult."

"Oh, I think I'll be alright."

"Look I do need to go there, and it would definitely be easier for you if I was there to accompany you."

"I suppose it might be good if the first time I took the India railway, I had someone who knows what they are doing."

"Well, Indian railways are a mystery unto themselves. No one really knows what's going on. But it might be better not knowing what the fuck is going on together," he laughed.

She smiled. "OK, but I would like to make it clear, as I did to Sin, that I am not travelling looking for sex. I can get it at home and no offence but if I was going to go on some middle-aged sex tourism holiday, I don't think I'd come to India."

Now he was insulted. "Why wouldn't you come to India if you wanted some sex? We know things here that Western men don't know. Indian men are very sensual, you know. Let me massage your back now and I'll show you. I know the seven-chakra points. Lots of Western women come to India for yogic influenced sex. I've had many women, from Sweden, Japan, France, Italy."

She rolled her eyes. "Do you know how many men have offered me massages since I've been in India? Every hostel owner, every IT manager from Bangalore whose wife is still sleeping in their hotel room, every hostel manager, motorbike guy and every tuk-tuk driver."

'We don't say tuk-tuk in India. We say auto."

"Ok, every auto driver then."

"Well, I noticed that when you walk your bum goes badonkadonk. I know you're trying to dress all modest and Indian style, but you can't hide your sticking out arse that easily."

She looked him in the eyes. "Shut up Vinny, otherwise I'm not going anywhere with you. I think I'm going back to my room to read my book. You're getting carried away, mate. You should think about how you talk to me."

She left the money for her meal on the table and walked out. Vinny wasn't sure what had got into him. He hadn't played that well at all. His uncle and his kitchen workers laughed at him from across the room.

"Oh dear. The famous charm didn't work so well that time. Auntie told you where to get off."

"Give me time uncle, give me time."

The next morning, he was at her guest house at nine. He had left his brother at the tent shop and told him to earn his keep and make some bloody sales for once. He asked the hostel manager, who was not a local man, if Kate had risen.

"Why should I tell you? Another guy just like you came by and asked the same thing."

"Who was it?"

"It was that good-looking guy with the long hair that all the girls go for."

Fucking Sin. He had to get Kate out of here and up to Kodi and away from Sin and his big muscles and six pack and his shiny thick hair. He had to show Sin that this time he wouldn't win. This older woman had taste. She wouldn't fall for Sin. He gathered from the way the man was speaking that Kate was still in her room. He was the kind of man who would have taken pleasure in telling Vin that Sin had gone off with her on his motorbike.

He only had to wait about ten minutes when she appeared looking sleepy with messed up hair in a blue tunic and her usual black leggings. She smiled sweetly when she saw him. She did not seem to still be angry with him.

"Oh, hello Vinny. I'm going to have some breakfast. Want to join me?"

He did not want to appear to be too much on the make, so he refused any breakfast and just had a juice. The manager frowned at him as he took his order of fresh mango juice with just a little lime.

"So, I had a good look, and we can get a train from Hospet to Bangalore and then a bus to Kodi. I think we should have a couple of nights in Bangalore before we get the ten-hour bus to Kodi. I would be glad to have you both on the bus and the train." She appeared to have forgiven him.

"I am going through a difficult time with the demolition. I'm quite depressed by it, the truth be told. It's affecting my purse and my mojo, and I'm worried about my mother."

"Don't worry I'll pay. I'm sure your mojo will recover but I'll reiterate that I don't need to bribe someone to have sex with me. It's a real turn off that I might have to employ some sort of financial transaction to achieve that. Call me old-fashioned but I would like to think that someone would be genuinely attracted to me."

Oh, it seemed she was going on once more about not wanting to have sex with him. He hoped she wouldn't go on like this the whole time they were together otherwise it would be very dull to travel with her.

"I'll book it all online if that's OK with you."

"No, no, it's best to book with one of the travel agents here. That way you are supporting the community here, not some travel app."

"OK, but I'm warning you that I have looked up the prices. I'm not going to pay some big markup."

"I'll book the tickets. They won't try and rip me off."

"OK, but check with me first."

"Let me go and talk to them. I'll come back to you with the prices. OK?"

"I'd like to leave as soon as possible. Tomorrow or the next day. Does that give you time to set things up with your friend in Kodaikanal?"

She knew her prices all right. When he tried to get a bit of a markup for the agent and himself, she said, "Leave it," and that she would use her travel app on her iPad. "Look, Kate, I don't see how an app can possibly know the timetables if the locals don't."

"OK, but let me come with you to the agents."

Much to his irritation Kate spent a good deal of time with the agents booking both the train ticket and the coach ticket. She told them that she had already booked a guesthouse in Bangalore that someone she had met had recommended. Adesh and Ganga had seen it all before. British women with their iPad showing them their fucking life's job. In the end pride overtook them and they found her prices for A/C two top bunks facing each other for less than her stupid app said.

"Are you going with Vinny? He'll look after you." He spoke in Hindi to Vinny. "I've given her a price less than the fucking travel app, but we have still made money. The travel app has tourist class prices but of course we haven't sold her tourist class. You understand? She will be travelling with you, so it won't really be tourist class. She will be travelling local but protected by you. Ok? I can bung you a little for bringing her to me."

Kate and Vinny spent a pleasant day at the reservoir. They both jumped off the boulders into the cool, clear water and watched the boatman in the conical boat hassling a group of tourists to take a trip across the water. They both laughed at a 'Beware of The Crocodile' sign - its smiling bright green croc with a swishing tail, bright red mouth and wide orange eyes. Vinny told Kate that it was put up to stop the locals swimming in the reservoir. Kate told Vinny that when she had been to OM beach, a policeman had stood by the edge of the sea and shouted dire warnings to anyone who tried to swim in it. Kate had enjoyed seeing the policeman's uniforms get wet with splashing waves as they whistled furiously at the men in their underpants who she said mostly screamed with delight and terror at the edge of the waves. Kate herself was threatened with arrest for swimming across the bay. One policeman with good English guilt-tripped her when she got out of the water. "You will encourage the locals and embolden them. They will drown in the furious current because of you."

Vinny couldn't help feeling that the policeman might have a point. He could imagine that the childish men might want to impress the western woman who was so coldly ignoring them and their requests for photos to show their friends.

"Did you learn to swim in this reservoir like those kids, Vinny?"

A group of postcard selling kids were diving expertly in the water near them.

"Yes. We always came down here even though our parents feared the crocodile."

"Are you sure there isn't a crocodile?"

"Yes. Well, no one has ever seen a crocodile."

As he said that he saw her eyes widen with terror and she started to thrash, and her head seemed to be pulled under.

"Kate? Oh…Kate."

His heart was thumping wildly in his chest, and he made his terrified body tip and dive underwater to look for her. He opened his eyes in the green water and saw her pale body in its stripy swimming costume. Her head was above the water. There was no crocodile.

"Kate?" he said, gasping.

"Oh, shit. Sorry. I couldn't resist. Sorry, did you…?"

"Oh no. Not really."

He spoke. He tried to laugh his lovable laugh, but it didn't really come out right. He could not tell her how much she had frightened him. That she had tapped into his long-held fear that there actually might be a crocodile that swam its huge form underneath their legs and would come up and drag them under. He started to try and coolly swim back to the side. He didn't want to be swimming with her anymore. She made him feel unsafe and foolish.

She swam behind him. "Vinny? Oh Vinny, I'm sorry. It was stupid. And not at all funny. That's not the kind of thing I normally do. I thought you would laugh."

"So why do it fucking now then?" he heard himself say. "I don't want to come away with you if that's the kind of stunt you pull."

"I'm so sorry Vinny."

"I know you are trying to be all nice and jolly with me and all, but I would appreciate you not talking for a while. I'm pissed off with you."

"Oh, come on Vinny. I'm sorry. I've said I'm sorry. I thought you would find it funny. I misjudged it because I don't know you well enough yet."

She looked really concerned now standing on the rock, face peering towards him in her swimming costume and her long-wet hair flapping around her face.

He started to enjoy the power he had over her. He had really got her attention now. He didn't feel annoyed with her anymore, but he wasn't going to put her out of her misery quite yet. He kept it up all the way back on the motorbike. He could feel by the careful way she held on to his shoulders and not his waist that she was concerned that she had really pissed him off. He kept it up right until they were sitting by the fire that evening at 'Shanti, Shanti' café, looking out over the river. A group of chubby rich Brahmin boys from Poona were playing the tabula quite badly.

"You know those guys are really quite shit at the tabula, right?"

"No. They seem quite good to me."

He was just about to tell her that was because she knew fuck-all about Indian music when he saw Sin striding over to them with his stooges in tow.

Sin stood over them and spoke in Hindi. "What are you doing Vinny? I hear from Ganga that you are travelling to Kodi with Kate."

"That's where she's going next, and I need to go. We decided that it would be good to go together. "

"Have you had sex with her?"

"That's none of your fucking business."

"Get up."

"Why?" Vinny stopped himself gulping.

"Because I want to fucking punch you in the face. It would look bad on me to punch you in the face when you are sitting down."

"What? In front of Kate?" Vinny said.

"Get up." Sin said.

"What's going on, Vinny?" asked Kate.

'Sin is angry that I'm going to Kodi with you."

Kate got up immediately. "Sin. I wanted to go to Kodi and so did Vinny. I'm a bit nervous on my own so I thought it would be a good idea."

"Kate, sit down, would you? This is between Vinny and me."

"I'm not going to let you hurt Vinny."

Sin reached down and pulled Vinny up, but Kate held on to his arm.

"Move away from the fire, Sin. Someone is going to get seriously hurt."

"Leave us alone, Kate."

Kate suddenly shouted at both as if she was shouting at her own children. "I said, get away from the fire, Sin."

Sin suddenly turned and pushed his face up close to Kate. He loosened his grip on Vinny at the same time and Vinny stepped away. "You know fucking nothing. Who do you think you are? The Queen of Fucking England? You're lucky anyone wants to fuck you at your age, you stupid old bitch. You're welcome to each other!"

Then Sin stormed off and pushed a couple of tables over. Vinny looked over at Kate's face expecting her to look upset, but instead she just shrugged and sat down again.

"That was a bit over the top, wasn't it? Thank God we're leaving soon. Have you two ever had a fight before?"

"We don't really get on that well. We have had problems in the past."

"Well, it looks like it's a good time for me to move on anyway."

He looked at her sipping her lassi and thought that it might be more fun than he thought travelling with her.

When they arrived at 'Gita's Guesthouse' in Bangalore, they were shown a room with only a double bed.

'I did ask for two singles." Kate said.

Gita was only slightly older than Kate. She wore her grey hair in a soft bun on her head, with an elegant, beige-coloured tunic and matching trousers. She looked at them both as if there was a bad smell in the room.

"I'm afraid that this room is the only one available. I seem to remember that yours was a last-minute booking."

"I suppose we will have to take it then."

Kate smiled at Gita and both she and Vinny set their luggage down by the large turquoise double bed.

When Gita left Vinny whistled his approval. "This is nice. That old woman has taste. She told me that she was responsible for all the décor."

Vinny immediately turned on the television, found a Bollywood blockbuster from a couple of years ago, flipped off his shoes and lay on the bed with his head in his hands, face close to the television. Kate had enjoyed the train journey and told him that he had made it easy for her. She appeared to be in a well-disposed mood with him.

"OK. We've got one day in Bangalore. What do people do in Bangalore?"

"Go to the shopping mall, maybe the Botanical Gardens but I'm not really up for that."

"I really don't fancy a shopping mall much. They have them in London too. Though I heard from someone that the art museum and art school are amazing. I'll ask Gita what she recommends."

Even though the Bollywood movie had medieval scenes cut with the present day and sexy Deepika Padukone in it, Vinny could not help being irritated by the sounds of laughter from Kate and Gita from the hallway. What were they talking about for so long? Wasn't it damn rude to leave him in the bedroom for over twenty minutes while they giggled and gossiped about whatever it was that middle-aged women gossiped and giggled about? His mood darkened as he thought of his poor, good mother and the pervy local government officer. His own mother didn't have the leisure to laugh and stand around in fancy hallways like this talking about shit.

Kate burst back into the room. "Gita has asked us both to go to the antique and clothes market tomorrow and then she wanted to take us to the art museum."

"I would rather go and buy a basketball cap. I need a new baseball cap."

"Oh," she said.

"I don't think Gita wants me at the antique and clothes market or the art school."

"Well, she asked both of us," Kate said.

"Yes, but I can imagine the kind of people that go to both those places, and you have to believe it when I say, baby, they sure wouldn't like me."

"Are you happy to go and get the basketball cap on your own at the Mall?"

"Not really." Vinny had to try and stop himself putting on a cross face.

"Do you want me to come with you in the morning and then I'll go out with Gita in the afternoon?"

It humiliated him to say it, but he didn't want to be in the Garuda Mall on his own. He liked being with her. He had hoped, too, that she might buy him the cap.

"OK, then I'll tell Gita that the afternoon is best for me. Oh, and I met this great girl from Bangalore in Hampi and she has invited us to see her band play tonight. I told her we were here on Facebook."

Vinny couldn't help sneering. "Where? Where has she asked *us* to go?"

"B Flat Bar."

"I've never heard of it."

"I'd like to go."

"Well, I'm not going."

Kate just did not understand that they would not be interested in him. They would look down on him for being a Hampi Boy, for travelling with Kate, for being of a different caste. They would assume that they were having sex together. He would get judged and sneered at for sex that he was not even having.

"Vinny, I'd really like to go. I'd prefer you to come with me, but if you don't want to go, I totally understand."

"It is too dangerous for a tourist woman to go out at night."

"I'll get Gita to ring a taxi company."

He looked at Kate with her constant enthusiasm and ability to make friends and felt full of hatred for her and her privilege and wild Shiva hair and her stupid fucking lone travelling at an age when she should be looking after her grandchildren. He snatched the remote control from the bed and turned the TV up louder. He enjoyed seeing her wince at the volume of the film music.

She went into the bathroom and got ready. When she came out, she was wearing a white tunic and white leggings with gold sandals, her hair was washed and falling about her face. It made him even more determined to stop her going.

"You are going to be so out of place Kate. These gigs are full of losers with black clothes and greasy hair. Everyone will try and trick you into buying them drinks by pretending to be interested in you. Oh, we thought you were younger blah, blah, blah. Oh, how brave you are travelling alone, bollocks, bollocks, bollocks."

"Will they? That's a very telling thing to say to Vinny. Anyway, I'm going to go. I'd like you to come but seeing as you don't want to, I'm happy to go out alone."

"Why don't you just stay with me? I'll give you an all over body massage and we will take it from there."

"Oh, for fuck's sake Vinny, just let me go."

Vinny soon got tired of the film and went to have a shower in the beautiful bathroom that had gold bamboo patterns all over the walls. He had never seen a bathroom like this. He tipped the small bottle of jasmine shampoo over his body making lather form on his chest and pubic hair. He looked down at his bobbing, shining cock surrounded by bubbles and washed it carefully pulling back the foreskin. He worried that his cock would not be big enough for Kate. He then wondered why he was thinking like that. He didn't even fancy her. He loved this shower though. He didn't care that Kate had left him alone anymore. Only when he stood in this shower did his anxiety lessen a little. This shower with its little gold and turquoise mosaic pattern. He had to say, the old woman had the best possible taste. He reached out and tipped the second bottle of shower gel over his hair and face and body. The stream of water was so strong and warm, and he tilted his neck up so that he got the full force of the water and rubbed his hands over his face and his hair. He kept thinking that it was probably time to get out of the shower, but he just couldn't force himself to get his naked arse out of there. The warmth of the water was the only thing that could possibly make him feel better, could possibly restore him.

He lay on the bed in the thick white towelling robe and when he looked at the time on his phone, he saw that it was nearly ten. He had spent nearly two hours in the shower. He sent her a WhatsApp message, but she did not reply. What if something did happen to her? Would he have to be the one to tell her children? He imagined himself flying over to London to break the news and consoling her beautiful, weeping daughter. What an irresponsible woman! She was out alone in Bangalore and didn't even think to tell the only person in India that gave a little bit of a shit about her where she was. At least women in India knew their duty and were not trying to behave like young women when they were meant to be caring for both the young and old. This time he tried to phone her. She didn't answer. Well, he would try to ignore her if she was going to be like that. He flipped from channel to channel from news to film and back. He turned off the light and tried to sleep. He thought he heard her come up the stairs and his heart leapt with relief which was quickly dashed as he heard the door of another of the hotel rooms open and close. He sent her a message on Facebook though he knew that if she had not answered WhatsApp it would be very unlikely, she would be on Facebook.

He was so anxious by the time she rolled in at nearly midnight that he didn't know if he wanted her to know how worried he had been or if he wanted her to think that he didn't care about her whereabouts at all and had had a perfectly fine evening on his own. She took off her clothes in the dark and he heard the slight twang of her panty elastic and felt his cock respond a little. He could not help faking a dry little cough so she would know that he was awake but not talking to her. She got into the other side of the big double bed moving slowly and quietly as she could. She had chosen to ignore his cough. He coughed again. The sound hit the walls of the dark room and came back at them.

She sighed and spoke. "Vinny? Are you awake?"

He sat bolt upright in bed. "Of course, I'm fucking awake! Where the hell have you been? You didn't answer any of my texts. Anything could have happened. You are so naive. So, fucking naive." Wasn't that what the sweaty corrupt official had said to him.

She reached out to him in the darkness and touched his arm. She stroked it. "I'm sorry Vinny. It was a basement and my phone didn't seem to work. Once I got in the taxi then I didn't want to wake you up. But I am sorry."

"It's fucking ridiculous how inconsiderate you can be," he said.

"I know I'm sorry. But can I just say something? You're not actually my fucking mother."

"Oh yes, I am fucking am," he said.

He felt the bed shaking. He thought that she might be crying but when he heard a snort, he realised that she was laughing. As first he felt a continuation of his irritation for her and then he caught it and saw how funny it was that he was telling her off and so disapproving and how she was a mother and he just a young man and he found the laughter just exploding out of him so that the tears were soon falling down his face and dripping into his ears and he was bellowing out into her direction and the darkness of the room. "I'm your fucking mother and you should fucking listen to me!"

He got one of the fat, silk, decorative pillows that had fallen on the floor and banged her on the head with it. She scrabbled around on her side and soon they were whacking each other as hard as they could with the slippery foam squares in the dark room. It took at least ten minutes for their laughter to completely subside and allow them to settle down to start to drift off to sleep.

To everyone that has been asking separately where I am and what I'm doing, forgive this Facebook post. I know that it is the modern version of a round-robin and I know round-robins are pretty unforgivable. I am now in Hampi, or to be more exact Tungabhadra or 'the other side' as the more hippyish area is known. Last night having been to see the palaces and temples I missed the last ferry over to the 'other side'. Luckily for me there was a conical shaped basket with four men in priest-like purple robes setting off across the river and they asked me if I wanted to get in with them. So, I was in a round basket with four Hindu priests and one of them tells me that he only became a priest because a woman broke his heart and at the same time, he is rubbing my leg. The basket starts going round and round as if in a whirlpool as we were going into some tall bullrushes on the other side and I decided to jump out. So, I jumped out in some tall grass to get away from this heart-broken lovesick priest and clambered up the side to my hostel. I saw a few snakes and so by the time I got to the hostel and arrived at the low tables and floor cushions that everyone was lying around on, and I was laughing and told them what happened. No one seemed particularly interested and went back to smoking chillums and playing board games. I do love India. The picture below is looking over the river from the other side towards the temple site.

THE INTERPRETOR ON THE STAND
May 2018

Billie and Charlie looked after her with a gentleness she had never felt from them before. Her son cooked delicious meals, and she shared a big white bed with her daughter.

"Mum. Stop tossing and turning. You must go to sleep. Do you understand? Empty your mind and slip into sleep. Go to the land of nod."

That was what she used to say to her daughter when she couldn't sleep, usually on a Sunday night when she got nervous in anticipation of the start of the week. Her daughter would stroke her hair just like she used to do to her, and it made her obey. Even though her mind was racing and her heart still pumping she managed to get to sleep most of the time, just to please her daughter. There was only one night she had to slip out of the bed and pull on her heavy grey jumper and some of Jenny's wellies without waking up either Billie or Charlie. She stomped down to the estuary shoreline at dawn. At first, she just stood there with her usual protective numbness, the hem of her nighty flapping around her. She had been unnaturally calm for the last eighteen months, because she didn't want to frighten Charlie, Billie or her mother. But it rose up inside her now and she screamed as loud as she could at the muddy green water and the seagulls trying to concentrate on feeding on the sandbanks. The tide was out and she was far enough away from the beach houses to let herself shout and sob as loudly as her lungs would let her. "I can't fucking do this. For fuck's sake! This is too fucking much. Shit, fuck, help! Fucking help me, someone." Not for the first time, she realised that she didn't call out to God in a crisis. So, she noted to herself that she was the real deal. A proper Atheist.

Some of the seagulls flew off with her high-volume yelling but most of them just turned and looked at her with disapproval. She turned away from them and looked into the estuary and wondered if she could just walk into the muddy water and drown herself Virgina Woolf style. She made herself snort with laughter as she looked out and realised that the shallowness went on for at least twenty minutes. She would probably get sucked into the muddy sand, before she managed to get to the water to drown herself. She thought of the way that villains on seventies children's TV quite often used to get sucked into quicksand, often with their horses. She and her friends would play getting sucked into quicksand in the playground. It was something she had been brought up to mortally fear and so she was glad to turn around and get back to the house and slip in to bed with a sleeping Billie.

Kate sat outside the court for lunch, her heroic friend Etta as usual supplying the thick egg sandwiches, fruit and flasks of tea for anyone that might decide to visit. There was a lot of love in those egg sandwiches. Thick cob slices with a generous amount of egg and mayonnaise in between. Kate had asked people not to tell her if they were coming to court or not. It was not a fun get together and she didn't want to give people directions to the courthouse or timings of the sittings. She told them that she would be grateful for their support but that she could not be involved with any logistics. Sometimes an old friend from school, a neighbour or a parent from the kid's school would be there sitting with her family on the bench outside or on the grass. Maybe a newer friend who she had met through work decided to hop on the train from London in order to support her, even for one day. She didn't tell anyone, but it made her feel that she was a witness to her own funeral. She found it so hard to speak to anyone and so just drifted around the courtyard, where her lot tended to congregate. They were all wearing unusually formal clothing, just like a funeral. Three of her ex-bosses had stood up and talked about her qualities – reliability, good judgement and kindness while she sat mute behind piss-coloured glass, which is what she imagined they might say if she had died and they were asked to speak at her funeral.

Some of the jurors sat outside in the same paved area as her family and friends. The young red-headed woman seemed to have made friends with the short attractive woman with a brown bob. Right from the start Kate had felt that these two might be the most sympathetic to the three women. Kate's mother nudged her and said a little too loudly – "I don't think it's going to do you any harm for them to see how many friends and family you have to support you, is it?" Kate didn't know. Perhaps they would think there were too many people on her side, that it was a deliberate ploy to make them think well of her.

When the day came for the first defendant to go into the box, Kate was glad it was Ranim. Kate had always known that Ranim was exceptional but now she found out that she trained as a physicist, had worked for *The United Nations* for women's rights and indeed had been arrested and tortured by the Assad regime. Her barrister told the story of her arrest by the army and her dramatic overland escape from Syria. Ranim's beautiful, sculptured face and large brown eyes were framed by her scarf, just a hint of her shiny black hair escaping the ornately woven cloth.

The prosecution lawyer went over all the texts Ranim had made to both Kate and the mother in the days before the Calais trip. When the tall, blonde, female barrister sharply put it to Ranim that she had been planning to help smuggle her friend's child into the country for weeks and had persuaded Kate to go along with her plan, Ranim kept her head.

"Ebeid is not much of a friend. She is more of an acquaintance, but I felt sorry for her that her son was in the camp and knew that she wanted to take him over some clothes and food, just as I would wish to do in the same situation. I have been to the camp five times and each time it is not only to act as interpreter but also for humanitarian reasons. Each time it has been important to give out clothes and food for the people who live in the most terrible conditions. Anyone that goes there would find it difficult to arrive empty-handed. It would be unnatural to talk to people for the newspaper and then not give some food or clothing to ease their suffering."

"Did you tell Kate what you wanted to do over the phone and get her to agree to help you to smuggle your friend's son into the country?"

"No, I did not. I have all my family over here in this country, my husband and my children. I run my own charity here. I would never risk my own family for someone else's however sorry I might feel for them."

"Did you meet Kate in person or at her place of work and ask her if she would help you?"

"No, I did not."

"You talk about your beloved country. It must be so hard for you to settle in a country which is so different from your own?"

"No, I love this country. I love this country for offering me and my family sanctuary and indeed life itself. While I have strong sympathy for all those in the camp, be they Syrian or from anywhere that suffers war and poverty, I would never jeopardise my own beloved children and my loving husband. My daughter had just started at Oxford University when we were arrested that terrible day. She had only been there two weeks. Why would I want to do this to my daughter for the sake of someone else's child, however much I sympathised? I am also an admirer of your great and wonderful Queen."

When Ranim came to sit down next to her in the dock, she was breathing hard. Kate dared whisper. "Well, done. You did so well."

Ranim stared straight ahead.

THE BASTARD DAUGHTER OF NEFERTITI AND HOMER SIMPSON
March 2016

Gita woke up and looked at her husband's naked back. It seemed that Sanjay had thrown off his pyjama top in the night so that she had to look at this ghastly sight first thing in the morning. Even though she was somehow still in the same bed as her husband, this act of informality shocked her. She had not seen him fully undressed for several years, nor did she want to. His shoulder blades were jutting out at what seemed to her a horrifying angle. There was a sprinkling of unattractive moles and freckles and some pitting from adolescent acne. She observed that he managed somehow to be both emaciated and flabby at the same time. She turned herself away from him, preferring to stare at her gorgeous little painting of a black and red frog. She had painted that over ten years ago and not for the first time she felt a small prick of pleasure at the study of her own work. It was good. She was good. She really could paint. It was only a small painting, but it was so full of life! It looked like that little frog fellow was only still for that moment. That it was about to jump out of the frame and onto her bed.

Sanjay had returned from his latest jaunt only a month or so ago and once again offered her little explanation as to where he had been. She didn't ask because she really didn't care. She had got so used to his going off for a few months every couple of years that she found that she looked forward to it, and even pushed him to go, making the marriage even more stultifying than usual, ignoring him when he spoke or walking out of a room whenever he entered, that sort of thing. She was no longer frightened of his fits of temper either. When she was younger, he used to absolutely terrorise her and the boys with his rages, and it was impossible to predict when they might happen or what might set him off. He could be such fun, running around the house, pretending to be a bear or a lion or whatnot, and then one of the boys would jump on him too hard, or shout out with excitement too near to his ear or kick him by mistake and Sanjay would just fly into a rage. His eyes would turn black, and he would shout so loud and lash out at them and the boys would run to find her and hide between her legs. They would then all move together like a nervous, shuffling six-legged creature and go and find Sanaya working in the kitchen and hang around her asking questions about her family and the cooking and just about anything until Sanjay calmed down. Sanaya knew exactly what they were doing and would play along with it, her eyes shifting to the door every so often checking that Sanjay was not there. She needn't have worried; Sanjay would never hit them in front of the servants. That would shame him and make what he did real. He knew that Sanaya would tell all the other servants and then everyone would know what a terrible brute he was, because the servants would tell all the other servants in the big houses nearby and their employers would overhear, and everyone would talk about it at the Bangalore Club or the tennis club. For someone who had so little control over his temper it was strange how much he cared about what other people thought of him. He didn't seem to care about what she thought of him or what the boys thought of him. As soon as she stopped being afraid of his rages because she no longer loved him, he stopped losing his cool over the slightest thing. Perhaps his testosterone level had taken such a dip with age that he was no longer at the mercy of his male hormones. Perhaps because the boys were no longer there to irritate him with their noise and - she had to admit - dominance of her affections. As far as she was concerned it was obvious that the children could not survive without a mother and a grown man of course could survive without his wife. He didn't even need to ask the question that was hovering about for those early years when the boys were small; "Who do you love more Gita, the boys or me?" The answer was patently obvious for all to see.

She knew that he had spent much of this latest jaunt in a little scruffy house that used to belong to one of the farmers on their land near Ooti. So, while he was trying to be all mysterious and Jack Kerouac, black jersey rollneck, *On the Road* beatnik crap, she knew that he had done very little except play at living the simple country life in her family's estate. She knew this because one of their estate managers had rung her and told her that Sanjay had been seen wandering around in a grubby dotti, swimming in the river and trying to catch fish with a homemade rod. All very Siddhartha, but it didn't impress her at all. My goodness she was tired of it.

"Madame, I have to tell you that he was not very successful. It was the kind of rod that boys would make when they were less than ten years old. It was terribly rudimentary, Madame, a matter of a stick and twine and a little wire. No fish with any sense would go near it and unfortunately for Sir there are no fish without sense in our river. Bad luck on Sir, but I would say that we probably have some of the cleverest fish in India, and that is why they are so damnably difficult to catch, particularly with such a hotchpotch rod."

The manager went on to tell her how Sanjay had also managed to set fire to the outside toilet of the little house and how two of the farm boys had to help him put it out. Sanjay had been forced to do his business in a bucket out the back. Gita apologised for her husband and mumbled something about Sanjay being run down from overwork, but she was pretty sure that the manager did not believe her.

"Sir said that he was trying to write a novel, Madame. He said…."

She cut him off before she took out the irritation she felt for Sanjay, on him and after all she was mildly grateful to the estate manager for having reported to her.

The first time he had disappeared the children were still in their early teens. How desperate and ashamed she had been. He had gone out to work at her father's pharmaceutical company on a Friday morning and just never come home in the evening. On Saturday she had phoned all his friends, but not his family because she hoped he would come back before they found out. She had phoned the police and hospitals, but no one knew where he was. The police of course tried to charge her a search fee, which she was tempted to pay but thought it was too much money and that they would probably take it and do nothing.

After two days of anxiety, she had finally told her mother, and she had responded down the phone with a shocking lack of sympathy. "Have you been your usual bossy self with him? Have you been undermining him with your famously sharp tongue? Oh Gita, how many times have I told you to bite your lip? You have gone and finally driven him away. For goodness' sake Gita, what on earth am I going to tell my friends when they ask?"

"Mother, I don't know he hasn't been murdered or kidnapped. I'm worried sick."

"Oh, he hasn't been murdered or kidnapped. I think he has just tired of you and your women's rights, burning bra nonsense. You are going to be a sad and lonely old woman, Gita, and you will only have yourself to blame. Do you think I looked at your father all the time all googly-eyed and thought everything that came out of his mouth was wisdom itself? No, Gita, I jolly well did not. Your father and I were progressive enough to let you marry for love, so you should take greater care of your marriage. If you are finding it difficult with Sanjay, you have only yourself to blame. It was your choice, Gita."

At one point, before his best friend Rupe had taken the trouble to come and see her to tell her where he was - in Kerala, in that hugging woman's ashram staying with some hippyish friends from university - she had worried that he had a lover and wondered what this other woman could possibly have been like to have wanted to get Sanjay into her bed. He was so lanky and awkward, but he did have a way with words. She used to love to listen to his stories when they met at university and remembered that he made her laugh like a drain the first six months they were dating. All too quickly the stories became repetitious. She started to resent the way he would try and get all the attention everywhere they went by launching into his near-death experiences, stories about chance and coincidence, or his barely believable encounters with Bollywood stars or famous singers. Women gave you all sorts of advice when you got married but no one told you that the greatest gift would be to learn how to handle your spouse's repetition of anecdotes and stories and childhood memories, the same jokes and puns, the same moves and responses and sounds during lovemaking. It was surely constant repetition that destroyed more marriages than infidelity, bad-temper, addiction or financial ineptitude. She found she could no longer cope, publicly or privately, with the tortuous re-runs of her husband's stories, now particularly bad, as there were always new audiences at breakfast at the guesthouse.

The guesthouse belonged to Gita. It was bought with her family money, and she had carefully designed the warm interiors and worked closely with the builders. It had been more successful than she had dared dream. A Canadian guest had said it had an easy going yet entirely respectable atmosphere, something that he said was difficult to achieve. Gita thought that was a very good description of both her and her establishment – *easy going yet entirely respectable*. Which is perhaps why she had been a bit put out by the British woman and her tag along toy-boy.

When Gita got up and went into the guest section of the house, she stayed away from the room of that UK woman pretending to be a young student with her hippy trousers and grubby T-shirts and the dark skinned Hampi Boy. She also knew that crusty old Indian men took advantage of young western women too, often with mental health problems or low self-esteem who went to places like Rishikesh or Goa. She had seen it with her own eyes.

Last year Gita had gone with her sister to Rishikesh to see the Ganges at its perfect and purest, just melted from the icecaps, a beautiful crisp light jade, full of mountain minerals and virginal freshness. The best place to visit the Mother Ganga before she became the army-green, rank, and dead-dog and human remains-infested cesspool of Varanasi. They had gone white water rafting on a whim and much to her own and sister's surprise she had copied the young German couple sitting next to her and suddenly thrown herself backwards overboard in her life jacket and bobbed along down the rapids in the sacred minty water. It was one of the most liberating, thrilling things she had ever done. She tried to think of that sensation every day and it always lifted her up for a few moments. The Germans were floating along with her, down the rapids, their heads held up by the life jackets, just marvelling at the bright ice blue holy water rushing all around her, looking up at the sky and clouds flashing past. She felt that she had become part of the river, part of the Mother Ganges, part of the world, and part of all that was beyond the physical realm. She and the Germans understood that they were simply flotsam and jetsam, and they were damn happy about that. It was something truly wonderful to realise, for that moment to lose physical self and understand that you were simply floating matter, passing through life lifted and held by Mama G, like the leaf or the branch bobbing beside them on the river. She and the Germans were just whooping and laughing and hearing the echo of themselves as their sound hit the rocky riverbanks and the mountains beyond. Her sister shouted shrilly at the men from the White-Water-Rapid company who were accompanying the boat in little canoes down the river. They responded by using their oars to suddenly turn and trap Gita in a two-pronged attack and absolutely force her to hold onto the nose of their craft. She was unceremoniously hauled back by the White-Water-Rapid guy into the main dingy. She sat violently shivering next to her sister, the Germans having also been forced back on board too. At that part of the river which approached Rishikesh itself, Gita and her sister had been appalled to see dread-locked, scabby, skinny-limbed old fellows in orange robes coming from out behind rocks on the side of the river with dazed-looking, wheat-haired western girls. Later too at the Ganga Aarti, where a wealthy looking women dressed in orange was leading the ceremony in a Canadian accent, they saw some particularly unsavoury looking holy men by the food stalls at and heard them say things like, "I want to put my energy inside you," and, "I can sense you have been very hurt by a man." Gita had been unable to help herself, intervening right there and then.

"Come on. Don't fall for it, girls. You could go up to any woman in the world and say, *have you been hurt by a man?* And they would say *Yes!* unless they were a monk or a nun or whatnot. It doesn't mean they can see into your soul or have any special powers. Energy inside you? We all know what that means. For goodness' sake. Don't let these old men anywhere near you. No Indian woman would touch them with a very long stick. I mean you'll catch some dreadful disease. I'd make a run for it if I was you!"

One of the so-called holy men with long, matted locks piled up on his head, orange tunics and a staff turned to her, his contrived spiritual face turning into one of twisted demonic hatred in a matter of seconds. "Leave us alone you old dried-up woman. You don't know who you are dealing with. I will curse you if you don't leave us be."

With that her sister pulled her away. "Come on. We don't need this. We are going to get in trouble if you don't calm it down a bit. What's wrong with you? You know how hard it was to get this time away from the husbands and the children. If we get into trouble, we will never be allowed to do a trip like this again."

She had told her sister off. "Get in trouble? We are not three years old. I'll say what I want, thank you very much."

But she had backed off for the sake of her timid sister, and they had walked back along the river to the guesthouse arm in arm. She made her sister double up with laughter when she stepped in a huge pile of sacred cow dung and shouted, "Holy Shit!" just like that.

"Oh Gita, you really are a piece of work."

Gita was just thinking how awful the British woman Kate was with her dubious, desperate sexual behaviour, when she was caught by her on the landing.

"Sorry to disturb you but I wondered if you could give me some advice about how to spend a day in Bangalore?"

"Well, I wouldn't know. It very much depends on what you and your, er, friend are interested in."

She couldn't help it. When she said 'friend', she could feel her upper lip curl in an involuntary mini sneer.

"Oh, Vinny and I aren't a couple. That's why I was a bit shocked about the double bed, I'd really prefer a room with two singles or even two separate rooms. If you remember you said that you did not have any and that you were extremely busy now. He is far too young for me. But he is travelling the same way as me and just had his family house smashed down in Hampi by the police. He wants to set up something in Kodaikanal so I thought we could travel together. I wanted to be kind to him. He's having a particularly awful time. His mother is so depressed."

"It's absolutely none of my business what you do. I am simply the owner of the guesthouse. I ask no questions. If you book on World-Wide-Wanderer there is nothing much I can do."

"OK, but I just wanted you to know. When you said 'friend' you did something funny with your mouth."

"I don't know what you mean?" Gita felt her lip curling up again. When had she started doing that? She started her sentence feeling stern and irritated by this woman's damn cheek and over familiarity but as soon as she looked at Kate and her mouth and saw she was trying to contain her laughter she couldn't help herself. She was mortified about her own lack of control and tried desperately to think of something terribly sad and swallow down the feeling rising out of her. It was a terrible feeling but also so delicious to be overtaken by an emotion. Gita had always been a giggly person; indeed, she had been in trouble at school and even university for laughing many times and although she tried to avert her eyes, she couldn't help it.

"Oh gosh, yes. Sorry. I was being judgemental. I can be awful sometimes, but it is one of the perks of owning a place like this. You can be snooty and sneery about whomever you like."

"It must be amazing. You must have had some interesting guests."

"Oh gosh, there's so many tales to tell."

"Go on."

"Well, there was a visiting professor, I think he was quite a well-known neurologist from Stamford University. First, he brought his wife to stay here whilst he lectured and then his mistress and the third time, he brought his wife again. He insisted on staying in the same room and asked that we booked the same restaurant for him in town on all three trips. He expected us to say nothing, but part of me wanted to just lean over to the wife and tell her. It felt rather disrespectful to me, that he didn't think anyone would give a damn about the way he behaved. It was almost as if he was flaunting to me that he could get away with it." Gita said.

"Cheeky sod."

"Cheeky sod indeed."

"And he sounds a bit weird. Perhaps he got off on it."

"Highly possible and he was such an unattractive, little man too, with huge hairy ear lobes. And both his women were so lovely, particularly the wife. Really elegant. Yes, he did seem titillated that he had forced me to be complicit in his deceit."

"What else?" This was fun.

"Well, there was a French woman that complained about everything. She complained about the noise of the honking car horns and about the spitting and clearing of the throats that apparently Indian men do in the morning but which I suppose any Indian cannot really hear. We are so used to it, you see."

Gita liked the way that Kate snorted when she laughed. "That is the sound of India. What on earth were you meant to do about that?"

"She complained about the décor too."

"Outrageous. It's gorgeous here. Just lovely. One of the nicest places I have stayed in so far."

"She also moaned about the food at breakfast which although I say it myself, is absolutely delicious."

"I can't wait."

"Oh, and she complained about the rain. The silly woman came here in monsoon and then complained to the World-Wide-Wanderer about the rain."

"Really Gita, couldn't you have organised the weather better for Madame's stay?"

"And she said that the bathrooms smelt odd."

"Did you answer it?"

"What?"

"Did you answer the comment on Wide-World-Wanderer?"

"No, not yet."

"Perhaps we should do it together."

"It would be jolly helpful if we could."

"And there was an English couple who stole the exquisite and really rather valuable bedspread from Rajasthan."

"An English couple. I'm so sorry. That's awful."

Sanjay came through from the kitchen, casually eating a Samosa he had swiped from the cook, saw Kate and put his long body almost between the two women. Kate had to step back into the hall.

"How long are you staying in Bangalore?"

"Well, I'm just here for one day, so I would like to see as much as possible. I was just about to ask Gita what she would recommend."

Sanjay started to talk, and Kate looked under his armpit and caught her eye. Gita immediately knew that Kate had known men like Sanjay. An insecure man whose romantic vision of himself turned him into a bore, unable to listen to other people's experiences, self-aggrandising at every turn. Gita had been to dinners and parties and events with Sanjay when he hadn't got a chance to tell one of his stories and on the way home, he would be low and depressed and pick a fight with her about the route home or the way she had flirted with someone. She never flirted. She knew that her height meant that she just could not get away with being coquettish.

"You know hardly anyone goes to visit the National Modern Art Gallery but it's rather amazing and has quite an interesting collection of Indian modern art. It's a bit of a hidden gem."

"Oh, I doubt she wants to go there. It's full of pretentious idiots sitting about talking about art in black clothes and too much kohl under their eyes."

"Oh, I do. It sounds just up my street. Tell me more about it."

Sanjay looked at them both with irritation. He opened his mouth to speak some more but decided against it. Gita was amazed to see him step backwards and then suddenly turn, fall slightly against the wall, mumble something about needing a cup of coffee and go downstairs.

"Look Kate. I'd like to go to the Modern Art gallery. I haven't been there in ages. Would you mind if we went together?"

"I'd love it!"

"And there is a fantastic little street market nearby that sells wonderful textiles and jewellery and leather bags. There's some gorgeous stuff. I'll tell you what. Let's take my little Beetle car and really make a super day of it. I could do with some time off. I've been working flat out for months. I honestly haven't had a break in so long. I was also thinking of getting my hair done."

"Oh, as you can see, I could really do with that."

"I have to say your hair is looking a little Goa-hippy. We can grab some lunch at a sweet little place I know and then in the evening go to the Bangalore Club. Oh, er and invite the young man."

They both looked at each other. Gita didn't even need to express that she hoped that the young man would not come with them. Kate knew that this was to be a lovely girl's day out and that this young fella wouldn't really be at home in any of the places she had mentioned.

When Gita went into the breakfast room the next morning Kate was sitting on the large round table with the couple from Pune whose chubby son was sitting an exam to get into Bangalore University to read economics and politics. Sanjay had managed to get up and out of the room by the time she had her shower and he stood with one leg up on a chair. *Who wanted his great big grubby old foot on the upholstery, and who on earth wanted to have to look up into the baggy crutch of his old grey trousers?* He was talking about the tiger that had walked into his math's class at school. Gita had to admit that it was one of his best stories, but she immediately felt a pang of possessive anxiety. She was really looking forward to her day with Kate and didn't want Sanjay waylaying her with one of his epic tales.

Kate smiled as soon as she saw her. "Hello Gita. I've just got to go to the Garuda Mall with Vinny and then I'll come back and meet you. Is that all right?"

Gita tried to hide her disappointment, only saying, slightly grumpily. "Better make sure that it is eleven as I have an appointment at the Nyara saloon for us both at eleven forty-five. What with the traffic and all I think we need to get off promptly."

"Oh yes. In that case I'll try and make it back here at ten thirty. Sorry Gita. I hope that's OK. I'll go upstairs and make sure Vinny hurries up."

'You know how to get to the mall?'

'I think Vinny knows. He says that he has been here before."

Kate complimented her on the breakfast. Gita had made sure that the cook tried extra hard because she knew that Kate would be eating it. She served creamy wheat Rava Upma with coconut chutney and lemon pickle as well as dahl and warm brown bread rolls and fresh figs. Unlimited amounts, and with lots of fresh coffee. Gita wanted her guests to be happy and they were. Her guests tended to come back time and time again. One American academic had stayed for six months writing a paper on Tagore and became rounder and rounder as he tucked into her breakfasts of Idli, enjoyed with Sambhar and Chutney, lingering around the breakfast table until mid-morning.

Gita was absolutely delighted when Kate walked in at ten thirty.

"What an awful place," Kate said.

"G Mall? It's dreadful. Come on. Let's go. Do you want to go to the loo first?"

Gita took Kate to Marilyn, her cream VW Beetle and they got in. Kate admired Marilyn's curves and her beautiful white leather seats. Gita smiled to herself because she knew her car was simply the coolest ever. The traffic was even crazier than usual, and Gita was forced to tell an auto-driver and a taxi what she thought of them in no uncertain terms. "You are fucking idiots. You nearly got us killed. I'm so sorry Kate. The traffic in this town has got crazy. Oh, it's all well and good that we are *the Silicon Valley* of India, but our roads are still fucking medieval. The roads are always meant to be fixed up, but the local big wigs are so corrupt that they never get done."

Gita couldn't help feeling rather gratified when she went over a pothole as if to illustrate her point.

Kate laughed. "You know in the guidebooks they say never to swear in India because it causes great offence in a way it doesn't in Britain."

"Is that fucking right?"

Kate laughed. "It sounds so much more shocking in a posh Indian accent."

Gita laughed. "I know. It's great, isn't it?"

They parked in the grounds of the Bangalore Club and walked down some broken stairs to the busy road.

"We're not really meant to park here unless we are members, but what the hell? I learnt how to swim here as a child and feel it is my second home. Look, I warn you, the salon looks like nothing. It is basically someone's parlour, but you know I've been going there for years and they know exactly what I want. So many of my friends come here now as well. It's a hidden gem."

Kate smiled. "It sounds good to me."

Gita and Kate sat directly opposite each other. Adiya, the young skinny daughter of Gariti, cut Kate's thatch of hair while Adiya herself styled Gita's silky grey hair. When she looked properly at the pokey lime green room with peeling paint and a smell of hair dye and damp, she worried that Kate would be horrified. Perhaps she was used to going to salons in London that must be so much grander than this. Gita looked at Kate and felt reassured. It was obvious to anyone how terribly low maintenance she was.

Adiya sighed ostentatiously.

The fourth time she sighed Gita was obliged to ask in Hindi. "What are you sighing for?"

"Well British Madame's big head is like combing out and cutting the hair of two women. There is so much of it. It will take more time Madame, so much more. I will need more money, Madame."

"Really? Look at how fine the hair I have on my head is. Together we surely balance things out between us?"

She felt her head going side to side, mirroring Adiya's head movements.

"No, Madame. It's not like that. Please inform the British Madame that I will have to charge her more. My arm is hurting."

"Please put it onto my bill. This is embarrassing for me. I must be one of your most longstanding clients. I brought her here and I think it's a bit much to suddenly increase her charge in the middle of an appointment. It's unprofessional. Put it on my bill, I insist. She is one of my guests. Anyway, is that all that the sighing is about? It cannot be just about the mop of hair. Are you lovesick?"

The girl looked up as if she was about to cry. The girl's mother started to comb her hair violently so that Gita was forced to wince and pull her head away. Kate raised her eyebrows. "I think the fact that they are quarrelling is making them quite rough with our hair. Ouch."

"Yes, yes. Ladies. Either you tell me what is going on between you two or I'm going to take my custom elsewhere. You are yanking my hair out and by the looks of things you are also hurting my friend. She appears to have tears running down her face."

"OK, OK," said the mother. She spoke in English now. "I will tell you. Adiya wants to study IT like her brother at Bengaluru University. She says that she is brighter than her brother and that she is not interested in carrying on helping me in the salon."

"I am brighter. I've already had so many app ideas and I'm incredible at coding. I could really do well. I know I could," Adiya said.

"We simply cannot afford to put two children through university. It is as simple as that. And if Adiya just goes and gets married and has children then it will be like throwing the money into the river."

Gita felt her hackles rise. "For God's sake. I'm jolly well sick of this country and its attitude towards women. You know I wanted to be an artist, Kate. I wanted to go to art school. It was the only thing I excelled in. And for some reason my family was dead set against it. So, I had to go and study business studies, which probably helped me with the guesthouse and all but so bloody frustrating. But surely there are grants these days? I heard of a girl from a less well-off family getting some sort of grant or funding or some such. We could investigate it couldn't we Kate?"

"Oh yes. Yes. There are a huge variety of philanthropic organisations which want to promote education for women and girls. Let's get onto it."

The Mother pursed her lips. "So, who would I get to help me here? That's what I want to know?"

"Come on. You're the most popular hairdresser with all my friends and you haven't given this place a lick of paint for decades. You might have to employ another hairdresser. You might have to think about that. Come on, admit it Garita, you're doing fantastically well."

Garita couldn't help smiling to herself while nodding her head from side to side. "Oh, I don't know about that."

It was getting quite exhausting having to peer over Kate's shoulder every time she showed an interest in an item of jewellery or a textile or item of clothing at the flea market.

"You're an absolute rogue. Do you think I don't know how much you are over-charging her? It's horrible the way you try to rip off tourists. No wonder so few tourists come to Bengaluru if there are people like you waiting to fleece them. You shame me, you really do."

Gita asked Kate to simply indicate with her eyes the bed sheets, or cushion covers she was interested in. The trouble is Kate would be opening her eyes wide and jerking her head, but Gita would start asking about the wrong thing and Kate would make a clacking sound in her throat. The stallholders were either charmed or irritated by them.

Kate took her time in the market. She bought a bright blue coloured tunic which she changed into immediately in one of the makeshift changing rooms at the back of the stalls. With the gold hoop earrings, she bought - not real gold, but nevertheless nice-looking - and the good haircut and blow dry she looked so much better. Gita enjoyed the fact that she had been the architect of this transformation and wondered if Kate's scruffiness had been a deliberate ploy as a female traveller alone. Before Gita had to admit that she felt rather embarrassed to be seen with Kate, but now she felt quite proud.

Gita's son Raj had phoned while they were having lunch in a nice little bar that had just opened. Gita had already explained to Kate that Raj had followed her example and opened a hip hostel in Pune that had orange walls and gold Keralan saris for curtains. It also had a tolerance for weed smoking - Raj had been totally open with her about this - and served delicious, locally sourced, vegetarian food.

"Mum, can I ask for your advice? I've overbooked. I got confused with all the booking apps and somehow, I totally messed up on one date. What should I do?"

"Oh gosh, love. Well, what's the second-best place in town for the age group you serve?"

"Well, I suppose Dev's place."

"What's it called?"

"Dev's Place."

"Well. Try to book a place there and pay for it. Tell them that you have had a problem with your computers and that you will pay them for their inconvenience."

"Really? I have to bloody well pay for them?"

'Yes. Otherwise, they will absolutely lay into you on World-Wide-Traveller if you leave them high and dry and you will lose business." She raised her eyes to the heavens for Kate to see and mouthed, "My son."

"Well, I think they were hoping to be both Mum, but at my place."

"Oh, very funny. Honestly that is what you must do. Overbooking is an absolute no-no. And do it super quick."

She put down her phone.

Kate smiled. 'That was amazing. The way you thought of a solution on the spot."

Gita answered modestly. "Oh, no. It's just I've been in this business for a few years now." But secretly she thought she had been fast witted and thought a way out of a problem which after all had never happened to her.

Kate and Gita sat drinking tea in the elegant café area in the Museum of Modern Art. They sauntered through the different galleries and looked at the art and laughed at some of it and admired some of it. They found the most famous paintings by Rabindranah Tagore, Raja Ravi Verma and Jamini Roy and talked about them in a light-hearted but intelligent way. Kate and she tended to agree about most of the paintings, and they had a passing art student take a picture of them both with their newly trimmed and blow-dried hair standing on the long modernist steps swooping up to the contemporary section. Gita taught Kate how to stand with one leg out and slightly turned to the side, "Didn't you have deportment classes at school?"

"God, no," Kate said.

Kate was suitably impressed by the elegant interiors of the galleries, and they took a shady stroll around the site of the sprawling

Manikyavelu Mansion next to the art gallery and sat on the edge of the modernist fountain pool where Gita spoke about her life with Sanjay. His wanderings, awful temper, bursts of violence and self-centredness. Kate spoke about her life with her ex who was quite obviously cut from a similar cloth to Sanjay. She told Gita that it was all about timing. That she had to wait until the timing was exactly right in order to get her ex to finally leave the family house. If she had got it wrong the situation would have been unbearable making her and her children's lives even more of a misery."

"It's bloody difficult here in India. Divorce is terribly frowned upon. But I have to say I keep dreaming about how lovely it would be if he went off for good. How wonderful that would be. If he just drifted off so that no one blamed me. In fact, they might be sympathetic to me. Oh, poor Gita, they might say, her dotty husband has strayed off again and this time for good. You know Kate, he doesn't help with the guesthouse at all. He just floats around trying to trap the guests with his endless stories and stealing food from the kitchen all day long. Did you notice his tight little pot belly? The thought of years and years ahead with him, makes me feel quite desperate."

"I was married to a childish, angry man who basically needed to be properly brought up all over again. No one had ever told him that temper tantrums are not the way to behave and so as an adult male he had an angry fit every time something did not go his way. And things rarely go completely your way, do they?" Kate said.

Gita agreed and continued. "The thing is, if you are with someone who flies into rages you end up hating them. Just because you might do what they want to avoid a scene or to placate them after a scene does not mean that you think that they are right. And no, you don't forgive them for the dreadful things they have said and done. You just store every single one in a bitter pool of hate and resentment. I don't know how people like my husband and your ex-husband can bear it. They must know that they are not truly loved. No one loves a bully. Even if you did once love them, it is eroded every time they insult you, lie to you, hit you, hurt you or humiliate you. Until you end up with nothing but hatred. Then that hatred turns into indifference, so that every cell in your body would like not to be bothered by the unpleasant sensations that the other person gives you most of the time. I am utterly tired of him, Kate and that's the damn truth."

There were people reading huge art books from the library, others working intensely on their lap-tops, whilst some had earnest conversations or simply ate together in silence. Everyone there could not help being affected by the perfect chicness of the environment. There was an air of quiet self-congratulation. A huge good old-fashioned modernist white space, half of which opened out onto the decadent colonial gardens which threatened to go to seed someday, but for now were happy to look ripely beautiful. There was a sense that everyone there felt they were in the exactly the right place at the right time and though no one spoke of it everyone gave each other slightly smug little glances and smiles as they sipped their tea and juices.

Gita had noticed two attractive middle-aged men in colourful kurta, both with thick salt and pepper, beautifully cut hair, chatting to each other, one of them speaking more than the other.

"Now is finally the time for the Indian artist to move away at last, and once and for all from the western gaze and turn his or indeed her vision inwards and take a good hard look there before trying to paint or sculpt or whatever it is he wants to do."

Gita found his voice rather overpowering but couldn't help wanting to hear what he had to say. Just as she was thinking of saying something funny about the men to Kate, she found that the two men were close by their table. They seemed to be asking both her and Kate if it was at all possible, they could join them. Before she had a chance to say no, Kate had accepted their offer. "Oh yes, that's fine." Kate looked at Gita and raised her eyebrows as if to say, "Well what else could I do?"

Gita felt a rush of irritation that these men with their expensive clothes and great hair thought they could just come and interrupt what was turning out to be a superbly enjoyable day.

"Hello there. I hope you don't mind. Rohit and I made a bit of a pact with each other that if we see interesting people we are to seize the opportunity. Too many times, you see people you wonder about and then you get home and kick yourself and think "Why the hell didn't I have the guts to introduce myself?"

He was doing well so far, Gita had to admit.

"So, introduce yourself. You've introduced your friend Rohit, but you forgot to introduce yourself." Gita surprised herself by being rather challenging and yes, a little flirtatious. It was very unlike her. She wondered if it had something to do with the haircut or the conversations and fun she had with Kate. Kate smiled at her in encouragement.

"Ha ha, yes, indeed. My name is Jay. But I'm more interested in your names."

"My name is Gita and this is Kate."

Gita expected Jay's eyes to turn to Kate and stay there. But his eyes kept coming back to her. Both men sat down on the white, Swiss-style chairs.

"Can I admit that I heard you commenting on one of my paintings in the Contemporary section?"

Gita felt her heart sink. Was it one of the paintings she had merely used as a tool to make Kate laugh out loud? Oh God, what if he was the painter of the portrait of a woman that Gita had described as "The bastard daughter of Nefertiti and Homer Simpson". Although she was proud of pulling that description out of her head and it did make Kate laugh - which was the whole point - that kind of comment could ruin someone's confidence for a while.

"Don't look so worried. Your description of my work thrilled me. Do you know what you said?"

"No, I'm not sure…"

"You said that it pulled you back into your childhood and then even further back to a precolonial India and then threw you violently forward into a time just beyond now."

"I said that? That sounds good."

Kate chimed in. "You did. About that huge red canvas which was abstract but then had a Shiva-like figure and a tiger in a jungle far into the background. Do you remember?"

"It was actually Vishnu, but yes, that was my painting." Jay looked admiringly at Gita. "Are you an art critic?"

"No, I'm not."

"Oh pity. Are you a writer?"

"No, sorry. I merely run a guest house."

"It happens to be the best guest house in Bangalore." Kate was perhaps playing the wingwomen role a little too hard.

"Anyway. Can I ask? Would both of you join us at the Bangalore Club tonight. It might seem a bit fuddy-duddy to you, but they do fantastic cocktails."

Gita was about to refuse when she saw Kate's face. It was nothing new for her at all, but for Kate, travelling halfway around the world, it might be interesting. It might be fun for Kate to see the posh club where they still had a chit under glass showing that Winston Churchill owed the bar money. To take her into the billiard room. To show her the portraits of the fat pompous Indians, show her the ridiculous colonial maps of India and take her to the impressive library where her friend Hita had been writing her novel for the past ten to fifteen years.

'Well, why not. In fact, that would be super. Kate is only here for the night so it would be great to show her the old place."

When she thought of Kate leaving the next morning it made her terribly sad. She wondered why an earth she had attached herself so much to someone she barely knew. It seemed to her that she and Kate were soul mates. That they understood each other perfectly. At the same time, she understood that Kate was probably someone very good at fast intimacy, but that she also found it easy to leave people behind too. It didn't make her think any less of her. In fact, in an odd way it made her like Kate more. She wished that she could travel with her but understood herself enough to know that she would not like it much. Something told her that her adventures were here, in the place of her birth. That her immediate mission was to find a new life within her old life, not to flee what she had so carefully built up, but to try and make her life take the shape that she wanted. No, she would leave the restlessness to Sanjay.

Her focus turned back to the man in front of her. He smelt wonderful, fresh and lemony. Simple but sophisticated at the same time. She told him so and he told her that it was 'Fab India'! Jay's smile was beautiful to see. His teeth were spectacular and for once she agreed with her mother that teeth were so terribly, terribly important. As she looked at him still, it struck her that she had not made a man smile like this for a long, long time. A smile full of expectation and potential joy.

THE MOTHER
May 2016

Ebeid's time in the stand was not the same elegant triumph as Ranim's had been. It was tedious to hear the translated phone texts - and every question and answer from the cross examination. The jury was fidgeting, and the bony-faced woman was asleep. As soon as she stepped onto the stand the anxiety overtook her, and she rocked and shook and seemed to gasp for air. She opened her mouth wide to cry out with a terrible wail that filled the courtroom and woke the skull-faced female juror. Judge Jeremy looked on in silence, his lips pursed. The interpreter stood by her looking as if he was also about to burst into tears.

"Could I ask My Lord if the defendant could be allowed to be seated in the witness box? She is practicing fasting for Ramadan, and I think it would help if she wasn't standing."

"I am well aware that it is Ramadan. I have been told a fair number of times."

The usher spoke softly to the mother. He also spoke gently to the interpreter who looked like he was about to have a panic attack too. Thanks to the sound and tone of his words both the mother and the interpreter seemed to recover themselves.

Seated she looked a tiny figure; her brown scarf tightly wrapped around her face pinching into the skin of her plump cheeks. Just a round face in the stand. Her life in Syria as a Biochemist fighting for women's rights was laid out to the jury by her barrister. The court heard that she had been arrested and tortured by Assad and had fled with most of her family and been given leave to remain, a couple of years ago. The court also heard that as well as the son who was found in the boot of the car, she had a young daughter with spina bifida who she cared for while her husband worked at London University as a lab assistant.

Her answers were muddled at times, and she seemed unsure as to where she and her son had been at any point and seemed to still be protecting her son, who it turned out had been given his French leave to remain six months previously. She insisted that he did not see the car but then said that he had come and picked up the bag of clothes as she waited for him by the car and the others had gone on ahead. Her barrister was a local one, because she had not wanted to be helped by Kate's organisation to find a lawyer like Jitendra.

Her barrister was surprisingly good. Of all the barristers there: the nervous prosecution women with her hesitation and soft voice, Jitendra with her London smoothness and the young over-eager man representing Ranim, Kate thought he was the only one that would appeal to the jury of Kentish folk. He wore a smart, slightly too well-fitting, expensive looking suit and let his robes fall from him so that everyone could see. He was well spoken and appealing. He had winked at Kate, when he had seen her sitting with her mother on the bench outside the court. Her mum had nudged her and said, "He's jolly dishy."

"Oh. for God's sake mum."

He tried very hard to lead Ebeid into saying that there was a possibility that the son had let himself into the car at the end of the day of his own violation, but she always insisted that she had been with him and that he would not have acted alone. Kate felt that familiar battery acid anxiety in her gut. It was totally natural to always protect your child, but Kate wished that Ebeid would protect not only herself but her and Ranim.

The prosecution barrister weighed in, when it was her turn. "I give it to you that you have exhausted all avenues. You had tried to get your son into the UK and had his entry refused twice. We have shown the jury copies of these refusals. You deliberately went to the Calais Camp to try and get your son into a car. Didn't you?"

The interpreter told her what the barrister had said. The interpreter in turn told the court what she had said, "No, No, No, No, No."

As Ebeid was raising her voice and becoming increasingly upset, Kate saw Detective Inspector Cookson turn towards the jury and make a dismissive blah, blah, blah gesture with his mouth, making a telling gesture, opening and closing his right hand. Kate felt a cold wave go through her. She was not sure if he sought to influence the jury or just assumed that the jury felt the same contempt for the mother as he did. Kate wasn't sure which was worse. Billie and Charlie saw his action too, and during the lunch break Billie wrote Jitendra an email complaining about the policeman's behaviour.

That afternoon, just before the jury came back from lunch, Jitendra stood up and cleared her throat.

"Your Honour, if I may? I received an email just now from someone in the court who said that Detective Inspector Cookson was making mocking and mimicking gestures towards the jury when Ebeid was in the witness box."

The Judge leant forward to speak into his microphone.

"Thank you, but I haven't seen Detective Chief Inspector Ian Cookson making any gestures. I'm sure he is an experienced enough policeman and has been in court enough times to know that he cannot do this."

Kate heard Billie make a sound of exasperation. Jitendra didn't push it, probably conscious of the fact that Kate was going into the witness box the next day and not wanting to get the judge's back up.

PARTICLES OF LOVE
June 2016

Atal tried not to go up to the communal platform area, where the hippy kids' piping voices and darting about got on his nerves. He liked to pass the day sitting and smoking his chillum, looking out over the mountain range, watching the vast sky spreading out before him, with the clouds and seams of light performing daily miracles on the top of the rocky peaks. He also liked to talk profound shit to whoever cared to drop by and sit on the yellow plastic chairs on his extravagantly long stone balcony. He had his own kitchen in his own private cottage and attempted to cater for himself as much as possible; giving anyone that was going into town in the Land Rover a bunch of rupees to buy vegetables, fruit, pulses and weed. The food served at the communal area in Luna Range was awful, just unspeakable. It managed somehow to be incredibly bland and terribly indigestible at the same time, giving him terrible farts and sometimes even the runs. He adored the little French couple that had taken over the kitchen for the month for free board, but their cooking was foul. He was unused to catering for himself but had managed to make some passable dhal and even managed to sneak in some chicken to make a decent enough curry though Govind strictly forbade meat. It said so in the long list of rules on the back of his front door, which also included *No playing of music on the veranda* - he had broken that of course - *No negative energy, only positive* - er, define negative please - and *Drugs will not be tolerated* - he presumed that they were just covering their backs as The L Range was known throughout India and the world beyond as a place where you could smoke weed and take magic mushrooms pretty much as you pleased.

Back home it was a different matter. His mother had a team of servants, or narc cops as he called them to his friends, following him around as soon as he took his first piss in the morning. "What would Sir like for breakfast?" and "What clothes would Sir like to be prepared?" or "Will Sir be in for Luncheon?" Atal felt they were in cahoots with his anxious, babying mother. They were her fussy courtiers watching his every move and very glad to report on any of his misdemeanours or slack behaviour. Last week as he was sitting blazing up by the pool, Mangesh came and stood in front of him and stared pointedly at the admittedly, very fat, ostentatious, joint he was smoking.

"Would Sir like me to bring out an ashtray for his, er, cigarette."

"I'm OK, thank you." And he took an extra-long draw from his obese doobie.

"I wonder how your mother would feel about ash, particularly ash such as that, being dropped around the swimming pool, Sir?"

"I don't think she would know about it unless you told her. Are you going to tell her?" Mangesh looked at him with his mean little Mongoose eyes.

"I'm not sure what the best course of action is, Sir, but I would strongly advise that you stubbed out your big cigarette."

Looking back Atal wasn't quite sure what happened. He thought he saw Mangesh and his shadow make a sudden jerky move to grab his joint and he reacted by standing up and pushing him sharply away. Did Mangesh step backwards in shock? Or did Atal shove him hard enough to make him take a tumble. Whatever had happened, Mangesh ended up in the swimming pool, falling backwards and into the water with a sharp, wet, smack.

"Mangesh? What happened? Do you need help? Here is my hand."

Atal leant in as far as he could to try and grab the skinny Mangesh, whose tunic had ballooned almost over his head. Mangesh carried on thrashing around and made a horrible girlish, high-pitched sound. Atal jumped in, put his hands around the small man's shoulders and swam for a few strokes until he could stand and pulled him face up to the shallow end, holding his head carefully out of the water. He was fascinated to notice how his hands were almost bigger than the man's whole face and realised at the same time that he was rather stoned. He held the man's trunk and pushed him up the ladder ahead of him, guiding his hands to the railings of the swimming pool steps. Mangesh seemed to be sobbing and gasping. Even though Atal felt sorry for the man he did think he was making a bit of a meal of it, but he guessed he didn't know how to swim and regarded water as something to fear, even in a swimming pool as shallow as his parents' one. Mangesh didn't even turn to look back at Atal but squelchily walked back to the house leaving a watery trail behind him like a huge, pathetic snail.

It took only a matter of minutes for his mother to appear, an elegant, flustered cloud of turquoise and gold, flanked by her two favourite servants. "What have you done? Are you mad? Mangesh says that you pushed him in the swimming pool. The poor man can't even swim. You could have drowned him and then where would we all be? You might have to go to prison. I know your father is good friends with the head of the police but there is only so much one man can do to save his son."

Carmela and Neela's heads moved from side to side to add emphasis to his mother's words and his mother's copious tears were starting to ruin her carefully applied make-up. When she rubbed her eyes the turquoise eye shadow spread onto her cheeks and chin. He felt love, weariness and disgust when he looked at her, making such a song and dance out of what was, after all, an accident. He guessed that she had little else to do except to give her servants orders and worry obsessively about him.

"Why are you doing this? Why are you never happy? Your father and I only want you to be happy and yet you reward us by looking like a ghost, smoking drugs and pushing people in swimming pools."

He wished he could just apologise and explain calmly what had happened, but he could not stop his usual bitter retort. "That's not quite true is it, Mum? You didn't marry me off to Raina because you wanted me to be happy, did you? It was because you wanted me to be connected to her fucking stinking rich Syrian family and now, she has taken my son away with her across the other side of the world and he doesn't know who I am. No wonder I smoke weed. I want to block out the pain. What were you thinking, Mum? Why did you do it? Why did you make two people be together who were not meant to be together? It goes against the laws of nature, doesn't it? And I don't make a habit of pushing people into swimming pools. It might be the first time since I was a kid. It was a fucking accident, OK?"

His mother started to twirl her wedding ring around her finger, something she always did when she was stressed. He could hear her taking a pause and trying to make her voice softer and more reasonable. He knew that he had spoken to her in a surly, sweary, adolescent way. His realisation of his own bad behaviour around her made him even more irritated by her.

"You need to talk to the Imam. You need a private talk with the Imam. We cannot go over and over this for the rest of our lives. We try to give you projects that interest you and keep you busy. We bought all those properties for you to manage but you still are not happy. When I think of what your father went through to get all this, to raise a family in comfort to have an only son who throws it back in his face."

Atal realised how drenched and uncomfortable he was and got up. It often shocked him how much taller he was than his mother. He could almost look down onto the top of her head.

"I'm not going to speak to the Imam. I'm going to check up on the gardens in the property in Goa. We got a *CoZyBed* review, which strongly criticised the gardens and the roof terrace in Patnam. We simply cannot afford to get any more negative reviews about that property. I don't think you understand how a couple of bad reviews will break our reputation in Goa."

His mother looked at him. "I'll get Theven to drive you."

"I don't want Theven to fucking drive me. I'm taking the Harley. I could do with a long drive to clear my head."

His mother put her head in her hands. "I hate it when you take such long journeys by bike. It's so dangerous. I think of poor Bitty who lost her son in Rajasthan. It ruined her life. Please drive safely, Inshallah."

"I don't think Dakash was too thrilled about being dead either."

His mother looked at him through her tears. "I don't understand what you are trying to say."

"Just that I want to stay alive for myself. It's not just for your sake that I drive my motorbike well and safely."

"What?" His mother was not in the mood to try and understand him.

"Never mind."

Atal went to his room to pack a small bag. He packed some jeans, a book of poetry, a chillum, computer, T-shirts, a couple of hoodies and a portable speaker.

As he was doing so his father walked in. "I hear you pushed Mangesh into the swimming pool."

Atal stopped what he was doing and looked up at his father. "Honestly Father, I don't know how it happened. One minute he was leaning over me and the next minute he was thrashing around in the pool. I'm sorry to have upset Mum again, I really am. I didn't mean to do it."

"Oh, he probably deserved it. He's really milking it with your mother. She has given him the day off tomorrow so that he can recover his nerves."

They both laughed.

"So, you are off to Goa again? Your mother would rather you didn't go on the bike, but I understand that a young man needs to take off on the open road sometimes. Before I met your mother, I used to take little adventures on a bike myself." His father opened his wallet, winked and gave Atal a thousand rupees.

Atal took it and put it in his army bag. That would come in handy.

"I have some motorbike maps of India I could let you have. They tell you places to stay where motorbike guys are welcome. I'll dig them out."

Why would he need those when he had his phone? Atal supposed they might be interesting but massively out of date.

"I don't suppose you want to come to the mosque with me, Son? For evening prayer?"

He looked up at his dad and wondered if he should go with him because of the money. He couldn't really cope with the thought of it even though he knew he probably should.

"Sorry Daddy. I'm a bit busy packing for the journey as you can see."

"OK, I'll find those maps after I have been to the mosque."

His father nodded and was smiling slightly sadly as he left the room. Atal knew that he really was a bastard to his parents.

On the fourth afternoon of mostly contemplating the sky at Luna Range he was called up to speak to Govind with grumpy Syama as the messenger. Judging the way the couple from Delhi with the home-schooled twins and all the other Indian hippy freaks looked at him with sliding hurt eyes when he walked through the communal area on the way to meet Govind, this was an unusual and enviable thing. Govind's house was quite a bit further up the mountain and Atal had to walk up what seemed to be more than a hundred stone steps to where *The Mothership* was perched over-looking them all.

It was a circular building with glass and wooden panels with the roof of a close thatch with red flowers draping around the edge of it. Atal didn't think he had ever seen a perfectly circular building before and admired it greatly, walking round the whole thing. Back at the huge front door, he turned to look at the view from this higher vantage point and found it even more spectacular than his own. This Govind dude knew what he was doing. Setting up a farm type thing for those who had tired of the rat race or the extreme hippy nuts that had got fed up with the alternative township of Auroville, near Villupuram.

Atal rang the satisfyingly huge cowbell that was in front of the massive door. An older European woman answered it. Atal reckoned this was Govind's Spanish wife Maria and he couldn't help being a bit disappointed that she was not better looking. When he had been told that Govind was married to a Spanish woman, he had immediately imagined Penelope Cruz and had been unable to put her image out of his mind ever since. Maria was small and slight with wispy orange hair and a beaky, bird-like face, thinnish lips and outsized multi-coloured glasses. Her hair looked like it could do with a good wash. He couldn't help noticing a greasy hen-feather like aspect to it.

Her smile was welcoming though. "Hey, you must be the famous Atal?"

"Well, around Pune I could possibly be considered infamous, but I don't think I've done anything of much interest since I've been here except look out at the sky. Great place you've got here, I must say."

He felt he was talking too fast and stopped himself. "And you must be Maria?"

She nodded and led him inside.

He stood in the vast circular room with long spider plants draping down from the balcony. Light poured in through the orange and blue glass sections in the domed roof.

Atal heard his name from above and looked up to where a serious looking Indian man in a cream tunic stared down at him. "Hey, Atal. Pleased to meet you. Come on up." The voice had an American drawl to it. He supposed that was inevitable for a cultish leader.

Atal started to mount the spiral staircase to the upper floor. Govind came to meet him and pressed his slightly clammy and cold hand into his. The sunlight through the roof hit Govind's round gold glasses so for a moment Atal could not see his eyes. When Govind moved his head and his eyes became clear Atal could see that he had gooseberry green irises. The contrast with his brown skin was striking.

Govind looked at Atal intently, letting his stare sweep up and down his body and back to contact his eyes. It was kind of creepy and a bit thrilling at the same time.

"So, what brings you here, Atal? I hear you have rented the whole of Jasmine Cottage. That's a nice big space for one young man, isn't it?"

"I just needed a break. I heard about this place from my friend Sav. He came here a couple of years ago. A dude from Delhi?"

Govind shook his head a little as if to dismiss any mention of his friend. He wasn't interested in Atal's friend. He was interested in Atal.

"Syama tells me you are Syrian."

"Yes, well, my mother is from Iran and my father from Syria. They met at Pune University where they were both studying physics."

"What an interesting mix of cultures. Do you practice Islam?"

"My parents do."

"And you?"

"I am open minded, you know. I went to DY Patil International School in Pune, where there were Hindus and Christians and a few Muslim boys like me. I'm really trying to get into Buddhism by reading

Bodhicaryavatara"- he wondered if he had pronounced that right, but he pressed on anyway – "by Santideva. I reckon I can relate so well to Buddha because I am a dissatisfied and spoiled little rich boy who wants to help people."

Govind put his hand on Atal's shoulder. "What is it you want to escape from Atal? Why are you here?"

Atal felt Govind's hand burn through his clothing. How did he do that? It felt like someone was resting a hot cup of tea on his shoulder. It was very disconcerting.

"From being served upon, from being watched and cosseted. From losing the ability to strive and work for myself. From becoming something passive and weak." Atal was not about to talk about his parents and Raina and his lost son.

Govind nodded his head. "OK, can I make a suggestion?"

"Yes, go ahead."

"While you are here, I want you to do things you would never do at home. I am going to put you on duty to clean the houses and the toilets. To serve those that stay here as you are served at home."

Atal was silent. He didn't want to clean people's crap from the rudimentary toilets. That's not what he meant at all. It would make him sick to his stomach. He was a paying guest and surely that didn't include cleaning toilets. He regretted saying anything about his mother's servants.

"I'm going to let you stay in that nice house of mine on the hill for now. I might send you to the shared dorm where those who are working for their keep. Let's see how you do. I think you want to feel some humility. I think it would help you. Don't you?"

Govind then sat down at his computer and started writing on his keypad as if Atal wasn't there. Atal mumbled a thank you and went down the stairs. He could not see the Spanish woman and so he stepped out of the Mothership, trying to close the huge wooden doors quietly. It didn't work and he could hear the door banging shut echo around the inner circular chamber of the house.

He came down the stone steps admiring his own ability to run jauntily down them and smelt some strong weed by the communal area. Pascale and Patrice were huddled together, giggling and chatting. Syama and her sister Ro, who were both exiles from Auroville, were both trying to be as officious and convincing as guesthouse managers as they could muster. They were booking in an older western woman and a young guy with his cap turned the wrong way around. Atal stared at the woman and felt as if he had seen her before. Perhaps she was famous or something, but he didn't think so. She wasn't looking around and clocking who was staring at her the way that famous people do. He really dug her thick eyebrows and her heavy sleepy eyes, though he wasn't totally sure why. He wanted her to look at him with her dopey eyes but as much as he stared at her she didn't look up from the long Luna Range form she was filling out. The boy next to the woman looked sullen and impatient for her to finish. At one point the guy in the cap seemed to notice Atal staring at the woman and looked at him with daggers in his eyes so Atal went to join the Frenchies on the bench.

Patrice smiled. "Hello Prince Atal. Do you want some?" He handed Atal a mean, spitty little joint.

"Hey dudes, I just went up to the Mothership and met Govind."

"Fuck you, we have never been asked up there and we have been here a month. What did he want with you?" said Pascal, in her thick and admittedly adorable French accent.

"He wanted to know what I was doing here, I guess. He was interested in meeting a Muslim boy."

""I suppose they don't get many Muslims coming to L Range," Patrice said.

Atal lent in. "Who is she?"

Atal jerked his head towards the Western woman.

Patrice looked at Atal. "You think she is hot, don't you? Even though she is old enough to be a grandmother."

"Well, as long as she is not my grandmother. I do find her hot. Am I a total freak?" Atal said.

Pascale looked at him with a little smile.

"How old do you think she is?" Atal asked.

Patrice shrugged. "Forty-something, maybe fifty, maybe older."

"God…. maybe it is to do with this weird and beautiful place we are staying in, but I really dig her. Do you know what I mean? I'm not embarrassed to admit it. I like her face and her insanely heavy blinking and why is her hair so big and messy? Did you see it? Her blinking? It's like the heaviest blinking you have ever seen in your fucking life, Dude. It's like she lives another life in each blink, like she goes to her parallel universe each time those heavy eyelids go down."

Patrice said, "I like the way British women speak, like Jane Birkin. It's very sexy for the French to hear an English woman speak."

Pascale looked annoyed and bit her pretty lip. "Well, maybe you can get to know her. She is coming to stay here,"

"Not with that little prick? I hope." Atal looked at the little guy in the cap, fidgeting around next to her with his slapped arse face.

"No. She has only booked for herself. She is coming here alone it seems." Atal smiled.

"Nice one."

When the woman and the boy left, Atal went to the front desk and asked for more details. "When is she coming?"

"When is who coming?"

"That older woman, who has just booked in."

"Oh tomorrow."

Ro put the form in the big old book, snapped it shut loudly and then looked up at him with her eyes narrowed and her lips pursed. "Why do you want to know Atal?"

"I want to be here when she arrives in the Land Rover and carry her bag down the steps, so she will like me. Where is she staying?"

"I haven't decided yet."

"Can you put her in that room connected to my house?" he said.

"Oh, I don't know. As I said I haven't decided yet."

Atal knew that Ro looked at him with longing doleful eyes, when she thought he couldn't see. He should not push it otherwise she would put the woman on the other end, right near the communal rooms. Women could be vindictive like that sometimes.

"Why are you so interested in her, Atal? The English woman is old and quite strange looking. Her head is far too big for her body. I can see from her passport details that she was born in 1964. That makes her fifty-two."

Fuck, that was old. Twenty-nine to fifty-two. That's quite an age difference. Twenty-four years. Jeez!

"Oh, I don't know. She just reminded me of someone,"

"One of your mother's friends perhaps," she said with a tight smile.

"Perhaps." Atal gave her a deliberately warm smile back. He hadn't felt so excited in ages.

Patrice helped him. It was very unlike Atal to make plans to get a woman. He usually let them come to him. Like Anouska. He hadn't made the slightest effort with her, but she had been bold and bought him a drink in that bar in Agonda. He had had a good time with Anouska, and she was probably the most gorgeous woman he had ever slept with. He had even invited her to come and stay with him and meet his parents, but after she asked the question, "How many servants do we have, darling?" in front of a group of her friends, he had felt compelled to end it with her, right then and there. Not only was her use of the word *We* a gross presumption but it revealed that she was probably unhealthily interested in his parent's wealth and status. That sort of thing switched the off button forever and he found it impossible not to be immediately revolted by her pale blond hair, careful make-up and long, thickly blunt, acrylic nails. The artifice that was perfectly fine a minute before became utterly intolerable to him the next.

Patrice told him that he had overheard a telephone conversation with the driver of the Land Rover, and it would arrive to deliver the new guests at around two the next day. The guests usually stayed for a night in the town of Kodaikanal because the Land Rover only came to the farm once every two days. Atal wondered where this woman had stayed and if she had stayed in the same room as that weird, twitchy little dude. He made sure that he was at the top by the road from half past one and hung about for an hour until he saw the dust from the Land Rover come into view.

He waited until she climbed out of the vehicle in a bright orange dress and black leggings and immediately took her bag from her before anyone else could. Annoyingly there were some other guests arriving, which hadn't been how he had pictured it at all. A large and gangly American man, a young Dutch girl and two giggling teenage Indian boys having their first time away from home and more than ready to puff like crazy.

The English woman was in a deep conversation with the Dutch girl and so she barely seemed to notice him taking her bag. The whole group walked to the communal area and Syama barked at him to take the quite heavy bag down to the Mini Jasmine Room. His heart leapt a little because it was the annex room to his cottage. Patrice had obviously persuaded Syama to let him have his wish. He let himself into the small room and set her big black bag on the little bed, and even though he knew she hadn't even been in the room yet, the fact that she was about to arrive and sleep in that damp bed made him feel excited. It felt kind of wrong having the big house when this older woman had this pokey little room with mustard yellow walls and a bad mural of a cornucopia of wildflowers. He didn't like to think of her having to use a hole in the floor outside toilet and bucket shower when he had a huge round bath and a pale pink western toilet which, rather oddly, was raised on its own pink concrete pedestal.

His rush of initial excitement faded. For the next couple of days, the woman seemed to be deliberately ignoring him and was even quite rude. When he was sitting chatting with Patrice and Pascale on his balcony, she came out of her little room and sat on the wall looking out at the view and thinking. She then took out a big, battered book and started reading.

"Hello. Oh, hey there. You are welcome to come and use my balcony. The view is so much better from here. Come and join us."

She smiled dreamily. "Don't worry. I'm fine here." She went back to reading and did not look up again from her book.

Atal tried his best to be really amusing so the Frenchies would laugh loudly and show how terribly funny and witty he was. When they didn't laugh loudly enough, he lowered his voice. "Hey, can you find me a bit funnier so that she will be interested in me?"

Pascale raised her eyebrows but did manage to laugh a bit louder, Patrice joined in, but Atal had to stop him by kicking his shin because he was going so over the top with such an insane bellowing laugh it would be obvious to the woman that he was faking it.

She still didn't look their way.

So, Atal tried next with some beautiful blushing mangos that he had got from the Swedish man who was building some sort of eccentric house type thing made of old glass bottles and found wood. He cut squares into the juicy sections of the sliced fruit and tipped them inside out, so they looked pretty and tempting. It was something he had seen the cook do at home and he was pleased at his first ever effort at doing it himself. He walked to where she still read in a chair and offered her some. She refused with the same distracted smile. He then wondered if she was a depressive, or a snob, getting over a torrid love affair or perhaps she was just not very nice. He felt very, very disappointed with her lack of response to him and it cast him down somewhat. It was very rare that women did not respond to him. Perhaps he had suddenly lost his looks and his charm? Perhaps his tall Persian, muscley thing did not appeal to an English woman, or perhaps that little toerag was more her type.

Patrice suggested that he made the woman, whose name they now knew was Kate, a cup of tea. "British people love to drink tea; they cannot resist tea."

"I fucking know that. The fucking British colonised India and made my Indian brothers and sisters work like slaves on their plantations just to serve them fucking tea all day long. Still make them work like slaves on team plantations. Have you ever been to Munar?"

"OK, it was just a suggestion."

"Why are you so bothered about this woman? It's getting boring. Why not try the Dutch woman. She is your age and kind of pretty," said Pascale.

"I don't know why but I am obsessed with this woman. I want to know her. I want to know all about her. I listen to her moving in that little room and coughing sometimes and I just want her to come and speak to me and like me. As I said, I'm obviously some kind of mother-complex freak."

So, he made her a cup of Assam tea in his increasingly messy kitchen. This time he went to her door and knocked on it. She let out a tiniest of sighs when she saw him. She awkwardly took the cup of tea. She sipped it while drawing in her breath, still standing in the doorway. "This is delicious. What kind of tea is it?"

"Assam tea."

"Aahh, Assam."

"Your lot annexed Assam and took over the plantations there. Then the British fucked the whole area, and it hasn't really recovered. I don't know if you know about that?" He wasn't sure why he said this. He couldn't help being annoyed that she had ignored him for so long. He wanted to punish her.

"Yes, nearly everywhere I've travelled the British are responsible for so much that is wrong. It's fucked up."

"That's OK. I don't hold you personally responsible. Well, I do kind of hold you personally responsible but I'm going to have to think of the most suitable reparations." Atal let himself smile and he tried to make it a bit sexy.

"Perhaps I should be bringing you a cup of Assam rather than you bringing it to me?" She said.

"As I said I don't really feel it is your fault. Stop putting yourself at the centre of everything."

She laughed out loud at that. She seemed to be warming to him. "My grandfather was in Burma though. My family benefited from colonisation I'm afraid. Are your family from Assam?" She looked up at him.

"Oh no, no. I'm not even Indian, but I was born here. I'm half Syrian, half Iranian. You won't catch me thanking you for the railways, schools or the law courts or the good old systems in the good old jolly old days though."

"Fair enough. I would be disappointed if you did." The woman paused. "Look, I'm Kate by the way."

They shook hands.

"I forgot to thank you for bringing my bag down. I know I should give you a tip. I've been feeling bad about it. It was remiss of me. Hang on, I'll just go and get my purse," she said.

"Wait. Let me just get this straight. You think that the reason I've been offering you things is because I want a freaking tip?"

"Oh, sorry. Have I got the wrong end of the stick?"

"What?"

"Have I misunderstood?"

"You think I work here?"

"Well, yes. Don't you work here? I saw you cleaning out my loo and doing the laundry and I thought, what with you meeting me to carry my bag and everything, you must be working here. I saw you chatting to the French couple that does the cooking and so I thought that I was living next to the house where the staff stay."

"What do you think of their cooking by the way?"

"Honestly?"

"Yes, of course honestly."

"It's awful. There is no seasoning. No spices. Barely any salt and pepper. I'm getting a bit desperate."

"Did it give you the runs?"

"Not so far but there's always time."

"Let me cook for you. I'll make some chicken and lemon dhal. I've got enough ingredients for both of us. We can eat on the veranda tonight."

She looked at him with her heavy blinks. Blink, blink. "That would be nice. Thank you. I was dreading the next meal and it's not as if you can go somewhere else or buy some food somewhere. You are kind of stuck here."

"OK, I'll make a start."

"Do you need help? I'm not used to anyone cooking for me. It seems strange not to help. I'm not sure how good I am at being looked after."

"I would love it if you came to dinner with me at seven."

"Great."

"Oh, and by the way…" Atal heard himself say.

She turned to look at him expectantly,

"I don't work here. I'm a fellow guest. I'm renting the cottage, and you are annexed to my cottage. I'm the rich guy bestowing my largesse onto you in your little shack which clings to my great big house like a pesky little mollusc. I just thought I would help you with your bag, because it was a nice thing to do to welcome you here."

She put her hand to her mouth. "Oh sorry."

"It's OK. I think it's funny."

"So, you were just being kind. Thanks so much. I am an idiot. Sorry, sorry. But why are you cleaning my toilets and washing my sheets? Is that just you being nice, too?"

"I'll tell you later, when you come around."

He had never tried so hard to impress a woman before. He wondered why the fuck she had such an effect on him. He ran up the stone staircase, counting each step under his breath and banged on the huge door of the Mothership. He told Maria that he had taken Govind's advice and that he was cooking for a woman that was not used to having people do such things for her. He asked Maria if he could borrow a cup with some spices in it, please, just to make sure the flavour blew her mind. He would very much appreciate it.

When Maria heard that Atal was acting on Govind's advice and trying to serve others, she ushered him into her kitchen on the lower level and let him choose. He took some garlic and onions too. He remembered not to tell her that he was cooking chicken and ran as fast as he could down the hundred stone stairs to his kitchen. In his house it was possible to get the internet from five until seven in the evening and he managed to look up a recipe for chicken curry. He carefully fried the onions and the garlic, the Marsala spices and then the chicken browning it on both sides. He tried to cook with Kate in his mind. The thought of her opening her mouth and taking in what he had made for her and it going over her tongue and down into her throat made him happy. He constantly tasted the meal. It was good. He could do this. It might even be better than the cook at home.

When the rice was boiling, he pulled out the little table from the kitchen and laid it carefully. He called out to her from the kitchen window. "Katharina. Oh Katharina. Your dinner is served."

Kate came into the kitchen with a bunch of pink and yellow delicate little wildflowers tied with straw. She gave the bunch to him. "I found these little flowers growing behind the house. I hope it is all right to pick them. I wanted to bring you something."

No one had ever brought him a bunch of flowers before and to see her before him holding them out made him feel a rush of intense pleasure. She had changed. She was wearing a white flowing long dress, with a gold leather belt around her waist and gold sandals. He was pleased she had made an effort. He thought perhaps she had even brushed her big nest of hair, but he couldn't be sure. He wondered what she wore when she was not travelling. He tried to imagine her in a businesswoman's suit and high heels. He took the flowers and found a vase in his bedroom.

"This is delicious," she said, and he believed her. She was not the kind of person who would fake enthusiasm, he didn't think. They smoked a couple of joints together over the evening and she did not seem particularly stoned even though they were strong. She asked him many questions. Questions about his life and about his parents and he quickly found himself telling her about Raina and about his son. He told her about the time his mother had slapped his young wife across the face and that he had not stood up for her and protected his wife and how he felt it was that evening that made her decide to leave and go back to her family. How he knew that he would never love her as soon as he saw her but that his parents were anxious for him to settle down young and start a family and to create a Muslim dynasty with what they considered to be the right woman. The *right* woman meant from the right family and so they found him someone who had never left Syria before. She was desperately unhappy from the start and all he could feel was a horrible guilt that she had been dragged there because of him. The unpleasant feeling made him resent her and so he started to be short and cold with her. It was still unbelievable to him that the second time he ever had sex with her, in the dark and with no words exchanged she had become pregnant. He told Kate how he had cried when his two-year-old son had been taken away from him back to Syria and only then had he understood how deeply lonely Raina had felt. He told Kate of his heavy shame. The shame that sat between his shoulder blades and weighed him down. Raina and his son had escaped the war and fled to Paris and he dreamt of finding them. He also told her about how he felt about his parents – about the love and the hatred which ran through every day he spent with them.

"Could you leave? Could you start a life of your own?"

"Oh, I don't know."

"But why not?" she said.

"That's just not how we do things here."

But he knew her method, because it was his own. He knew, like she did, that to listen to people disarmed them, and that to be really interested in other people gave you considerable power. Most people had never met someone that was so deeply interested in them, that would prefer to listen than to speak. Someone that was not waiting for you to finish a sentence so that you could get in your own anecdote or remark. He then started to ask her questions which at first, she batted back at him but he gently persisted, and, despite herself, she revealed to him that she was divorced, worked with refugees, had two grown-up children who she adored beyond measure and that she liked good music and to dance. He also learnt that since her divorce she had had a quite few boyfriends but that she had not loved them enough or they had not loved her enough.

He felt shocked at how much he didn't want her to go to bed when she got up, stretched herself and said, "I'm afraid I have signed up to do that yoga class at the crack of dawn."

"With that shy guy with the acne from Kerala?"

"Yes."

"Are you good at yoga?"

"I'm so bad. I know people say you can't be bad at yoga. They should see me."

"Really, what time is the class?"

"Six-thirty."

"Fuck."

"I know. Atal, thanks so much for the delicious food. It was amazing. I feel so full! Once again you have shown me how incredibly kind you are. I really appreciate it. You know I'm going to do the washing up don't you?"

She went to go to the kitchen, and he leapt up and stood in the way of the door into the house.

"No, it was my absolute pleasure."

"Hey, let me contribute please. It makes me feel bad if I don't at least do the washing up."

He reached out and touched her forearm. It was soft. He liked its fullness.

"Sorry. I can't let you do that."

"Oh yes. You never explained why you are waiting on me hand and foot. Even cleaning the toilet which I find rather embarrassing."

"That's for tomorrow, I think. I will explain tomorrow."

He found the idea of making any sort of future arrangements with her encouraging.

Once again, he was acutely conscious of the sounds of her moving around in her room, probably undressing and putting on a night-dress. Damn, he wished she was in his bedroom now. He didn't know if he wanted to have sex with her, but he did want to lie down on his big double bed with her and carry on talking to her. He wanted to plump the bed cushions and put them under her bottom.

Before he slept, he put on his alarm. He would show her his OK yoga moves and get to check out her body when it was not covered in tunics and western over the top modesty dressing that all the women who travelled around India always wore – arms and legs covered all the time. Maybe he would be put off by what he saw and so he could stop obsessing over her. Once again to be allowed to think of higher things and get back to his reading and meditating and staring across the mountains.

In the morning, he brushed his teeth and ran his fingers through his curly hair. He threw on some track suit bottoms and a T-shirt. He thought it was a T-shirt that made his muscular torso look particularly good. He called out her name, got no answer, saw her pink flip-flops were not there on the outside mat as they usually were and ran down the stone steps to the scruffy yoga hall into which he had never actually been but passed a couple of times on his wanderings around Luna Range.

The class had already started. Ro and Syama were there. The mother of the twins and the Dutch girl were doing the cat pose. The yoga hall was painted in different rusty tones and there was obviously a major leak from the roof in the recent past because there was a large damp patch on the wooden floor which everyone had avoided. The view through the long slightly dirty window showed a lower variation of his magnificent view over the mountain peaks and then another range beyond that as if the world consisted entirely of impressive mountain ranges and nothing else. He grabbed a smelly mat and took a place next to Kate.

Kate was wearing a yellow, slightly stained T-shirt and tight-fitting knee length yoga pants.

He looked at her and smiled. She smiled back and rolled her eyes as she started on a quite sloppy salutation to the sun. She was not particularly bad, but he noticed an expression on her face which at first, he couldn't recognise but when he saw how slow she was to change position he realised that it was boredom. She was finding it hard not to drift off and think of something else. He wondered what she was thinking about. He wanted to know what was making it so impossible for her to concentrate on the gentle instructions of the teacher.

Halfway through the class the teacher told everyone to do a headstand. Ro and Syama did theirs with elegant ease. He was just starting to think about attempting a headstand himself when he saw Kate kicking herself up into a precarious position, managing to balance for a minute and then flip right over down on her back with a loud slam that echoed through the empty hall.

Immediately he moved over to her where she lay. "Are you OK?"

She was laughing. "Ooooffff, bloody hell."

The shy yoga guy must have been freaked out by the only Westerner being the one who whacked her back so fucking hard because he shouted out. "What are you doing? Why did you even attempt something you know you can't do? What a stupid move."

"Yes, we can all do it here because we have practiced yoga for years. It is in our blood because we are Indian." It was Syama, getting a dig in.

"Hey dude, maybe you should ask her if she is all right before you get angry with her. It's not very yogic of you, is it?" Atal said.

Kate sat up pushing her arms behind her back.

"I'm fine. Sometimes it is great to have a bit of padding on my bottom."

"Ok, well next time take it easy. Try to be a bit calmer in your movements. It is all about quiet control, not about showing off to other people in the class."

Atal took the opportunity to whisper to Kate, "Let's go," and she nodded. They rolled up their mats without looking at the others and then ran up the steps to his house laughing.

They spent most of the next four days together. If she tried to go back to her room to read, he would shout out her name until she came back – "Katy, Katy, Katy!" She tried to be annoyed with him and called him a 'needy bastard' but he could tell that she loved it really because she spent more time with him.

He gave her a tour of the K Range, and of the Mothership. Govind and Maria let him show her around the interior briefly but made it clear that they did not want to be interrupted for long. He took her to meet the crazy Swedish man Lars who was making a house of rubbish. Lars could barely hide his contempt for Atal. Atal supposed it was because someone had told him that Atal's family were rich but seemed to want to talk to Kate about his childhood and why this project was so important to him. Lars did not ask Kate a single question about herself and after fifteen minutes Atal mumbled something about a tight schedule. Lars cast Atal a look of resentment and then carried on sorting bottles from tins.

Atal took her to the cowshed where the Irish vagrant seemed to live with the cattle and had been doing so for at least four years according to Syama. He never came up to the communal area. The Irishman also wanted to talk to Kate about his life, and how this was the only place where he had found peace. He told Kate that he might stay there with the cattle, if Govind let him, at K Farm, until he died.

"What is it with you?" Atal asked Kate as they walked away. "Why do men want to tell you all about their sorry lives? You should start charging for this. And I notice they don't ask you a single question."

Kate shrugged. "I'm used to that. You just sort of switch off."

They went to the dorm which housed the Frenchies, the Dutch girl and two ex-IT managers from Bangalore who wore long leather coats, listened to industrial Indian techno and smoked weed all day long. One of the ex- IT managers had started painting a mural on the side of the dorm. He had taken magic mushrooms a couple of days before and was attempting to depict the mechanical *but incredibly wise* little creatures he had seen.

Atal couldn't help saying, "Everyone sees mechanical creatures, Bro."

"Which means that they really do exist."

"Or, that we are all incredibly dull and imagine the same shit."

The ex-IT manager shrugged his shoulders.

"Hey, does Govind know about this painting, Dude?" The ex-IT manager looked up at him.

"Who's Govind?"

"He's the ruler of K-farm. He's the leader that lives in the mothership. Never mind, he probably won't find out. I've never seen him mixing with us lot down the mountain, anyway, but Syama or Ro might tell on you. You had better make sure they are on your side, Dude."

Atal and Kate went for a swim in the deep, green rock pool with the small waterfall and she sat in her wet bra and knickers on a mossy boulder island, and he looked at her out of the corner of his eye and thought she looked like a European painting. He asked her if he could sketch her in the notebook, he always carried around with him, and she said that she felt too chilly to sit like that in her wet underwear. She got up and narrowly avoided slipping back into the rock pool. She jumped on the bank and went behind a rock and put on her creased blue dress. He made a fire from leaves, his lighter and some dry wood he had collected to warm her up after her swim. They sat around jumping up to sit in different spots trying to avoid the direction of the smoke and he talked about his search for a higher consciousness. He spoke about his experimentation with magic mushrooms – with micro-dosing, eating a small quantity and having a slightly altered, but not uncontrollable state for days at a time- to develop his senses. He spoke of his lack of patience with the way religions promised an existence beyond death. He spoke of his difficulty with his parents and their inability to understand that he did not want to go to mosque and pray. He thought that they believed that he would come back into the faith once they had managed to get him to stop puffing. He also told her that he was interested in medicinal plants and fantasised about travelling around the country treating people who were sick with natural remedies.

She asked if he would ever want to come to the UK.

"What? With a name like mine? I hear they hate Muslim boys there, even more than they do here. No way, darling."

When they sat at Sunset Point later in the day, she referred to their previous conversation. "Well, I think there is great comfort about death in quantum physics from what I can understand of it, which isn't a great deal, mostly what I've read in my son's New Scientist magazine. There is something called granularity, which means that everything in the universe is made up of tiny pieces whether that's atoms, quarks, higgs or packets of energy, and then think of indeterminacy which means that electrons actually disappear from existence until they interact with something and then think on relationality which means that the universe is not how things are, it's how things interact and occur. Everything that is real is only real as a measurable distance to something else. Without two points to compare, there is nothing to measure."

"I think I understand." He did like looking at her olive-coloured eyes though. Just like the green olives they sold in the market most local to his home.

"So, hold onto that because there is a further concept which comes from something called *Loop Quantum Gravity* which basically states there exists a smallest amount of area that space can be reduced to. This stems from an idea that any part of space is essentially an interwoven fabric of tiny loops. Are you still with me?"

"Yes, I think so. I mean my parents both did physics, so I suppose this stuff is in my blood."

"So, the universe is an expanding and finite system of a massive number of particles. Eventually the universe will reach its expansion limit and shrink back down into a minimum area, at which point it will bounce back into an expanding state. It seems to me that death does not exist in a timeless, spaceless world. Immortality doesn't mean a perpetual existence in time but resides outside of time altogether. The particles that we are made up of have existed, will exist and exist now even beyond our birth or death. I find that immensely comforting. Don't you?"

He found himself leaning into her as she turned to him with the magnificent view behind her.

She put her hand on his chest and pushed him gently away and looked into his eyes. "Atal, you know that I'm going to the Philippines in a couple of days. You know that I have to leave?"

Atal felt a sharp pain in his sinuses. He felt a similar, searing pain when Raina had left with his son. He also could feel that tears were leaking out of the corner of his eyes, and he quickly put his hand up to stop them. "Why would you want to leave all this? Are there mountain ranges better than this in the Philippines?" He gestured towards the sky and the mountains. Also, why would you want to leave me? Haven't you been exquisitely happy these last few days."

"I bought the ticket long before I met you."

"I will pay you to stay. How much did your ticket cost? I'll double it."

"Don't be silly, Atal. I arranged to meet my kids in the Philippines before I left. They want me to go diving with them there."

"Are you sure it is your kids you are meeting?"

"I'm sure."

The Frenchies were also leaving the day after Kate. They suggested that a small group of them should go and spend the night on the top of the mountain and watch the sun come up. They took lots of water and fruit and nuts, torches and blankets. The IT guys, the Frenchies, Ro and Syama and the shy - but it had turned out quite angry - yoga guy all set off in the dark, using their torches and phones to light up the narrow mountain path. Atal set himself right behind Kate,

"I'm obviously shining the torch at your bum every so often, if that's all right? It's keeping me going."

Kate laughed.

The IT guys were the first to arrive and by the time the rest of the group had reached the top they had already put on their industrial Indian house music and started a fire. A chillum was quickly passed round, and the yoga guy was encouraged to try it for the first time. They danced round and Atal and Kate echoed each other's movements from the opposite side of the fire, the Frenchies going crazy with their expressive dancing. The next thing he knew everyone appeared to be lying down except for him and the yoga guy. He felt that Kate would want him to engage the yoga guy in conversation, that Kate was telling him in her head to engage with the yoga guy.

He made an effort. "I was wondering. Have you ever considered stepping your yoga career up a notch and trying astral projection? It might be just what you need to get on the next ladder of your career."

He heard a snort of laughter from where Kate lay.

The yoga guy looked worried and Atal realised that the poor man was stoned for the first time in his life and finding it hard to follow what anyone was saying, let alone hearing him talk about "taking off the external body as if it were a cloak and using the astral body for experiencing the inner world of the astral and for groovy journeys though the atmosphere."

“Have you ever gone on an astral journey, Atal?” the yoga guy asked.

“No, as a matter of fact I have not. Although I would very much like to.”

For some reason this got Kate going again and he could see her body rocking with laughter. This got him and then even the shy yoga guy going so that they were all three joined in loud, hooting laughter.

A moment later everyone seemed to be asleep except for him. He could see Kate had curled up into a foetal position. He took his blanket from his rucksack, put it over her to keep her warm and lay next to her.

He whispered to her, “Kate. These past days have been some of the happiest I have ever known. I have loved being with you. I have loved caring for you Kate. I love you, Kate. I really do. I love and respect you so much.”

She seemed to be fast asleep, or if she had heard him, she had decided to ignore him. He dared put his hand underneath her T-shirt and onto the warm skin of her stomach, which moved up and down with her breathing. He smelt the depth of her hair. He listened to the rustling of the eucalyptus trees behind them and the popping of the dying fire.

Delicate, tiny thing that she was, Ro was snoring like a huge and very ancient man. One of the IT guys lifted his head up and shouted out grumpily “Who the hell is making that terrible noise?” He looked accusingly at Atal.

‘It’s not me, Dude. It’s that little girl over there; would you believe it?’

His cock was pressing hard against Kate’s back. He dared put his hand inside her leggings and touched her pussy. It was wet and that encouraged him to stroke her clit and then slip two fingers inside her. She pushed her arse against his hard-on, and he moved his hands and pulled down her leggings. Making sure the blanket covered them both and keeping his movements to a minimum he slipped into her and moved slightly back and forth, playing with her clit all the while.

"It's nearly our last night together. We just had to do this Kate. We had to do this."

Atal and Kate fell asleep for a while, but they were woken up when they saw that the sun was starting to rise from behind the mountains and shouted for everyone to sit up and see. Slowly each of them pushed themselves up into sitting and looked out into the orange light. He watched Kate as she looked out over the new day and she turned to him and smiled. "How beautiful is this?"

"It's really beautiful but would you be happy about going down the mountain and into my bed pretty soon so we can fuck each other's brains out."

"OK," she said.

They spent the whole day in bed, only getting up to eat boiled rice and some oranges which is all he had. When he first took off his clothes and stood in front of her, she touched the tattoo across his chest. The name of his son.

"You like it?""

"I hate tattoos. Jibril is the Arabic version of the name Gabriel, isn't it?"

"Yes."

"I was pregnant with a child and had a late miscarriage. We had decided on the name Gabriel."

"So, we both lost Gabriel."

"I hope you will see your son again, Atal. I think you will."

And he lent down to where her mouth was and kissed her for the first time. Then he tasted her pussy for the first time and wondered what it tasted like when it didn't have his come in it. He supposed he would never know that. As they knew they would never see each other again they did everything that they could think the other might like. If one of them started to drift off to sleep, the other woke them up with more touching and licking and fucking and sucking.

The twins burst in the next morning, shouting for Kate.

"It smells awful in here. Yuck, what is that disgusting smell?' Kate sat up with the sheet around her.

"What's up you two?" Atal said to the twins.

"Syama said to remind you that the Land Rover is coming to take Kate to town so you can take the bus to the airport."

"When is it coming?"

"In an hour. You only have an hour to pack. Syama said you'd better get a fucking move on."

"I'll tell your mother you swore," Atal said.

"We will tell everyone that you two were sexing in bed together."

The twins ran off laughing.

He didn't beg her to stay as he wanted to. He wanted to lie on the floor and hang onto her legs, so she couldn't walk. He watched her get up quickly and put on her clothes. His nose filled up with terrible pain, and it started to bleed, dripping bright red blood onto his chest and onto his tattoo. She ran and got him some toilet paper, held it against his nose and pinched it until it stopped and then she cleaned up the blood on his chest with a wet cloth. She kissed him on his bloody chest and then on his lips so he could taste his own blood. He explained to her softly that he couldn't get up otherwise he might cry like a baby as well as bleed and that was too much liquid coming from him what with all the coming he had done. He told her he was going to stay in bed and put a pillow over his head. He hoped she wouldn't think him rude. She kissed him on his forehead and told him that she understood. As he watched her go, he knew they would never be in the same room together again in this life, but he felt certain that like two particles they were entangled forever, mirroring each other beyond the distances of time, place and space.

Sara, sorry to text you so late. I think I have fallen in love with a prince on a mountain top. Classic late middle-aged woman travelling on her own for the first time huh. The trouble is that he is twenty-four years younger than me and his family are practicing Muslims. I will probably never see him again and yet, I know I will never forget him. He was the sweetest tasting man I have ever met.

KATE ON THE STAND
May 2018

Kate's name was called out - God, she got tired of her name in those days in court – every time she heard it, she got a shock of fear. She got up from the dock and started to walk to the stand. Her stomach lurched as if she was going to be sick and that high-pitched ringing in her ears came back. She somehow got her legs to work across the blue pattern carpet and up then up the three wooden stairs and into the wooden witness box. She was surprised to see there was a badly fitted square of the ugly carpet in there.

She looked up towards where her family and friends sat, for the first time able to see them all clearly. She could see how pale and pinched Bille and Charlie's faces were. Charlie had his arm around Billie. She could see that Billie was trying not to cry, biting the insides of her cheeks, but her eyes were almost pleading. She didn't want to see her mother or anyone else but the children's faces. They were all that mattered. Then she looked across at the jury, for the first time from this face-on angle. It was the seventh day of the case, and they were tired. This morning, they had been shown a video of Kate's sweet car, impounded since that day, with a man showing that you could only lock the door manually as the key fob didn't work, and unless you locked it twice, the boot could stay unlocked. They had paid for an ex-policeman to make this video, and although Kate and Jitendra felt it an important bit of evidence which showed how easy it was to leave the car unlocked, the jury hadn't seemed particularly impressed and hadn't written any notes.

Kate was wearing her best navy shirt dress saved for this day and had her hair done at a local Maidstone hairdresser yesterday after court was adjourned. The hairdresser had asked if it was for a special occasion and when she had told her that she was a defendant in Maidstone Crown Court the conversation came to a halt. She tried to stand in a way that seemed respectful, yet confident, her hands in front of her, resting on the witness box ledge. She had practiced this in front of the Jitendra and her kids She tried to convey that she was a mother, a professional, grounded and stable person, but that she, in certain circumstances, could be a bit careless and scatty. How had Juliet described it when she was in the witness box? That Kate was the kind of person to lead a trip to the Calais camp, remind everyone to take their passports and then forget her own. Kate thought that was fair. She was to address her answers to the jury. That's what Jitendra had said. She was to project. She was to speak carefully and clearly.

The prosecution barrister stood up eagerly as if she had been waiting for this moment for the last few days. Kate had only seen the back of her head and was surprised to see what a pleasant open face she had, with a slightly too long fringe she had to brush away with her hand. She wondered why she had become a prosecution barrister. Once again, they were taken through the sheets of texts between Ranim and Kate, just as the prosecution had done when Ranim was on the stand.

"I refer to text number thirty-two on page four."

She waited a moment for Kate to get to it.

"Can I ask why you called Ranim 'Love' here. Why did you text- 'Hey love, I look forward to meeting you at Brixton station?'"

"That's just the word I use to address people."

"You use the term 'Love' towards someone you say you have only worked with. That's intimate for a work colleague, isn't it?"

"Yes. That is a word I use a lot. I think if you went through all my texts, you would see that I use the word to address all sorts of different people even if I have only worked with them."

"I suggest that you had a deep, loving friendship with Ranim. The kind of friendship which would make you plan to bring in her friend's child in the boot of a car."

Kate felt a calm wash over her. Surely the barrister was seeming a bit desperate focusing on the word 'Love'. Is that all she had?

"No, I had a working relationship with her, but I do admire her hugely. I don't admire her so much that I would help her to do something like this. I also can't imagine her ever asking me to do something like this."

The barrister then took Kate through their movements within the camp using the fucking, shitty old map. She could see that the jury were beside themselves with boredom at the repetition, either looking half asleep or fidgeting.

"So, when the journalist was interviewing in the bus at the end of the trip with the Eritrean interpreter, where were you?"

"The journalist was on the bus with Ranim, the Syrian interpreter, not Faven, the Eritrean interpreter. The interview was with a Syrian woman, so the journalist needed Ranim in there."

"The photographer saw you walking away with Ranim, Ebeid and her son. Did you leave with them so you could put Ebeid's son in the boot?"

"How could I leave with Ranim if she was in the mother and baby bus with the journalist?" Kate said. *Come on, how many fucking times do we have to go through this?*

"Why did you leave the area and go to the car then?"

"Because I needed to go to the toilet urgently. The last time I went to the toilet was when we met the photographer at the petrol station."

"And you thought it was a good idea to relieve yourself between two cars."

Then Kate turned her head briefly towards the judge but addressed the jury.

"There were thousands of people living in desperate conditions with a row of ten portaloos to serve them all. They were never cleaned. Who by? We had been told that women had been attacked when they had gone into them. So, for those two reasons any women visiting was strongly advised to pee between cars if they could. We had been there a long time. I also urgently needed to change my tampon."

The women leant forward. Kate could see that her mouth was twitching.

"You knew that you had your period on the morning you left?"

"Yes."

Where was she going with this?

"So why didn't you take extra precautions?"

Kate let this sit. What did she mean? "I'm sorry, I don't understand what you mean."

"Why didn't you take precautions to er, serve the fact that you were menstruating?" Again, Kate paused.

"What kind of precautions?"

The woman flushed. A couple of the male jurors shifted uneasily. Some of the women in the jury smiled. "Why didn't you wear a thick sanitary towel?' the prosecution barrister said.

Kate thought she heard a titter from the gallery.

"Because I use tampons, but I'm not sure of the significance of my choice of sanitary product."

Truth be told, Kate had never been the most organised person when it came to her periods. Perhaps a different type of person would have thought to have used a tampon and a sanitary towel for the long day, but Kate had never thought like that.

The prosecution barrister bent her head and looked at her notes. Her lips twitched again. "Can we move onto your interview?"

Here we go, thought Kate.

"When you were asked if you knew if anyone you were with had a relative in the camp you said, 'I don't know'. I suggest that you did know and that in fact you had been planning to help Ebeid bring her eldest child through to the UK for weeks before you went."

"I said I don't know because I was very confused about what had happened. I had never met Ebeid before and hadn't been told that the person coming with us had a son in the camp."

"But right at the end you met the son, didn't you? She introduced you to her son."

"Yes, she did."

"So why didn't you tell the police that?"

Kate breathed in and out. She took her time. That's what Jitendra had said, *but not too much time, otherwise it could seem like you are overpreparing.*

"It was a highly stressful day. I was responsible for the safety of everyone I had asked to come with me. At the same time, I was trying to get the best possible story whilst protecting the identity of the women we met there. When I saw that boy in the boot, I didn't know what had happened or who had known about it and I didn't want to get anyone into trouble by making assumptions. I regret being vague. I should have said that I had discovered at the last moment that Ebeid had a son in there, but I didn't. I wasn't sure that the boy in the boot was her son and so I didn't want to imply anything that I didn't absolutely know to be true."

"Was the reason you said, 'I don't know' to cover for your agreement weeks before to hide this young man in the boot?"

"No. Why would I risk my job, my life and my reputation to help someone I had never met? My job relies on me having a calm character with good judgement so that I can work with refugee women. Why would I risk that for this one person who I had no contact or relationship with? What would my motive be?"

"Perhaps you thought it was the right thing to do. That it was his last chance."

The prosecution barrister sat down. No one else asked her any further questions.

At lunch her children hugged her and told her she had done well. Her old friend Jim O'Leary had turned up. He was wearing a white crumpled suit, and a lime green shirt. Nearly elegant, but due to his innate scruffiness, never quite that. His thick white hair made him so much more handsome than he had been as a teenager. He hugged and kissed her and said that he had seen her from the gallery and that he had sat right at the back, which is why she hadn't seen him. That he wished that he had been able to come from the start but that he had only just come back from visiting his mum in Ireland. She had known him since she was fourteen years old and was deeply touched by his support, particularly when she knew that he could be so fragile emotionally. When he had his nervous breakdown a couple of years before, one of his delusions was that he felt that he was going to be put in prison. That he deserved a long sentence in prison. What for, he never said.

"Well, done. You did well there. It was like a television courtroom scene." Jim said,

"Yeah, well. If it's a television show, then I want to change the channel. How about a sit-com," Kate said.

"I think it is a sit-com," Jim said,

"How about when she said that thing about sanitary towels? It certainly made Granny laugh." Billie said.

"Was that Granny laughing? I thought I heard a woman laugh."

Kate suddenly felt overwhelmed with irritation that her mother had laughed. Perhaps she wouldn't have felt so irritated if they hadn't had that little scene with her mother and Patty in the beach house last night.

The evening before she was due to appear in the stand was a crucial one. Charlie and Billie cooked her a simple meal of pasta with tomato sauce. They did breathing and stretching and walked along the estuary front. Her mother was staying with her old friend Patty in Whitstable. Just after they had eaten her mother texted her, asking if she and Patty could pop by the beach hut. Kate was grateful to Patty for driving her mother the thirty minutes to court each day, but she didn't particularly feel like seeing either her Mum or Patty when she needed to be calm and focused. She didn't need her nerves jangled by their constant reminiscing and nostalgia.

When her mother and Patty came to the beach hut, Kate moved so they could sit on the sofa and Billie offered them both a cup of tea.

"How are you feeling about tomorrow, love?" her mother said.

"Well, Charlie and Billie are doing a great job of keeping me calm."

"Oh, you'll be fine darling. I was just saying to Patty that it reminds me of my court appearance when I tied myself to the railings outside South Africa house in the 80's. I think it was 1985. I used it as an opportunity to speak out against Apartheid in court. I used it as a platform. Do you think you might speak out about the appalling conditions at Calais?"

For fuck's sake, Kate thought.

"Mum, I don't think you were tried at a Crown Court, for something you might be sent down for seven years for."

"Wasn't it at Crown Court? I think it was!"

"Sorry, Mum. I really doubt it was. I don't think you can compare going to a magistrate's court and getting a fine with what I'm going through. I'm looking at a seven-year sentence here."

Billie spoke to her Gran. "Hey, Gran. We're trying to make sure Mum feels relaxed."

"I'm not trying to make your Mum, unrelaxed. I was here to gee her on. Inspire her even. I thought she might like to hear that her old mum had been in a similar situation."

Bille was now standing by her. She could see how upset her mother had made her.

"I've heard about that fucking speech in a court, a magistrate's court, by the way, so many times. Could you please stop putting yourself at the centre stage? I would be so happy to swap places with you and for you to go into the witness box tomorrow, but I'm afraid it's got to be me. It's like I'm starring in a play that I never even auditioned for. Just for once, can you be the supporting actor? Please."

Her Mother then burst into tears, as she always did whenever any one dared answer back. Patty rubbed her arm. Patty had been rubbing her arm like this for decades.

"I would love to go into the witness box instead of you, but I can't. I feel so powerless."

Kate looked at her mum weeping and pulled herself back from her fury. "It's alright mum. I know it's hard for you too, but would you mind if you and Patty go now and us three can continue just winding it down now. I really want to try and get some sleep."

They went back into the court for the closing speeches. Jitendra had asked her to read the summing up she had written in their little room. Kate got her to change the bit in which Jitendra reminded the court that Ebeid was the last person to touch the boot, when she removed the bag.

"So, you are implying that she deliberately didn't shut the boot so that her son could get in anytime?"

"Yes."

"The prosecution hasn't proved that she knew about it. I thought they were meant to prove their case."

"Her evidence seemed very muddled Kate. She didn't come across well at all. Anyway, you are being too nice. It's important that we differentiate between you and the mother in the jury's minds."

"Jitendra, my children are there watching me. I don't want them to see us throwing the mother under the bus to save my neck."

Jitendra looked at her. "I think the kids would mind a lot more if you went to jail."

"I'm asking you not to do that."

CALAIS CAMP
October 2016

"Right, let's go to the official mother and baby unit. I've got a couple of texts from Faven saying that the meeting will go on for hours."

The group all walked fast with Ranim and Kate at the front, down a road with tents and protected shipping units which some of the people in the camp described by an Ethiopian man as 'prison cells' the last time Kate was there.

"You go in there for the beds and heat, but they take your handprint, and you are not free to try and jump the lorries and cars at night. So, you are really stuck, not just camp stuck."

This time there were queues of children outside the shipping unit area. Priya asked Kate what was happening there and Kate asked Ranim if she knew.

"Unaccompanied children have been told to register and get a wrist band. If they do not, then they will be arrested and detained just like everyone else."

One of the children who looked about ten years old ran to Valentine and made a praying motion. "Please, please. You are a good English man. Take me to UK. Take me with you."

Valentine looked uncomfortable and quickly backed away from the boy.

"What about the children here? What will happen to them?" Priya said.

"Well, Lord Dubs tried to make the government promise to give sanctuary to some unaccompanied children – there are meant to be a thousand children who are alone here."

Kate lent down to the boy. The boy lifted the leg of his filthy tracksuit bottom. There was a deep purple oval shaped bruise.

"The police hit me with bullet."

Valentine looked at it. "That does look like a rubber bullet bruise. I've seen them before."

"Bad men come to the camp. Some of the French police are paid by the bad man."

The child started to make a loud, wailing, sobbing sound. Valentine responded by walking away with a stony expression and the three women looked hopelessly at the child.

Ranim and Kate knelt and embraced him on either side.

"You must register with the French." Ranim said. "He must try and claim asylum with the French. It is too, too dangerous here for a child. Europe should be so ashamed. This is a humanitarian disaster. How can they let little children suffer like this?" she started to cry.

Priya handed the child a Kit-Kat from her rucksack. He snatched it, scoffed it and asked for more. Priya shook her head and showed her hands to say that she had no more. The boy looked at them all quickly, decided that they weren't going to help him and then ran away from them as fast as he had approached them.

The group walked on in silence for a few moments. Then Ranim turned to Kate.

"Kate, I didn't like the questions the journalist woman was trying to make me ask my friend in the caravan."

"Why, what was she saying?"

"It always seems as if she was trying to make my friend cry. How did it make you feel when you thought you were going to die on the sea? How does it feel to not know where your husband is? Pushing, pushing until tears fell down her cheeks."

"I'm sorry, she's usually alright. I think of Priya as a good person. I think she is tense, not helped by the photographer. I think he's putting pressure on her. I've never seen her like this before." Kate said.

"He hates all of us. What is his problem?"

"He seems to have a lot of problems. While he is boasting about having been in Syria, he seems the most terrified of all of us. I couldn't think of a worse person for *The Daily World* to send here. What a total arsehole he is. Sorry Ranim I know you don't like swearing," Kate said.

"You are right. I don't like swearing but, in this case, I cannot help thinking you are justified. He is an arsehole! A total arsehole."

Kate and Ranim laughed a bit too loudly and Priya and Valentine turned back to look at them.

Ranim received a text. "It's my friend Ebeid who was in the car. She just texted."

"Can you get her to come to the Kid's Café? We need to start gathering together to leave."

Priya managed to get through the French official security and into the makeshift building where the home office meeting was taking place because they thought she was a refugee woman. Once again Valentine and Kate were left together. Men with flak jackets came over to them, both with walkie talkies.

Kate understood one of the men saying in French, "It looks like there are some fucking journalists here."

"OK, Valentine. They don't seem to want journalists in this area. Please don't take any photos. Leave this to me please."

Kate went up to the angriest looking man in a flak jacket. "We are from a British charity."

"We don't want any fucking British people in this area. We don't want any journalists or British people. This is a French controlled part of the camp. You choose Brexit, and now you can fuck off."

"Well, I didn't choose Brexit but OK. We are waiting for someone from our charity to come out of the UK home office meeting. I hope that is alright. Will you let me try and call them?"

"Please move over there now. We are not interested in what the British have to say about the camp. It is their fault. All this is their fault."

Kate wasn't about to defend British immigration policies to anyone. "OK, we will stand there." She texted both Priya and Faven.

Please come out of the mother and baby unit as soon as possible. The French demolition men don't want us here and it's all getting a bit tense.

OK, just coming. I'm with Faven, I'll bring her, Priya answered.

The group of them walked fast back towards the main drag where the Kid's Café was. Priya was nervy and irritable.

"I suppose we will have to go into the Kids Café. We have only got one interview despite being here for hours and at least there we know there are people willing to talk to us."

"But you really need to speak to women. This is meant to be about women's experience of the overland journey and Calais."

"Well, I'm afraid that you haven't provided me with the interviewees that you promised. I'll have to expand the piece to talk about everyone's experience."

"Christ Priya, you've seen what it's like here. Everyone is absolutely terrified."

"Yes, I know. I'm terrified. It's not worth being that terrified, for stories that are just not going to have an impact."

Kate stopped herself arguing with Priya as she knew it would make things worse. There were a couple of trestle tables outside the Kids Café with huge piles of bags of cheesy Whatsits and hula-hoops that some British charity must have donated. Kate wanted to have a packet of hula-hoops more than anything. She suddenly realised that she was desperate to do a pee and that she was incredibly hungry. She saw that Valentine was lingering by her side as if he wanted her to protect him. Faven was texting and eating some cheesy whatsits.

"I'm just phoning my boss. You go in," Kate said.

He hesitated. She saw that he wanted to go in with her. She crossed the path so he would not overhear what she was saying to her boss.

Juliet answered quickly. "How's it going?"

"Not great. It's a bit mad here. The French police have started demolition. It's hard to get the women to speak. Faven's OK, I'm just looking at her now. We're just by the Kid's Café. Priya's being really stressy and difficult. She has been wanting women with more gruesome stories, and the photographer is such a dick. I can't stand him. It's made it so hard having him around."

"Oh God, no. I'm sorry. Look leave as soon as possible. It will get dark soon. If you can't get interviews, you might as well get out of there."

"Yes, I think you're right. I'll get everyone together now."

THE MIRROR LAKE
July 2016

Keith had seen the same mask as the face on other female visitors to their guesthouse when they first met him. Keith was laughing loudly to himself in anticipation of one of his icebreaker jokes as he walked up to the new guests. Only the occasional Aussie traveller ever seemed to really appreciate his humour but still he couldn't help himself. He had to come out with it even though Mary-Joy had told him not too many a time and particularly when people had just arrived.

"Darling, you are so funny. You make me laugh so much. But not everybody gets you. They find you over the top. It's their loss, but that is the way it is. The world is not ready for your humour yet. It will be one day - maybe not in your lifetime - but it will one day."

Keith could tell that the women and her two grown-up kids were not going to be receptive to him in the slightest, but he had to crack his latest favourite joke anyway. It was a bit rude, but he thought he would give it a go. "Hey, do you fancy a joke after your travels?"

The three of them looked at him wearily. The older woman said, "Go on then."

"OK, then. An old man is given a session with a call girl for his birthday by his nephew. She arrives at his door all dressed up as a French maid, very sexy, with frilly whatnots and pinny and such and suspenders."

The middle-aged woman nodded quickly as if she wanted him to hurry up and finish. He deliberately slowed down his voice.

"She says all sexy like, *I'm here for Super Sex*. So, the old man takes his time to think and finally says – *I'll think I'll take the soup thank you*."

The son at least let out a little giggle. The middle-aged woman and her daughter rolled their eyes.

"Geddit? Soup or Sex sounds like Super Sex? The old bloke would rather have soup."

"Right," said the middle-aged woman.

"Sorry, was that a bit blue for you, love?" Keith said.

"No, not too blue," the woman said.

"What do you laugh at then? What tickles your fancy?" Keith asked.

"I don't really laugh at jokes."

"Even this one? Now, don't worry. It's not at all blue."

The woman breathed out sharply through her nose as Keith told his next new joke. "So why did the scarecrow win an award?"

"I don't know," said the son. At least he had the decency not to just ignore him.

"Because he was outstanding in his field," Keith said, looking at them all, his eyebrows raised as high as he could push them. Daring them not to laugh.

"That's pretty funny actually," the pretty looking daughter said without laughing. The other two forced out a titter.

"Blimey, you're a serious bunch. As I asked before, what do you laugh at then? What tickles your fancies?"

The mother sighed a bit. "I suppose when people say funny things or tell me things that have happened to them that are funny, or funny things just happen in front of your eyes, or the way someone says something. Spontaneous funny is the funniest."

"Does that mean you don't like stand-up?" Keith asked.

"Yes, I do like stand-up. I think we all like stand-up. All three of us have been to stand up together."

"Well, that's planned funny."

"Yes, I suppose it is. But I suppose it sort of seems spontaneous if it's done well enough."

This stuck-up woman was talking absolute bloody rubbish and so easy to catch out. It wasn't even that fun catching her out because it was so easy. She didn't know what she was talking about. Keith got the feeling that she knew that he liked a bit of banter and for that reason she was being deliberately non-committal. She didn't want to engage with him at all. Perhaps she was a man-hater or something. You sometimes get them coming out to Coron.

"OK, guys, when did you last find something funny?"

The woman looked at her kids for help but then spoke before they had a chance to help her. "Well, we all went to a yoga class on El Nido yesterday morning because I wanted to show the kids that I had done a bit of yoga in India. I've been away from them for quite a few months, and I wanted to impress them. We all laughed a lot because the teacher kept telling us to pull up the muscles of our paginas. Even Charlie, who hasn't got a pagina."

"Particularly Charlie," said the daughter.

"A what? What was this woman talking about?"

"Well, you know, rhymes with..."

"What?"

"Well, it rhymes with vagina. The woman was mispronouncing the word and saying pagina. It seemed funny at the time, although it seems a bit infantile now. You did ask us when we last really laughed."

"It was really funny to be fair. But you had to be there," the grown-up son said.

Keith wondered why he said, *to be fair*. What did being funny have to do with fairness? It made him wince a little to hear her say vagina, especially the way she said it. Not sexy but like a doctor or a biology teacher or something. "Now who's being blue," Keith said.

"I didn't say you were being blue. Also saying the word vagina is not being blue."

"What does being blue even mean? I thought blue meant you were sad."

The woman explained to her daughter. "Well, it means being a bit risqué, a bit saucy. It's a bit of an old-fashioned word."

"I'm not that much older than you, you old frump," Keith thought. Keith didn't like the way this woman looked at him as if she were better than him. She was very sure of herself. He bet she hadn't had sex in years by the look of her, sort of sturdy and dried up at the same time if that was possible. Dry hands and a few brown marks on her face, already. Menopausal.

Filipino women didn't seem to get the menopause or certainly never talked about it in front of men. He didn't have that many friends from back home, and only one or two were still with their first wife, but those that were spoke with horror about their wives' menopauses. All anger and sand-paper fannies.

"Look, sometimes I'm a bit much for the English people who come here. No wonder I had to come and live in the Philippines because you might say I've got a bit of a quirky personality. Here everyone knows old Keith and just accepts me for who I am. Not everyone understands my off-the-wall humour, so don't you worry. You'll get used to me during your stay, no doubt. Most people do. They learn to love me. Mark my words, when you leave here, you'll think I'm the best thing since sliced bread. People usually do."

Keith could hear Mary-Kay's flip-flops behind him. She walked up beside him with her lovely perfumed, sweet jasmine, coconut smell. Pretty much all women in Southeast Asia smelt as sweet as that. Even Mary-Joy's fat old Mum, as wide as she was tall, smelt delicious. Good enough to eat, although the thought of doing that to Mary-Joy's mum made him feel seriously ill. He put his big old arm around Mary-Joy's neat waist and squeezed her a bit too tightly, probably to offer himself reassurance in front of this cold and uppity crew. He could feel by Mary-Joy's bracing muscles that she wanted him to ease off a little but couldn't wriggle away from his paws because she knew that wouldn't make a good first impression. He released his hold a little and she stepped away.

"May I introduce my better half? My very good lady wife, Mary-Joy. I just call her *The Boss*. Just ask her anything. She knows everything about Coron, even though she's a Manila girl. She also knows everyone, and everyone loves her. Perhaps a bit too much if you know what I mean?"

Keith saw that all three; the mother, the pretty daughter and the tall dark son were trying to hide their shock at the age difference. He felt like just saying, "Yes, it's thirty-eight years between us before you try and guess."

He knew that Mary-Joy would see it too and that it sometimes upset her but instead she just warmly welcomed them to the island of Coron and asked them if they would like a fruit juice on the veranda of their house before she showed them to their stilted cottage on the hill with the glorious view over the bay. Mary-Joy had the uncanny knack of knowing what guests were going to be like just by their first moments at the cottages. If they were going to be fussy and difficult, or if they would just hole themselves up in their cottage and keep themselves to themselves without asking a single question throughout their stay. She just knew. She knew if couples were happy together or if they were having problems, or if one was keeping a secret from the other or having an affair back home or something. He wished that she wasn't so sensitive to how others were feeling because it made her anxious sometimes and she could become snappy with him. She wanted people to enjoy their stay, and it wasn't just for business reasons although she had a good business head on her too. Mary-Joy was the whole package all right. A top bird. He knew that as soon as he clapped eyes on her in that girly bar in Manila. She was gorgeous of course, flatter chested then, before the op he paid for, but gorgeous, nevertheless. Keith resented that everyone always assumed that the breast augmentation was anything to do with him. It was all to do with Mary-Joy. Apparently, she had always been teased about her flat chest, although Filipino women were not known for their huge boobs or anything, but he went along with it and paid for it at a top clinic in Manila and he wasn't complaining with the results. He wasn't complaining but to be honest they were perfect as they were. A perfect handful. Now they were a bit porno and although it got him going it sort of bugged him that the porno feeling had overshadowed the purer, small, pretty tit love feeling which in truth he preferred.

Anyway, what he really loved about her was that she was as sharp as a tack. Nothing got past her. Neither he nor anyone intimidated her. In a quiet and gracious way, she knew her worth. Very unfortunately for everyone involved her family had always disapproved of their relationship and although her mother had softened, her father certainly had not and probably never would. The first time the family met him her father had launched into the nastiest tirade in front him, perhaps not realising that Keith had been living in the Philippines for thirty years and naturally enough had picked up decent Filipino.

"Not only is he far too old but he is an idiot. It's plain for anyone to see. No money in the world is worth being tied to this one. I suppose the best thing is that he will die soon. Make sure you feed him rotten food and give him as much fuss and fighting as you can so that he will fall over with a heart attack as soon as possible. Fucking sex-pats, they are ruining the whole of Southeast Asia with their pig faces and bodies sweating all over our women and children. He's ugly. So ugly. Did you have to get yourself such an ugly one? His face is so long, it is like a horse. You don't have to do this, a smart woman like you. I don't want people thinking that you had to marry a big, hairy, pink, pig, horse-face, giant because your family wanted you to. And mark my words that is what they will think. And what about children? Poor kids with that old waste of space as their dad. He's hardly going to run and play with them, is he? You'll be wiping his arse and the kid's arses at the same time."

Mary-Jo had waited until her father finished and then got cross, "Where do you think I was working when I met him? In a bar. It was a hostess bar. Smart as I am, it was the only job I could get. You know that. Most of the other girls were sleeping with the Western men but I was not. I was the manager of the bar. Keith is a decent man. He treats me so well. Better than Jose ever treated me. He loves me so much. I would be a fool to turn down such love and devotion because I doubt it will come again for me. And Keith does not have much money. I am marrying him for love."

Her father had pushed his body even further down into his velour sofa, so that his football belly shot up. "I never took you for a fool Mary-Joy. You were always the smartest of my kids, but you have really disappointed me."

Even though he and Mary-Joy were more than fine and got on like a house on fire whenever Mary-Joy got a little upset he wondered if she thought of what her father had said. Maybe she secretly hoped he would hurry up and die so she could move in with a handsome Filipino who was more her age. And the topic of kids. She had said that would only want them if she was well off and the cottages were going well. She said that her sisters had more than enough kids for this generation of the family. She didn't really bring it up and he didn't want to in case she suddenly wanted them. He couldn't at his age. It wouldn't be right, and he didn't want it and he didn't care what Charlie Chaplin had fucking done.

He wished he hadn't heard all that from her father because it wasn't the kind of thing that helped on those occasional times when you were feeling a bit unsettled in your marriage. He should know. This was his third. First to Jackie when he was too young to know his arse from his elbow and then that grasping bitch Sonya in Manila and of course now to the lovely and smart Mary-Joy. His best wife by far. He couldn't believe his luck. Brains and beauty next to him on the pillow every night. And he wasn't a rich man.

It was easy even for him to see that these three new guests were not interested in luxury and would be happy with the simple cottages. The mother seemed content for her kids to make the decisions and every time she looked at them her eyes went all shiny and full of love. It was a bit much to be honest, to see how much this woman doted on her kids. Later that night Mary-Joy said that could not imagine her own mother letting her grown-up children tell her what to do the way this woman did.

"She said that she has been away from them for a long time and they obviously get on together, but even so. She is being a bit too relaxed with them I think, letting them boss her around."

The brother and the sister gently bickered about where to sit on the veranda and whether they should ask about diving. Keith pretended not to hear them speak about diving perhaps because he knew that Mary-Joy would speak on his behalf.

The brother spoke up. "Our Mum has been travelling, and we got her to PADI up before meeting us in the Philippines. None of us has done loads of dives but we heard that Coron has some incredible diving spots. Can you recommend any diving centres here?"

"Well, you've really come to the right place as Keith is a very experienced dive-master. Keith is taking a French couple out to the Japanese wreck today and he took them to the lake yesterday. This is a fantastic spot for diving. Totally fantastic. Do look on World-Wide-Wanderers and have a look at Keith's diving reviews. The internet passcode is JoyandKeith2 – J and K are capitals.

The son got onto the travel site on his phone, and it only took a few minutes for him to read the reviews. He nodded his head. "Glowing reviews for you, Keith." He looked at Keith with a slightly quizzical expression as if having to rethink his first impression of him.

"Listen mate. I've been a dive-master for forty-years, so I should be good. What I don't know about diving isn't worth knowing and what I don't know about the Coron dive sites really isn't worth knowing."

All three darted a look at each other. Keith couldn't work out what they were trying to silently convey.

"I know that my daughter's going to be too shy to say but it is her twenty-first birthday the day after tomorrow and she thought it would be really good fun to dive on her birthday."

Mary-Joy smiled one of her beautiful smiles. She clapped her hands. "Twenty-one. Oh congratulations. Keith, did you hear that? Billie's going to be sweet twenty-one."

"Of course, I heard. I'm not completely deaf yet."

Some guests loved their banter and bickering. He wasn't sure about this lot. They were so very tight with each other. There was obviously no man in the picture even waiting back home. It was hard to imagine a man being able to squeeze himself in between them. Perhaps that's why they were a little bit hostile to him. Anyway, the feeling was mutual, truth be told. Grown-up kids always made him feel uncomfortable because it got him thinking about Simon and Jenny, his children with his first wife Jackie. They must be in their forties now. How long ago did he see them? Ten or fifteen years? Twenty? He hadn't been the best dad in the world he supposed, but the trouble is that their mother had turned them against him from the off, so he felt that even if he had hung around and seen them every Wednesday and every weekend like some dads, they wouldn't have had a much better relationship. It was too much heartache to hang around and be mugged off and slagged off by Jackie, for her to leave him waiting out in the rain at the agreed meeting spot outside the Wood Green Leisure Centre for an hour, or changing plans at the last minute so that he had to turn back from coming to pick them up with his throat all tight from the upset. She rubbed his face in it when she found a new fella who she invited into the home within three months of meeting him. Keith felt she delighted in his obvious hurt that another man had just replaced him. He had shouted into her face, "How do I know who he is? He could be a paedo? You must find out more about him."

She split up from that one two years later and it turns out he was a heavy drinker. She wanted Keith's help then, when she was trying to get him out, but by that time he was already off and out of the UK making a new life for himself. That's why he decided to come to the Philippines to work as a diving instructor in the first place. And of course, the idea of beautiful, feminine women rather than the ball-breaking, wide-waisted Jackie types was something of a draw too. He wasn't the first western guy to have got sick to the back teeth of women taking over the fucking world with their women's rights and over-reactions to a bit of knee-touching or bum patting or whatever to long for a society in which women were sweeter and softer and yes, kinder.

"Well, would you want to go out to a birthday meal or something like that? On Saturday nights there's always a local dance in the square. Everyone goes there. It's not a touristy thing, though tourists are welcome. So, you can go out on the Saturday night before the birthday and then for Billie's actual birthday you can dive and maybe have a lovely meal at the restaurant on the beach. We are going into town on Saturday night so we can give you a lift in. Otherwise, you could get a tricycle in." Mary-Joy said.

'Yes, yes. That would be great. Thanks so much. It would be good to go out and celebrate Coron style."

Right, so they would be lumbered with that holier than thou cow and her stuck-up brats on their Saturday night. Great fun to be had by all then. *Thanks Mary-Joy!* He was really looking forward to that then.

Mary-Joy brought them fresh coconut juice, and they all drank it with enthusiasm.

"I'm what you might call a bit of a diving maverick. I used to work for the biggest diving shop in town, but let's just say I disagreed with the way they treated the dive masters and the clients, and they gave me the boot. So, I've got all the equipment and a place to hire the tanks, so I think that you'll have a great time with me. Ever been wreck diving?"

All three shook their heads.

"There are only some of the best wrecks in the world out there. I'm surprised you haven't read up about them. And I've got a few other treats in store, but I'll leave it as a surprise."

Mary-Joy sat on the end of their bed and brushed her silky black hair. Her beauty sometimes brought him close to tears, but he never let her see it. Her youth already put him on the back foot without her knowing that he thought himself the luckiest man alive.

"Why did you invite those Brits to the restaurant with us? Great Saturday night that's going to be."

"You know how important World-Wide-Wanderers reviews are. A couple of bad reviews and people just stop coming. It doesn't take much. We've had a few complaining about the cottages being too rustic or the sound across the field from the Karaoke Hall."

Keith knew that there had been quite a few complaints about him too, but M-J didn't want to upset him by reminding him. One German woman said that his voice was the loudest she had ever heard, and a Canadian girl had called him *a deeply unpleasant man.* M-J had stopped him from responding to the reviews the way he wanted to which was probably for the best.

"I just wanted to make sure they gave us a good review, you know. And besides, I kind of like the three of them. I think the Mum is interesting."

He looked at her and wanted her to just lay her soft, oily body on top of him with her big hard boobs pressing into him like she used to. She used to hold his face in her little hands and tell him that she felt safe with him and his large body to protect her from anything and anyone.

"Imagine travelling on your own to all those countries. She's going to have been to ten in nine months. It's quite brave and a bit foolish." M-J said.

"Don't you get any funny ideas? It's all right for a battle-axe like that to travel alone but imagine you going off. There would be no end of trouble, a beautiful woman like you. The men would be falling over themselves to help you every time you rocked up somewhere. Besides which, I want to travel with you. We have a laugh travelling together, don't we?"

She turned her head to smile at him. "We do. We had a wonderful time in Thailand on our honeymoon., But that was five years ago now. It's about time we went on holiday."

"But who would look after the cottages?"

"I don't know. Joan and Larry?"

Joan and Larry were another British and Filipino couple. They were closer in age than Keith and MJ but they all got on well as a foursome, although Larry had let the booze catch him these last few years.

"Larry's a lazy arse pisshead, although I agree that Joan could handle it. She's one efficient lady."

MJ started to rub his big old gnarly feet with some of her body oils.

"Oh, thanks darling. That feels nice. You're good to old Keith."

And she kept on circling her thumbs and fingers until he must have drifted off because he was none the wiser until the morning. She could have slipped him a mickey for all he knew.

M-J wasn't the type though despite her witchy perceptive voodoo powers. The foot massage was probably developed by the women of Southeast Asia to put men to sleep rather than demanding sex.

Even though it was a Saturday he had worked hard all day, trying to fix up the roofs of the upper cottages, pushing the new bamboo into the areas where there had been some rot. Over the years he had got quite skilled with bamboo. He thought of himself as almost as good as a native. These guys you saw fixing buildings were so skilled with bamboo because it was in their blood. You saw whole houses woven out of bamboo branches and leaves. Bamboo was a wonderful thing. In the Philippines they had ladders, scaffolding, boats, bridges, furniture – in fact just about everything you could think of - made in this tough, light-weight material. And it grew so fast. If he was a different sort of man, he would think of a business that involved exporting bamboo products to the West.

He moved to the main house and tried to fix the outside pipe to the bathroom which had come loose from the wall. He was up the ladder when he heard women talking. He could hear M- J because she always spoke so loudly because of his deafness and from working in nightclubs. He could just about hear the other woman. He thought it was the English woman.

"I know how he seems. He is a great big bear, and he can often say things that make people uncomfortable," Mary-Joy said.

"He doesn't have much of an edit button, that's for sure."

"My family doesn't approve of him. They are very unhappy about the age gap. They begged me not to be with him."

Keith cupped his hands around his ears and pulled them forward while holding onto the top of the ladder with his elbows. It was a method that he had been taught all those years ago in the Scouts and it always amazed him what a difference it made to the clarity of sound. He had to be careful not to kill himself by falling off the ladder trying to hear what the women were saying. He decided to hold on with one arm and cup his ear with the other and twist himself forward. It seemed that MJ was doing most of the talking and the London bird was doing most of the listening.

"I could see you were shocked by the age difference, Kate. I've got used to being able to see what people are feeling about us."

"Not as shocked as you would think. I told you I had been travelling. Well, I fell in love on top of a mountain with a man who was twenty-four years younger than me. Obviously, I haven't spoken to my children about it. Perhaps, if I hadn't just had that experience, I would have been more judgemental."

The dirty old bint, Keith thought from the top of the ladder. It was disgusting the way these old women travelled around taking advantage of young men looking for money. It was enough to turn your stomach.

"What was he like?" he heard MJ asking a little too eagerly for his liking.

"Oh, he was half Iranian, half Syrian and very rich and spoiled. He was interesting and beautiful. I left him just before this to come and meet the kids. It's very hard to be Muslim in India now and Atal was obviously searching for something."

"And he found you?"

"Yes, he found me. He was so attentive to me. He decided that I needed to be cherished and although he had never looked after anyone in his life and always been served on hand and foot, he wanted to care for me. It took a while for me to let him."

"That sounds lovely."

"It was. I really learnt something from him. He really made me feel that I can let someone care for me as much as I care for them. It might not sound like much, but it's made me feel good about myself somehow. I'm grateful to him and I wrote a letter just before I left India to tell him so. But let's talk about you. I suppose it's not just an age thing people react to, it's that there are so many red-faced old men – *Gammons*, we call them back home - from the UK, Australia and US who take advantage of women and children in Southeast Asia. And can I be honest with you? We are never going to see each other again after we leave, so I'm going to just say, - you seem like a super smart and beautiful young woman who could have your pick of men."

What a bitch. He would have preferred for her to be straightforwardly disapproving. This concerned middle-class way was a total mind fuck. Keith gripped the top of the ladder so he could see his knuckle pressing white through his red skin and heard his own breath get heavy. He reined himself in and got control and calmed himself down.

MJ laughed her beautiful laugh. "You wouldn't be the first person to say something like that. But here is the surprising thing. Underneath all the stupid jokes and long stories Keith is such a good man. He is the only man who has ever made me cry with laughter. When I wake up in the morning, I am always pleased to see his big old face. Unlike your young man, he is not a rich man, but he is hardworking, and we have so many ideas together and you know what? We work so well together. Our ideas bounce off each other. We fit together."

Keith felt himself grinning from ear to ear. Like a Cheshire cat on top of a flipping ladder. It was at that moment of giddy happiness when he swayed and nearly tipped the balance of the ladder.

"Mary-Joy, if you've found happiness with Keith then I'm glad. You really don't have to explain anything to me anyway. Why should you?"

"I know I don't. But I wanted to talk to you about it. My close female friends are all in Manila and you seemed like the kind of person I could talk to."

Keith felt anxious. If he came down the women would realise that he had been eavesdropping on them. But he couldn't wait up there forever and he knew that women could talk for hours. He decided to just descend the ladder and front it out. He climbed down the ladder and walked jauntily up the stairs to the veranda without a by-your-leave.

"Hello there, ladies."

"Hello Keith love, where have you been?"

"Oh, just on the roof fixing it up. Job done. That should keep the rain out when the rainy season comes."

"Well, help yourself to some calamansi juice. We're just drinking some. I made it fresh."

"It's absolutely delicious," Kate said.

He deliberately didn't look at Kate so that she wouldn't know if he had heard her or not. Let her sweat a bit.

"Don't mind if I do. Thanks Sweetheart."

They managed to squeeze Kate into the pick-up truck along with them while the kids were more than happy to bump around in the back. Keith could hear them laughing and shouting as he drove along the coastal road, so it was obviously a bit of a novelty for these city kids to travel in the back of a pick-up truck.

"So, I ordered the cake for your daughter as a surprise. I'll get them to serve it up after supper."

Kate smiled at Mary-Joy. A big smile, the like of which he had not seen bestowed on him since she arrived.

"Thank you so much Mary-Joy, that's so kind. How much do I owe you?"

"Oh, just settle with the restaurant. They quoted thirty dollars. I hope that's OK."

"Yes, that's fine. I am so grateful."

"I remember my twenty-first. I was ten years ago now. My Mum threw me a party and made me a huge five-tiered purple cake. It was beautiful," Mary-Joy said.

When they were all sitting around the table at the restaurant it surprised Keith that old Larry seemed quite taken with old Kate, even though she didn't seem the slightest bit interested in him. Perhaps he and Joan were going through a rough patch. Come to think of it Joan was looking a bit fed up with her *used-to-be very-attractive-but-now-a-bit-fucking-old-face-even-though-fillipinos-don't usually-crack* sulky pout. Pity, when they were thinking of asking them to take care of the guest houses while they had a well-deserved second honeymoon. They would have to make sure Larry and Joan were getting on a bit better before they asked them. It wouldn't really be on for them to create a bad atmosphere around the guests.

Larry was busy telling a story with a face a bit too close to Kate's. Kate was leaning back on her chair towards her son to get away from Larry.

"They have a strange practice in the Philippines. If someone is hurt and you take them to hospital, and they can't afford the fees then you must foot the bill. Last New Year's Eve a man came off his motorbike by the side of the road just outside town. He was in a bad way. A very bad way. He appeared to have broken his leg at least."

"Oh no. That's terrible," said Kate.

"Well, Joan was saying, 'Oh no, we will have to pay if you help him' but I was thinking in God's name and all that is good and human we just have to. Well, I scooped the poor guy up and took him into the hospital. I told them I had never met him before, but they were adamant I paid. In the end I paid the fees for the poor fella but that's just the kind of person I am."

"Well, that's very nice of you." Kate smiled.

"Oh, I think I was the one who made you help him. You were too mean to want to help," Joan said loudly so that everyone at the table stopped their separate conversations.

Mary-Joy could obviously see where this was going and asked all the guests if they were enjoying their food. The son answered,

"It's really good. We haven't had much luck with Filipino food, so we're so pleased to have fresh fish with some spice and a nice salad."

"Oh God, why do the British always say that Filipino food is bad. Is it because they know that everyone says that British food is the worst in the world?" Keith couldn't help saying.

"Well, maybe we have been to the wrong places, but we couldn't find any food that wasn't completely bland. So strange considering that some of the food in Southeast Asia is the best in the world. We thought it was because the Philippines was an American territory." Kate said.

"Well, the Americans didn't rule over the Philippines for that long compared to Spain. So perhaps you don't like Spanish food?"

"Well, I do like Spanish food actually."

Keith couldn't help defending the cuisine of his adopted country some more. "I think the best food in the Philippines is home cooking. I don't think they are an eating-out kind of country. Mary-Joy is an incredible cook."

"Yes, I'm sorry. You're probably right. Sorry," said Kate, "We've probably been unlucky."

The town square was packed, blasting the kind of Korean Pop music that made Keith's chest hurt. A pack of fishermen with peg teeth seemed to jump for joy, when they saw Mary-Joy, Kate and her daughter. Joan had gone home in a funk and Larry was lurking in the sidelines with a vacant smile swaying his bony hips. Keith was surprised to see Mary-Joy dancing with Kate and her kids and Kate's boy dancing a bit too enthusiastically with her.

Keith didn't like dancing. His body was too big, and he didn't know what to do with his arms and hands. The second wife Sonya had encouraged him to dance with her on New Year's Eve in a Karaoke Hall in Manila and then once he was up on the floor had laughed and said, "Oh my God Keith, you are right. You are a terrible dancer. You go one way; the music goes the other."

Mary-Jo had always stopped dancing when he tried to join in, although she was too much of a good girl to say anything mean. So, Keith just stood on the side of the square looking on.

He could see the British lad writhing closer to Mary-Joy and her slim body and large bust was wriggling a bit too close to Kate's son's body while Kate and her daughter were being danced with by the two oldest fishermen in town– the ancient mariners Keith liked to call them, flanked by four lady boys who were giggling and simpering. What a sight! Keith wondered what an earth they thought they looked like.

Keith had to step in, pretend to dance a bit and pull Mary-Joy towards him.

"Oi, Oi. Calm down Missis. Don't show me up."

"What's the matter?" She looked up at him, the multi-coloured lights flashing from all around the square in time to the pulsating music, lighting up her sweet face in coloured beats.

He could see that she had her best totally puzzled and completely innocent face on which annoyed the hell out of him at the same time as touching him. The confusion of those feelings made him even crosser.

"Come on. I wasn't born yesterday. I saw the way you were dancing with that young lad from the UK. You were really enjoying yourself, weren't you?"

"I was dancing with all of them. Not particularly with him. I love to dance Keith, and you do not love to dance which means that I must take the opportunity when it comes."

'When it comes. You mean when it comes." M-J looked at him quizzically. "You said it wrong. Never mind."

"What? What did I say wrong? Is it the right time to give me a grammar lesson? When I am just trying to let go and have a laugh? I work very hard for us and all the things we want to achieve; I should be allowed to have some fun sometimes."

"Anyway. Carry on."

"No. You have ruined the night for me now. Let's go home."

"What about your British best friends?"

"Oh, they won't mind taking a tricycle home. They are enjoying themselves."

Mary-Joy went up to them and said something and then walked past him and he followed. Before he turned, he saw the British lad give him a stare. And he gave one right back which said, *I may be old, but I'm not a fucking idiot mate and I'm not so past it that I can't give my luscious wife a good seeing to.*" At least he hoped his stare said all that.

Keith couldn't help enjoying telling the woman and her kids that they would have to climb up the wooden steps and then back down to Barracuda Lake with their wetsuits on and with the full tanks on their backs, perhaps because of that moment in the square.

They were liking him a whole lot more than they had done after the morning's dive in Croon Bay exploring the Akitsushima wreck. He showed them a rudimentary map he had made and told them that the majority of the shipwrecks of Coron Bay resulted from a sustained air-attack on the Imperial Japanese Navy that took place on the twenty-fourth of September 1944 by the US Navy. Their bored, barely polite attitude towards him had changed once they had swum through the large crack in the hull and seen the dials of the machinery that operated the crane, the ferocity of the American bombardment still so shocking, even though the ripped metal had been softened by bright orange bushes of black coral, crimson sponges, sediment and coral. They were relaxed divers, and it surprised him how well he and they worked together in the water despite their on-land dislike of each other. It seemed that they shared the sense that underwater was a place of utter tranquillity, even though they were exploring a huge testimony to a hit of such violent impact.

The three of them had not been on many dives and this was their first altogether, but he felt sure that they would be able to squeeze through the hole from the engine room to the control room to show them the panels still with the gauges and dials. They seemed to give themselves to his direction, following him completely, giving in to his experience and knowledge in a way that pleased him. It felt right, their reverence of his experience and their essential passivity. He judged that they could follow him into an even smaller hole to the second floor, passing the bank of what looked like giant corkscrews- the machinery for raising the shells onto the deck to feed the guns. Keith showed them by pointing his long finger close to their faces that it still had holes in it and their eyes widened behind their masks. They were a good little diving team.

Once they were back on deck and had taken off their tanks they debriefed. "Guys. That was meant for experienced wreck divers only but because you were really, really cool down there so I knew that it would be OK. Excellent work guys!"

"It was incredible," said the birthday girl, Billie. "I loved it."

After the climb with their tanks, which had all three of them huffing and puffing, Keith had them sit on the edge of the turquoise water surrounded by two mountains and spoke to them as seriously as his naturally jokey and fun persona would allow.

"OK, this limestone-cased lagoon was formed by a karst sinkhole which has separated the lake from the open ocean and the volcanic activity beneath the surface heats up the saltwater trapped inside. So, on this dive it is not what you see so much as what you feel. You are not going to see the most amazing fish you have ever seen but you are going to have a unique experience. This is a dramatic thermocline which means there is saltwater and freshwater. There is a real difference in temperature between the saline and the freshwater, and it is important that you relax into that difference, rather than resisting it. Follow me closely just like you did in the wreck dive, and everyone will be just fine. I think you are going to really love this, and I promise that I will not let you boil to death. Do you trust me?"

'I'm pretty confident in you after our amazing wreck dive this morning." the daughter said. I don't know if you both feel the same?" She looked at her mother and brother. Both Kate and Charlie nodded.

Keith took them straight down through the freezing top water close to the jetty and down and down through the different temperatures to the intense heat at the lunar landscape bottom of the lake. He showed them how to sink their hands into the silt and push on through what seemed to be the bed of the lake to another dimension beyond. They started to move like astronauts on the moon, obviously delighting in what they were doing, climbing up mini cliffs as if without gravity. He knew that his big awkward body was now elegant and sleek as he glided through the water and they followed him, man, woman and children. He showed them the tree growing in the middle of the lake and allowed them the time to let the strangely bold catfish and shrimp surround them and nibble and feed from their faces and hands. And then he started to make his assent up and through the thermocline to carry out their safety stop in the colder water and there it was! It didn't always happen, but it was perfect today. He signalled that they should all look up and he saw their shock in their widened eyes through their masks when they saw themselves reflected at themselves, deep underwater, their own images. There they were, the water family, big man, woman and two grown-up children staring back at themselves in the sheet of mirror-like glassy divide between the hot salty water and the cold freshwater. The prefect underwater family unit who saw in this silvery moment the sudden beauty of themselves and the surrounding sun-lit water.

Dear Charlie and Billie,
I'm writing you a postcard old school style so God knows when it will get to you. I will probably be home from Japan already and trying to get used to life in London. Still, it doesn't matter because I did want to write to you both and say how much I loved being in the Philippines with you and diving with you. The total twat Sexpat turned out to be the dream Dive Master, didn't he? How weird. What a surprise? Thanks so much for making me PADI up and learn how to dive. I think it is going to be one of the great pleasures of my life. I love you both like mad and miss you like crazy.
SO MUCH LOVE
Mum,

CALAIS CAMP
October 2016

Kate wondered what she should do about her need to pee when she walked into the Kids Café. The Kids Café tent was full of the same crowd of mostly Afghan teenagers as when they first walked past. It was quite dark inside with the intense blue light from the tarpaulin roof. The air was heavy with weed. She saw that Ranim was speaking intently to two of the teenagers while Priya seemed to be involved in an argument with a middle-aged woman with letterbox red hair.

"Your dirty newspaper had me arrested. I was held by the British Police for two nights after one of your fucking journalists wrote about me diverting funds. I haven't done anything except run these places and feed these kids for the last two years. Get out of here. Go on, Get out. Fuck off. How dare you come in here?"

Priya tried to defend herself. Kate tried too. "We are trying to get the readers of *The Daily World* to understand what is going on here. Priya is the one voice of reason in the newspaper."

"I don't care. I just want you out of here. Now!"

Ranim beckoned to both women to come outside with her. "A Syrian woman who lost her daughter in Libya will speak to us. She wants to tell the UK what she has gone through."

Priya looked pleased. "That seems interesting. So, where do we have to go?"

"Back to the Mother and Baby bus I'm afraid."

"Well, I was about to gather us all up to go back across the channel. Can you please get your friend to come to the Mother and Baby Bus if that's where we're going? We have to leave quickly as soon as the interview is finished," said Kate.

Valentine had not come into the Kid's Café. He was still waiting outside. When he was told that they were going back to the bus his face flushed red under his pale beard.

"Look, I'm feeling as if the young men are going to target me and take my equipment. I'm going to be fucking pissed off if I've come all this way and got no photos and have my equipment stolen."

Priya pleaded with him. "Come on, this one sounds very interesting. What if we ask if you could photograph her hands or the back of her head?"

Valentine looked cross.

"Or you could go back to the car?" Kate said.

"I'm not that happy walking on my own."

"So, come with us. It won't be long will it Kate?" Priya said.

Kate nodded in agreement.

They walked back the way they had come. Kate thought she felt some leaking from her tampon and some considerable pressure against her bladder. Once on the bus Priya and Ranim went inside. Valentine was refused. Favela stood outside chatting to a couple of women holding their babies.

Kate was relieved to see Ranim's friend with a young man. They walked over to Kate and the woman said, "Son. This is my son."

"Oh, I didn't realise you had a son here." Kate wondered why she didn't know that. Had anyone told her? She didn't think so.

"Right, OK. You have a son here," Valentine said, eyeing the young man suspiciously.

The young man spoke, looking at them with heavy, weary brown eyes. "Six months I have been here. I don't know what to do now. My family all in UK."

"That's awful. I'm so sorry."

Kate now felt that she was about to wet herself and flood at the same time. She couldn't wait until they got to the Eurostar entrance where she knew there were some toilets. She knew she had to get back to the car quickly so she could go between the cars without Valentine following her.

"Look, I'm sorry. I must go to the car. Can you all join me when they have finished?' She spoke to Valentine. "They said you might be able to photograph the woman from behind her, so you had better stick here."

"I thought you said that we all had to stick together. How do we find our way back to the car?"

"Ranim and Faven know the way back to the bridge better than me. Faven, you'll guide them back won't you?"

Faven looked up from her phone and nodded.

Kate had to stop herself running down the main drag, back past the Kid's Café, across the wasteland with the one-man tents, past the police vehicles and back under the bridge. As she walked briskly, she felt into her coat pocket and tried to find a tampon. Where were they? She could feel the stickiness of blood in her jeans. They had to be in the car. She had a rucksack in the backseat of the car, which held her jumper and another pair of trainers. They were probably in there. She opened the driver's door and then reached into the back and found two tampons at the bottom of the bag. She took one and then walked four or five cars away, looking anxiously at the groups of men milling around the cars but deciding that she had to deal with what was happening to her.

She squatted down and saw that her blood had gone through her pants and onto the crotch of her jeans. She peed and was amazed at how much came out of her and flowed down the sandy slope. She hoped the men wouldn't see it and know what she was doing. She then pulled out her used tampon and inserted the new one. She quickly dug as deep a hole in the sand as she could in the sand next to her and buried it, covering it with impacted sand. She thought about what the women who stayed in the camp did. *Where did they pee? How did they change their sanitary towels or wash their cloth pads when they had their periods?* She wiped her hands on the tufts of grass that grew out of the sand.

She went back to the car, found some wet wipes in the glove compartment and cleaned her hands. She was pleased with herself that she had left them there. It was very unlike her to have wet wipes. Perhaps they belonged to her son who had looked after the car when she was away for all that time. She got in the driver's seat and texted her boss.

"All's well that ends well. We were about to leave but then got an interview with a woman that Priya seemed interested in. Phew. Catching the five o'clock train."

The door opened and Ranim's friend came in and sat in the same place she had sat in the back, the furthest away from her.

Kate turned and smiled at her. "The others. They are coming?"

"Yes, yes. They come."

Kate tried to ring Ranim and got no answer; a second later Faven opened the car and came and sat down.

"Where is everyone else?" Kate asked.

"They will be here in a few minutes. They were walking just behind me."

Kate got out of the car and looked out. She was happy to see Ranim, Valentine and Priya all walking and talking together. She shouted out to them, "Come on. We really should get going. We've got a train to catch."

Priya told her that in the end she had got a good interview and apologised for getting really stressed. She was now as anxious as Kate to get home. She said goodbye to the photographer. Kate nodded to him, and he barely nodded back. Rude.

When they got to the Eurostar terminal Kate leant out at the French border patrol.

"What time is the next train?"

"Je ne parle pas Anglais." The man in the booth barely looked at them.

"Le prochain train? S'il vous plait?"

He waved her through without answering her.

Kate stopped at the English control, and she passed her ticket to Ranim and each person gave her their passport or ID cards to give to the woman in the booth. The uniformed woman peered down into their car. Kate saw her expression pinch a little at the sight of them. She looked at them all from her point of view. Two women in hajib, an Eritrean woman, an Indian woman and a scruffy white woman.

"Where have you come from?" The woman asked.

The last time Kate had come her colleague Rosemary had simply said, "We have been shopping in France." And they had been waved on.

Ranim said, proudly, "Helping women in the Calais Camp."

The woman spoke into her mike. "Can someone come and open the boot please? We've got a car from the camp."

A border control man asked her to roll her window down. "Can you step out of your car and come with me and open your boot please?" Kate got out of the car, and she and the man walked round together.

Kate leant down to pull the boot up and immediately locked into the eyes of the person curled up foetus style in her boot. "Oh fuck!" she shouted.

The border control man looked at her rather than in the boot. "Have you hit your head?"

Kate pointed to the boot. She couldn't understand why he couldn't see what she could. "No. Look, there's someone in the boot." Kate looked deep into the young man's frightened brown eyes and thought of her own son.

The uniformed man by her side immediately shouted, "There's one in here! Got one!"

Men in black uniforms started running towards the car. Kate walked quickly and sat back in the driver's seat because she couldn't think of anything else to do.

"There was someone in the boot."

Faven laughed. "You're joking, right?"

"No, I'm not joking. There's a man in the boot."

Ranim started shouting at Kate. "You idiot. Why didn't you check the car boot before you left?"

"What?"

"Why didn't you check the boot? You are so careless. You are such a stupid lady."

"I didn't think so. It was all such a rush. I haven't been here as many times as you. Why didn't you tell me to check the boot if that's something the driver always does? Is that something the driver always does?"

"Yes, well. No. I'm not sure. I'm not a driver. I don't have a car. I don't know if the driver always does that."

"I didn't do it when I came before."

"Well, didn't Juliet tell you to do that? Didn't she take you through what you must do before you left? A man got in contact with the other woman who drove us here a few months ago. It was in the main bit of the car though and they could see him."

"No one told me that. Why did no one tell me that? And no. I've never been told to do that."

"It's common sense. You are such a foolish woman. What have you done?" said Ranim and turned away from her.

Ranim started to speak to her friend to tell her what was happening and Kate heard her take a sharp intake of breath.

The uniformed men surrounded the car and told the women to get out. They were told to walk ahead and were taken by two black uniformed men into a neon lit room. They were told that they should stay sitting around the table and that if they got up or got too close to the walls an alarm would go off. The women started to talk amongst themselves.

Priya whispered to Kate. "Is it a man or woman?"

"It was a man. I think it was Ranim's friend's son. I can't be sure. I didn't see him for that long. I think it was though."

Priya looked shocked. "Do you think Ranim's friend knew? Do you think Ranim knew?"

"I don't know about Ranim's friend, but not Ranim. She would never risk what she has in the UK. Her children are doing so well. When could it have happened?"

"I don't know. Did you leave the car unlocked.?"

Kate thought about Faven telling her that she had not locked the car in the forecourt, and she thought about going back to the car to get the tampon locked in the camp all day? She didn't trust herself to have locked it at any point of the day. Didn't you have to turn the lock twice to make sure it was locked these days?

"Oh, God. I don't know. It might have happened when I went to the loo between the cars. I went to get a tampon from the car first. That car doesn't always lock."

The door of the room was open, and through it, Kate could see her car being forensically searched, by men wearing gloves. What had happened to the man? Was he still in the car? Two other men appeared to be taking photos of the boot of the car. Kate stood up to get a better look at what they were doing, and the alarm went off.

A plump police officer and bottle-blonde policewoman came into the room. Kate thought that they had come to turn the alarm off. Instead, they stood in front of Kate. "We are arresting you on the serious charge of suspicion of facilitating the entry of an illegal immigrant into the UK. You do not have to say anything, but it may harm your defence if you do not mention when questioned something which you later rely on in court. Anything you do say may be given in evidence."

Kate felt like laughing. They looked and acted like bad actors in a shit police drama. Kate thought of her kids. They had been worried about her going, particularly her son. As she left that morning, he shouted out. "Mum, be careful. Why are they sending you there on the day of demolition? You've only just gone back to work."

DANCING IN THE PARK
September 2016

Mr Hamasaki stood so close to Yumi that she could smell the cigarettes and whiskey on his breath. She saw, when politeness forced her to look up at him for a second, that his eyelashes had a kind of dandruff on them close to the roots. It gave her a little shock of revulsion.

"What's your name then?"

"Yumi?"

"How long have you worked here, Yumi?"

That kind of question made her heartbeat faster. It was the same kind of question as, "How do YOU think you're doing Yumi? How would YOU rate your work progress?" This kind of question usually came before being asked to leave before her contract was up.

"Nearly four months. I am on a temporary contract for six months."

Her upper body was bent a little in deference to his much higher and more permanent status.

"Mmm, I thought I hadn't seen you around before. So, you are temporary? Well, can I give you a bit of advice for free?"

She nodded as enthusiastically as she could.

"If you want to advance beyond being a temporary Office Lady, then you will have to socialise much more with your colleagues after work. I don't think I've seen you at any of the work drinks and socials and after four months of working here I think I should know who the hell you are."

Yumi felt her phone buzz in her skirt pocket. She felt sure that it was the woman that was coming to stay with her tonight. Her first ever booking on *CoZyBed*. She desperately wanted to answer it. She regretted ever having got up from her desk to go to the toilet. She should have gone downstairs. That's what she usually did. The toilets on her floor were in view of Mr Hamasaki's desk, which meant that he was on the perpetual look out for women to intercept.

"You're quite cute. Who knows, if you came out more with us then you might find yourself a husband or at the very least a boyfriend. Then you could kick back, stop working and have a couple of kids. At your age it's obviously time to get on with it. Don't leave it too long, little Missy, otherwise it will be too late, and you'll be sorry."

"Thank you so much for your advice, Mr Hamasaki. I very much appreciate it. I am not actually an Office Lady but still I am thankful."

"What are you then?"

"I am a copy writer and an editor. I write all the in-house reports, web sites, and publications. I'm a senior editor. We have been liaising via email about some internal comms stuff. I'm Yumi Tanaka, Senior Editor."

He licked his lips with a pale-yellow tongue. He didn't seem to know what to say next. She thought she saw his upper lip quivering.

"How can you be a senior anything? You are so young. I thought that the Yumi Tanaka that kept telling me to rewrite stuff was some old woman."

"I am senior editor because I am good at my job, and I have a lot of experience.

Well, I like to think that I am good at my job." Mr Hamasaki let out some of his sour breath. She tried not to breathe through her nose, but she found it difficult.

"Who's that calling you, huh, again? Is that your boyfriend? Is that why you are so anxious to answer it? Maybe that explains why you are so standoffish? You've got a secret Sugar Daddy none of us know about? Who keeps you in shoes and handbags? Go on, answer it. Tell your precious boyfriend that you are going to be late home tonight, because you are coming out with the boys from work. I wonder how he will feel about that?"

He put his hand on her forearm and stared into her eyes in a way that made her look down at her shoes to get away from his gaze without insulting him. Mr Hamasaki had a bad reputation for being mean as well as pervy with all the women that worked here.

Yumi was happy to hear someone coming up quickly behind her and calling out to Mr Hamasaki. She turned her head to see Mr Chiba.

Mr Chiba was younger than Mr Hamasaki and she had never heard of him pushing up against any of the girls or getting them to come to his desk so that he could make comments about their appearance in front of his work colleagues or sending them disgusting video clips or talking to them about finding husbands or coming out to drinks. She wondered if Mr Chiba, with his unusually wide apart eyes, moon face and small thick legs had seen what was happening and had deliberately interrupted them.

Mr Hamasaki answered Mr Chiba grumpily and took a step backwards. Yumi took her chance to get away and as she did, she looked at Mr Chiba with a glance of gratitude and slipped off, walking fast to her desk, grabbing her bag and quickly making her exit out of the office and onto the busy subway.

There were, in fact, new employment rules about not working late on a Friday since last November's death from overwork of that poor woman who worked in a digital advertising agency. Even so in her office she knew that going home before seven or eight was frowned upon, even on a Friday night and was seen as a sign of lack of commitment to the organisation.

Walking fast she looked at her *CoZyBed* message from the woman *Kate Mancini* and saw that she thought she would be at her apartment at seven-thirty. She had to get back. She had arrived in the office at seven this morning so she could put the hours she needed into finishing the introduction to the financial report, but she knew that she would be disapproved of for leaving and that a number of her colleagues would note it and perhaps mention it to her boss. For once she had to risk it. This *CoZyBed* App had the potential to give her a second income and perhaps she would be able to pick and choose where she worked a little more and not always have to go wherever the editorial agency sent her. She was also excited that this woman was from London, England.

She had sent the woman a map made of pictures of all the landmarks to guide her when she came out of Roppongi railway station to reach her apartment block. She had enjoyed making this visual map for the foreigner with pictures of shop-signs and buildings she had to follow, sort of like a treasure hunt. It was fun to make, and she hoped it would be fun to follow. Yumi knew she was very lucky to have a tiny apartment in the smart area of Roppongi. Her brother-in-law had rented it five years ago and passed it on to her when he and her sister had moved to Osaka for work.

It was her friend Simo from her dance group who had suggested that she go on *CoZyBeds*. "As long as you keep it from your nosey, stuck-up neighbours you should be all right. You will do so well. All the tourists want to stay in Roppongi Hills. You are sitting on a golden egg there, Yumi. I don't know why you haven't taken advantage of it before. It's crazy. Maybe we should get married, and I can stop work and raise the kids and just dance with them all day long."

Simo was probably the best dancer in the hip-hop troupe. He worked in a clothes shop in Shimokitazawa and wore his hair in a shiny ponytail with the sides shaved either side, and his ears were pierced many, many times right up to his scalp. He could make her laugh so much that she cried. Great big tears that were embarrassing because she knew that it made her mascara run down her face. Yumi sometimes fantasised about what it would be like to be living with Simo, so when he said the marriage thing she couldn't help her heart flipping right over and pushing right up so that it pulsated in her throat and she had to turn her face away from him. How wonderful it would be to have a family of hip-hop dancers! It would be heaven on earth. Maybe they could make a family video and put it on YouTube, and it would become amazingly popular, and people would pay to advertise on their channel and that is how they would live. Just hip-hop dancing all day long.

Once Yumi got into her apartment, she set about trying to make the small space look tidier and put her make-up and nail varnish into some plastic bags and threw them under the kitchen sink cupboard. She had already made a bed up right next to hers where she slept in the sitting room. She hoped that Kate would find this all right. She put a pink fake fur blanket down on the futon and then a sheet on top of it. She thought that this would make a lovely, soft bed for her. She sprayed some of her most expensive perfume in the air, just in case her apartment did not smell nice to a foreigner. She then worried that she had sprayed too much and opened the small, grated window out onto the stair well. Then she heard the buzzer, and a voice. "Hello Yumi. Is that Yumi?"

"It is Yumi. Please take the lift to the sixth floor. I am number sixty-seven. OK?" Yumi shouted into the intercom.

"See you in a minute," the woman said.

It was not a minute. It was two and a half minutes long.

When Kate stepped into the room with her big hair and dirty green rucksack she seemed to fill it. Yumi felt that she looked like a western cartoon of someone's messy mother and she was older than Yumi had anticipated. She wondered if the photo on the *CoZyBed* profile had been taken some years earlier.

"Where do you want me to put this?" Kate said.

"Oh, is it OK if you put the rucksack on your bed?"

Yumi thought she saw her eyes flicker to the fold-up beds so closely side by side. She knew that British people had bigger apartments from watching so many British television series and wondered if it seemed strange to her to sleep so close together. But Kate smiled and placed her rucksack on her bed.

"Thanks, so much for your photomap. I had a lovely time following your pictures, although I did get a bit lost. Maybe there were too many photos that looked a bit alike."

"You are very welcome. I enjoyed doing it." Yumi noted to herself the need to make the next map have more distinctive photos.

Both women stood. There was only one chair by the small table and the only spare space in the sitting room had been taken up by the fold-up bed.

"Look, I know it is a Friday night, and you are probably going out but I am going to meet a woman I met in Myanmar who is here attending a conference in Tokyo. I am meeting her at the bookshop *Tsutaya.* Someone recommended that I go there. I have heard it stays open late on a Friday. Is that right?"

"That is a good place to meet. That is the best meeting place in Rohingi Hills. You get many, many foreigners and people from Tokyo who want to practice their English. It is very close to here."

She saw the woman look at her for a minute. Then she asked, "Would you like to come and meet her? I'm sure Su-Su would love to meet a Japanese woman who is close to her age. I think it would be very interesting for her. She speaks very good English. Like you, your English is amazing."

Yumi had been hoping that Simo was going to contact her and tell her about things that were happening at Yoyogi Park tonight. She didn't feel comfortable contacting any other members of the dance troupe to find out what was going on tonight and yet she didn't feel confident enough to ring him. He always contacted her. That was the way it was. She felt that if she contacted him, it might somehow reveal the way she felt about him.

She decided that it would be good to practice her English with these women and Kate had already made her feel so happy about her spoken English. She could always go to Yoyogi Park afterwards, but she would be careful to make sure that she didn't seem rude to Kate or her friend from Myanmar. The idea of being rude to the women gave Yumi a pinch of anxiety in her stomach.

Yumi replied that she needed a few minutes to change out of her work clothes and that she would be very pleased to come, thank you so much for the invitation.

Kate walked fast and seemed to know the way to the late-night bookstore and coffeehouse from Yumi's apartment. She asked Yumi about her job and her family, turning her head to meet her eyes even as she strode along. Even though it was early evening, Roppongi Hills was already filling up with people wanting to enjoy themselves in bars, restaurants or nightclubs. Girls dressed up as schoolgirls, frilly maids and Little Bo Peep were standing on the streets and calling out to the salary men who made their way home.

"I have been in Tokyo five days now and I still find it hard to get used to the sight of girls enticing middle-aged men on the streets."

"It's not so much here in Roppongi. It's a thing that happens very much in the area of Shibuya. I don't know if you have been there?"

Kate wrinkled her big nose as if she had smelt something bad. Yumi pretended not to see it.

As they approached it, the bookstore was already buzzing with a mix of foreign and Japanese people. Sitting at one of the only spare tables outside the busy store was a girl with her hair scrapped back in a traditional costume of some sort, with a long red skirt and a close fitting bright blue jacket. She smiled and awkwardly waved when she saw Kate. Kate went up to her and embraced her. Yumi could see that the young woman was a bit taken aback by the embrace but that she tried to reciprocate Kate's enthusiasm.

"Su-Su meet Yumi. Yumi meet Su-Su. I am staying at Yumi's lovely apartment right in the centre here."

Yumi bowed slightly and shook Su-Su's hand. Su-Su laughed and did the same. Kate asked them both what they wanted from the coffee store, and she went off with her order of two green teas and a cappuccino for herself.

Su-Su turned to her immediately. "Do you speak English?"

Yumi's father worked for a business that exported horseradish sauce mainly to America and so he made a point of taking advantage of the free tutoring offered by the company. In turn he made sure that all three of his children were given conversational English tutoring from a very early age. He always said that it was conversational English that the Japanese found such a challenge and with all three of his children it had paid off. All of them worked to some extent in English. Yumi's eldest sister had moved to Toronto and was trying to get Yumi to visit her and her children and her brother lived in Singapore working for an American bank. She hadn't spoken to her brother for months. He was always so busy and apparently, he had an American girlfriend who worked with him.

"Yes, I work in English, quite a lot. I am an editor and copywriter at a Branding Agency."

Su-Su smiled a toothy grin. "That sounds very nice to me. Tokyo is such an exciting city. There is so much to see. I have been visiting so many things when I am not busy at the conference." Su-Su told her all the tourist places she had seen, and how beautiful the hotel she was staying in was and how kind everyone had been to her. "I like the way the inside of Japanese buildings are very calm, just like I hear the countryside of Japan is. I wish I had seen it, but I think it is very peaceful, with the sounds of a small river very often and birdsong. It is very crazy in the street in Japan. Very crazy, but when you go inside somewhere the way the rooms are designed makes you feel peaceful and relaxed. It gives you the space to get your head into order from the crazy street. I like that."

Kate came back balancing their hot drinks and both Su-Su and Yumi thanked her profusely.

"What is the conference you are attending?" Yumi asked Su-Su.

"Oh, it is a big tourism conference, it is one of the biggest there has ever been. Today I gave a speech to more than eight hundred people."

"Oh, my gosh, your big speech was today. How did it go? That's such a massive audience," asked Kate.

Again, that smile that went right across her face. Yumi thought that Su-Su had one of the loveliest smiles she had ever seen.

"Well, I gave the same speech yesterday but today was in the big conference hall with a very big audience. Oh, it was very, very good. You see, I live on a beautiful lake." Su-Su turned to look at Yumi. "The lake is where Kate and I met. It is a lake where women make silk out of lotus and I spoke all about the challenges of tourism to the lake and the eco-structure. I spoke about how tourism had changed the culture already but that if carefully and thoughtfully handled it could benefit the community so that it thrives in the long-term. I also spoke about the way that foreign textile companies and fashion houses like to say that they created lotus silk and had the idea of making it. I make sure they know that the women of the lake started it more than a hundred years ago. It is a skill that belongs to us. It makes me so angry when foreign companies try and claim the skill. All our beautiful colours come from jackfruit, seeds, flowers and bark. All from nature. All-natural dyes."

"Did your audience like what you had to say?" asked Kate.

Su-Su smiled again. "Most of them clapped and clapped for so long when I finished. Some of them even stood up and clapped. The head of my tourist company said that it was the longest clapping that he had heard the whole conference. He was very happy with me. He asked me to come to another conference in New York, America next year!"

Kate and Yumi both beamed at Su-Su.

"Well, done. It sounds like you absolutely smashed it."

Yumi and Su-Su turned to look at Kate. Yumi asked with a puzzled expression. "Smashed it? What is this?"

"Oh. It's just an expression meaning that you did very well. It means you took the task and tore it apart. Sorry, it's a stupid expression. It's what young people say."

"Is this lotus silk?" Yumi reached out to touch Su-Su's beautiful turquoise jacket. It was so soft it seemed to slip between her fingers before she had even touched it and at the same time it had a dampness to it, making it seem alive and breathing somehow. "Oh, but this is so soft for me to touch."

"When I was with my mother at Lake Inlay Su-Su took us to one of the cooperatives and we watched the women spinning the lotus stalks, weaving the cloth and dying the cloth. We bought each other scarves. I got her to take mine home with her because I was frightened, I would damage it on my travels. The colours Yumi! Such colour. I have never seen such deep colours." Kate said.

"Japanese people love lotus silk very, very much. Some very big designers buy silk directly from our women's cooperatives on the lake. I have been speaking to these fashion houses while I am here, on behalf of the women. I have had to be very strong sometimes to get the best for the women. This is the most labour-intensive weaving technique in the world. Women must be very patient to do it. Which is why many of the women who weave the lotus silk are older. The younger women are too restless and have too much on their mind. The older women know how to go into a state of meditation. I am happy to say that I have fought very hard for all three cooperatives I represent. I hope they will be pleased with my effort", said Su-Su.

"Wow, Su-Su. So not only did you come and give the best speech at the biggest tourism conference in the world, but you also battled against some big designers. What a trip you've had!"

Yumi could not help touching Su-Su's jacket again.

Kate and Su-Su laughed.

"It does feel good. I wish I had known that I was going to meet you Yumi. I would have brought you a scarf from the lake," Su-Su said.

"Your women weave some magic cloth. I would love to see this lake." Yumi said.

"Many Japanese travel to my country. Perhaps you could visit? You would be very welcome to stay in my house with my mother and I."

"Su-Su lives in a stilted house in the middle of the lake. She showed us as we were going past in a boat. There are stilted schools, temples and shops. It's amazing."

"I would like that."

Yumi immediately thought of going travelling with Sumi. She thought that he would be interested in Myanmar. He was interested in everything. He always asked many questions. His enthusiasm and curiosity were the two best things about him.

"I have to make some more money and save it up and I would have to find someone to travel with also."

Su-Su laughed. "Look at Kate. She has done her journey mostly alone."

Kate smiled and nodded her head. "I am sad that it is ending. I want to see my family of course. But I'm sure it will be very hard having to go back to work and settle down and not just wake up and decide that I am going to do something, and just do it without even speaking to anyone. I have had such a brilliant time, so much better than I would ever have imagined. I wonder if I'll ever settle down again when I know there are so many places to see, people to meet and happily live. I thought it would calm my restlessness but perhaps it has ruined me for life."

Su-Su looked at Kate with a side-long glance. "You are different from the woman I met with her mother."

‘I was just starting out wasn’t I, when you met me? It’s all the things I have seen. It’s all the people I have met.”

Su-Su laughed and put her hand up to her small mouth. “No. It is more than that I think. I think you fell in love. Am I right?”

Kate smiled shyly. “Yes, I did. On top of a mountain in India. So much younger than me that I don’t even want to tell you because I’m afraid you both would judge me. But young as he was, he taught me so much in a few days. Perhaps more than my husband taught me in eighteen years. He made me feel that I deserved to be treated well and with consideration.”

“Will you see him again Kate? If you love him so much.” Yumi asked.

‘No. I don’t think I will ever see him again.” Kate smiled while her eyes misted with sadness.

“I am in love, I think,” said Su-Su and giggled. Kate looked at her with a smile.

“Is it with the man who rowed the boat that day?”

Su-Su giggled and covered her face with her hands. “Yes, yes. It is. How did you know?”

“I remember that my mother was very taken with him. He wasn’t only handsome, but he had such a kind face,” said Kate.

“He is so clever as well. Not just handsome,” said Su-Su. “I can talk to him for hours and hours, like no one else. I admire him very much. And we were at school together and I think we always loved each other.”

“Oh, that’s lovely Su-Su,” Kate said.

“So am I!” Yumi found herself blurting out, louder than she had meant. All three women laughed at her exclamation. Yumi had not told anyone about Simo. Not even her closest female friends. There was something about these two women that made her feel both very free and very safe. She wasn’t sure when she had felt like this before. It felt good to be with a woman her age and an older woman, both with very different lives but with so much in common. “I am in love too.”

The two women smiled at her with shining eyes. The waiter came and cleared their table and smiled at all three of them.

"Who is it with? Are you going to tell us? Tell us about him?"

"His name is Simo." Yumi paused.

"What is he like, then?" asked Kate. "Tell us a bit more."

What was Simo like? He was beautiful. Beautiful to see and to hear. Beautiful inside and out. "We dance together in a hip-hop troupe. We are meant to be dancing tonight in Yoyogi Park. He is the best dancer ever and when I see him, I feel so happy. Just like Kate says he makes me laugh and laugh. He is so funny. And he is so interesting. He is very important to me."

"Are you together," asked Kate.

"I'm sorry. I don't understand."

"Is he your boyfriend?"

"No, no. I would like that, but I don't want to ruin our friendship." Yumi couldn't help laughing some more because she liked the sound of Simo being her boyfriend. "He does not know that I am interested in him in a love way. He knows that I am interested in him in a friendly way."

"He probably feels the same way as you. He probably feels scared to say anything in case it makes things awkward for your friendship. He is probably frightened of rejection too."

A schoolgirl walked past in her uniform; there were two businessmen in suits walking behind her laughing.

Kate's face became serious. "Japan has taken me by surprise," she said.

"What do you mean?"

"I have been to India and Malaysia and Indonesia these last months, which are all places that don't have the best reputation for the way they treat women. I just was taken aback by the way women are expected to behave and look here."

"I don't understand," Su-Su said.

"Well, the first day I arrived here I wondered what was going on. I was on the underground train, and I could see a woman of my age wearing ankle socks and almost a schoolgirl's outfit and then when I went into the shops there were so many frilly, dolly outfits but for grown-up women. It was really strange. What does a grown-up woman do if she takes herself a bit seriously? If she doesn't want to dress or act like a baby or a doll?"

Yumi's head and heart hurt. This woman had made her feel very uncomfortable. She also had a picture in her head of Kate dressed as a baby-doll and it wasn't a nice image. She wouldn't look cute at all. "Seriously? If a woman takes herself seriously? I don't understand."

"Yes. A woman like you. A woman who works hard and does not want middle-aged businessmen to stare at her and to have to giggle at things a man says that are not that funny. I sat next to a woman in Kyoto with a man on the next table in a restaurant and she laughed and laughed behind her hand, but I knew she was not really laughing. She was not really finding it funny at all. It was fake giggling. I felt like tapping her on the arm and saying *No one's that funny. No one's ever been that funny. Nothing has ever been that funny. Stop it. It's not good for him to pretend he is so funny.*"

Suddenly it seemed as if Yumi could not understand what this woman was talking about, as if she didn't understand English anymore. She saw Kate's lips moving but she didn't know what Kate was trying to say. She looked to Su-Su for help.

Su-Su looked at Kate and at Yumi. There was an awkward pause between the three women.

"I think what Kate is trying to say is that women are expected to look and act like young girls here. I went to that area by the temple and there was a group of middle-aged businessmen grouped together by the entrance of the park and when I looked to see what they were watching it was a small girl who was wearing make-up and singing into a microphone. It made me feel very worried about that child. I could see her mother standing at the side and looking at her daughter and the men. I wondered what she was thinking. I can't imagine my mother dressing me up so that old men could look at me as a child. It made me cry on the way back to the hotel."

Kate nodded,

Yumi felt as if she was going to burst into tears. What were they saying about her country? She thought that tourists were meant to love the maids, the teen area of Akihabara, the geisha girls and the pretty, giggling girls. This was not what she expected when she came out to meet and talk with these foreign women tonight. She wished she had stayed at home and waited for Simo's call. She felt as if Kate and Su-Su were waiting for her to answer.

"I have not travelled outside Japan. I do not know how women are treated in other places. But I do watch American and English films and television, and I listen to the BBC and the World Service. I think they prefer young girls there too. I don't know about Myanmar. I am sorry, I don't know much about Myanmar." Yumi nodded towards Su-Su.

She continued. "A lot of times you see young women in films whose boyfriends are old men. Is it so different in your countries, then? It seems to me that people like to come to other people's countries and make criticisms when they have only been there for a few days. It makes them feel better about what is going on in their own country. It makes them feel as if their country is superior. But perhaps it is not. Maybe it is more obvious here."

Both women looked at her.

Kate spoke first. "Yes, you are right. I am sorry to have upset you. Japan is a very beautiful place. The countryside and the architecture of the temples with their sloping roofs and the kindness of the people have impressed me. It is the only place I have visited where I can go out at night on my own and feel safe, so that perhaps tells you something more important than my observations. I apologise." Kate leant over and touched Yumi's arm.

"My sister left to live in Canada, I hope very much to visit her one day. She felt that she wouldn't get as far as she wanted as a journalist if she stayed here, because she was constantly being overlooked and she isn't very cute, like me. Maybe it's a family thing. She was sick of it here anyway and has done so well in Canada. I don't know why men in Japan want women to act like children so much. I wish I could tell you more about it and why it happens, but I can't." Yumi didn't really know what was happening to her, but she felt a tear running down the right side of her face. She used her sleeve to wipe it away.

The two women looked at her with even more concern.

"Maybe it is because they don't want to give up any power to anyone, just like the men at the top in any country. Women who are like little girls are not threatening," Su-Su said.

Yumi liked Su-Su even more.

"I think that the real question we need to look at is why this happens in so many countries. Rather than Kate asking why men in Japan seem to have sexual feelings for very young girls we should be asking why does this happen all over the world? When my mother and I visited Thailand, we saw western men who were only coming to Thailand to have sex and there were many English and American men. I have heard from my Facebook friends in Vietnam and Cambodia that it is very bad there too. Very terrible men from the UK and Europe and the US travel to exploit young children for sex. I can see that as our country is opened out it will become like that too. Maybe it already has. We have many poor families in our country, and it is that poverty that these men will take advantage of."

Yumi felt her phone vibrate in her rucksack. She was pleased to look at her phone to break this difficult conversation. It was a text from Simo. *Where are you? Ill-effects are playing. I need you to partner with med! Right now! I won't wait all night. Hurry up!*

She felt a surge of joy and then thought about her guests. It would be so rude to leave them now. She wanted to be polite to her first *CozyBed* guest and she knew that it was important to get as many stars as you could along the way. It wouldn't be good for her if her first review was bad either. She also felt embarrassed that their observations made her cry in front of them. She couldn't remember the last time she had cried.

"That is Simo, the man I told you I was in love with." It felt great to say that. "He asks if I would like to go to Yogungi park to dance. There is a hip-hop DJ there called Ill-effects." And before she could stop herself, she asked. "Would you like to come?'

When they were standing on the subway in a little huddle Kate told them, "I really apologise for the way I spoke about Japan. I think it is because I am quite a disorganised, chaotic person and I keep getting the rules wrong and I was being a bit defensive and hard. I've been told that I'm doing the wrong thing quite a lot in Japan. Japan doesn't seem to like me much."

"What rules have you got wrong?"

'In Nara I met a lovely Italian TV weather girl at a hostel right by the Tōdai-ji temple and we decided to take ourselves off in one of the public bathhouses. They are called Sento aren't they Yumi?"

Yumi nodded.

"Well, we had been told certain rules and being the only Westerners there we were really careful to stick to them. We were very glad that we didn't have tattoos as we wouldn't have been let in if we did. We showered thoroughly and washed our hair and tied it up because we had been told that it is rude for the hair to touch the water." Yumi nodded. "We also showered before we entered each different communal bath, and we made sure that the towels didn't touch the water. We thought we were doing well and although the other naked Japanese women were staring, they seemed fine with us being there. We felt that we were really getting into our stride and had been in most of the baths, when the Italian girl noticed that there was an outdoor bath area. I went in front of her through the glass doors enthusiastically and seeing a shallow outdoor pool I immediately flung myself in. The Italian girl just watched me splashing about and rolling around and telling her how lovely and warm it was and that she should come on in even though it was a bit shallow. We both noticed at the same time that the women in the other outdoor pools were staring at me angrily and tutting and the Italian girl was looking about helplessly and trying to work out what was wrong. A couple of naked old women stood up out of the hot bath and started to shake their heads and walked back indoors as if it was because of us. The Italian girl started laughing and could hardly speak because she was pointing to some signs about my head. *It's a footbath. You idiot. You're meant to sit on these high-up stone benches and dip your feet in there. You're splashing around like a mad woman in the footbath. That's why they are so upset. It's for feet only and you've splashed a fair amount of the water out.* We left soon after that because we had become a bit unpopular."

'I would like to have seen that." Yumi said. She and Su-Su were laughing.

Before the three women had walked out of the subway station Yumi said, "Don't look at the streets over there."

"Why?" said Kate.

"You will not like it. It is the area where teenage girls go to shop for sweets, and cute clothes and toys and businessmen line the sides of the pavements because they like to look at them shopping, and quite often give them money so they can buy the things they want, and they can carry on watching them."

"OK. Well, we will try not to look." Kate said.

They turned into the main entrance of the park. There were lights in the trees and the bushes and many people walking down the paths towards the shrine of Meiji. Two women in elaborate kimonos walked past them arm in arm.

"Wow" Kate said and stared after them.

"Have you ever been to the shrine of Meiji?" ask Su-Su. "We came here with my British boss, and it was wonderful. Kate you should visit."

"You realise it is my last day tomorrow? My last day of travels. I have to go and get some presents for my family. My daughter has asked for a kimono. Maybe I will be able to fit in a shrine visit. I'm not sure. I can't believe this is it. What a lucky person I am. I feel as if I will never forget a minute of this. It doesn't matter if the rest of my life is shit, if I have had this. If something bad happens, I will have this."

As they followed the path into the park it became much darker. Although there were park lights, they were spaced quite far apart, so there were patches of darkness in between the bright lights. Su-Su put her arm through Kate's. Yumi put her arm through Su-Su's and Kate's.

Already, Yumi could hear Ill-effects' sound system and it excited her immediately. She turned to the two foreign women and was surprised to see that they were excited too. Not nervous of walking in the dark park in a strange city but just happy to be led by her to a new experience; to be guided by her and she was enjoying showing them this part of her life and her city.

There were more people than usual in front of the huge sound system. Maybe more than a hundred. Before she had a chance to wonder where he was, Simo rushed towards her. He took her by the hand and pulled her to him. "Where have you been? You almost forced me to dance with Tomo and it just wouldn't be the same."

Yumi just wanted to dance with Simo. She was glad that he didn't dance with Tomo because she felt that Tomo was a great dancer too, and super pretty and smart. She and Simo immediately fell into one of their routines. Their bodies mimicked and inspired each other's in total dance understanding. They knew each other's moves and bodies so well. A clearing was made around them to give them space. She could see Kate and Su-Su on the edge of the circle of people looking at them and they were smiling so widely and clapping and moving to the music too. *How surprising that this evening had turned out this way,* she thought as her body and Simo's pushed each other on. This was what it must be like to make love to somebody, to make love to Simo. When the track finished, she knew that Simo wanted her to jump up and put her legs around his waist. They laughed delightedly into each other's faces while she wrapped herself around him and everyone clapped and cheered including Ill-effects. She had never seen Ill-effects clap. She had rarely seen him look up from his deck or address anyone. He was one of those grumpy DJs that just let the music do the talking. "Did you see? The miserable bastard just clapped for us."

Simo kissed her on the mouth before setting her down on the ground.

With their beds side by side and the light from the streets coming through the slats in her sitting room blind, Yumi could see Kate's sleeping face. The lines and dips that covered her face in the daytime were softened. She felt real tenderness towards this older woman. It had been a magical evening. They stayed in Yoyongi park, dancing and drinking beer until three in the morning.

Su-Su said that she had only once stayed up that late before and she had sent pictures of the night to her boatman boyfriend.

It turned out that Kate loved hip-hop and danced with Su-Su and some of Yumi's dancing friends while Simo had never left Yumi's side and had asked her if she wanted to go to a real hip-hop club with him the next night. Of course, she accepted and wondered if it was a date. She thought it was.

Yumi was so glad Su-Su and Kate had come. She felt that they had brought her luck. She was sad that Kate was leaving. She would have liked her to stay a few more nights. She was glad it was Saturday. She would take Kate shopping and find her daughter a lovely second-hand kimono in a vintage shop she knew. Kate let out a sigh in her sleep, mumbled something, laughed and turned away. Yumi told herself to try and sleep. She had a busy day tomorrow and a date, yes, a date, with Simo.

Instagram
This is a photo of a hip-hop event in Tokyo. What a great night. The end of my amazing travels
These are the top ten things I've learnt while I have been travelling

One – that just sitting in a room and staring out onto an unfamiliar view and thinking without anyone interrupting is a blissful thing. Sometimes hours could pass just staring out of the window or out of a balcony.

Two - Humour and laughter is the most powerful connector between two human beings, even more than sexual attraction perhaps. I could be the best friend of an Indian woman in her seventies and the next week I would be doing everything with a twenty-year old German man and what made us like each other so much? Not a shared religion, shared class or race or experience or background but because when we first met, we made each other laugh.

Three - a big black scarf is the most useful thing a woman traveller can have. It can keep you warm when you might be cold, keep you modest in countries where you must be. Place it on your head, put it over your shoulders to cover your arms or round your waist, over your mouth when you are on a motorbike, or the back of a jeep, on your head in a plane or a train or a bus when you need dark to sleep.

Four - very few people are interested in others. Even if they have travelled far away from those, they know to meet others they don't know, most people are just waiting for people to stop talking so that they can talk about themselves. If you meet someone who is genuinely interested in other people, befriend them immediately.

Five - religion is both a comforter and a suppressor of change. The rigorous daily religious ritual makes sure no one has time to stop and think and do anything about their living conditions or the unfairness that is all around them, but a belief in God can make the unbearable tolerable I suppose.

Six - a lot of people around the world believe in dumb luck above any God and are always doing strange things to increase it, particularly their financial luck. They are touching wood, buying goldfish to let into the river Mekong, throwing coins in fountains and wells, burning paper replicas of mobile phones or fancy cars in front of shrines of their ancestors, and in Bali, standing in a cold stone temple pool for hours in order to achieve high grades at school. I couldn't help thinking that these shivering young people might get better grades if they used that time to study rather than freeze their arses off.

Seven - corruption and nepotism is everywhere, even in the smallest village.

Eight - people are only so rich because people are so poor,

Nine - the shortest of loves may endure for a lifetime in your heart.

Ten - tiger balm really is the best medicine in the world – it clears your blocked nasal passageways, gets rid of muscular pain, clears headaches, repels insects and if you do get bitten then it stops the bites itching so much."

October 2016

They asked Kate to get up, and each one held onto an arm each and took her into another room. They put her rucksack from the car on the table in front of them. They went through each thing and recorded it, one of them naming what it was and the other writing it down - the jumper, the trainers, two tampons, a few coins, a muesli bar and some crumpled receipts, lots of crumbs, an apple core. They took her phone and asked for the telephone number and pin number. Kate was ashamed of how messy her bag was. They took the laces from her trainers. She could hear loud crying outside the room and presumed that the other women had also been taken off into little rooms by more stern-faced police officers.

Kate was handcuffed with her hands to the front of her body.

"You will be taken in a police vehicle to a police station in Hythe. You will be held in a cell until you have been questioned by the police."

"I need to phone my kids and my family."

"Once you get to the station then you will be allowed to make one phone call."

Kate thought that the only number she knew off-by-heart these days was her mother's landline. She would have to phone her and get her to tell the kids. Both men took her outside into the forecourt and into a large black vehicle with smoked windows.

"Why do we need one vehicle each? That seems a bit wasteful, doesn't it?"

The man driving didn't speak, but the man sitting next to her said, "We don't want you conferring about what to say in the interview. Also, people react strangely to being arrested."

Kate knew what he meant. Having her hands in cufflinks made her feel like she might suddenly lunge at one of them and whack handcuffed hands and metal down on the neck of the driving policeman.

"I'm fifty-three years old. I don't think I pose much of a threat for you."

"You'd be surprised," The policeman next to her said.

"Is it possible to dim the lights at all?" Kate asked the on-duty officer. She thought she had been in the cell for a few hours and even though she knew she wouldn't sleep on the blue thick plastic bed with the rough blanket because it was so bloody cold, the neon lights were making her feel like she might throw up. A drunk sounding man a few cells away had been banging and thumping his door and screaming ever since she had been put in the room. Kate hoped that Faven wasn't in the cell next door to the drunk.

He said, "We need to see you on camera. I don't suppose you've ever been arrested before?'

"No. Does the camera show the toilet area?"

"We have to make sure you are safe, but the toilet area is pixelated."

"Are we given anything to eat?"

"You won't like it?"

"I'm so hungry I would eat anything."

The way he was standing with legs apart in the doorway of the cell, was as if she was about to make a bolt for it.

"Well, there's shepherd's pie, curry and rice or toad in the hole."

"Is it like school dinners?'

'No, it's much worse."

"Can I have shepherd's pie please?"

"Yes. This is not a hotel though so it might take a while." He closed the cell door.

"Officer? Officer? How are the other women? You know that the Syrian women have been imprisoned in their own country, so it's so much more traumatic for them to be in a cell. They were both tortured."

"One of the women has requested that the door be open, and an officer watch her. She has explained why. The smaller lady is in hospital in France. She had a panic attack."

"Oh no. And how are the other two? The other two women I was with?"

"They are like you. They are calm. They are reading."

"Are we allowed to read books? Can I read please?"

"I'll send an officer soon."

"Why is it so cold here?"

"As I said, this isn't a hotel."

And he went out, closed the door and locked it.

What felt like a couple of hours later a policewoman just let Kate follow her out of the cell and go to a small stock room where there was a cupboard box of battered books.

"We haven't got much of a library," the officer said. There were a couple of terrible looking thrillers, with lurid covers, *Oliver Twist* and *Your Rights as a Prisoner in Custody*. "Your young friend took the bible. She's been reading it ever since she was put in a cell."

Kate took the legal book and the Dickens. The police officer was reluctant to give her two but then she relented. Kate didn't like Dickens except when he was dramatised. She just didn't like the way he wrote. It had always irritated her ever since school. But it was the best on offer.

First, she read the legal book and noted that they had to let her out after twenty-four hours unless they applied for an extension of thirty-six hours. She read *Oliver Twist* and still didn't like Dicken's writing. At some point when she thought that nearly a whole night had passed another policewoman came in and dimmed the lights. She never got her shepherd's pie.

"I was told the lights had to stay on all night."

"Oh, that would be PC Plowden. He can be a bit naughty like that."

It was hard to know how long she had been in there. Her head was buzzing with the day. The safety of the women was her responsibility, and everything had gone horribly wrong. She felt both failure and fear. How the fuck had the young man got in the car? Was it definitely Ranim's friend's son? Perhaps she had left the car unlocked from the beginning and one of the men who had been milling around looking at the cars had tried it and found it open during the day. No, it must have been when she went and peed. She looked up at the camera as she pissed on the metal toilet and tried to stick a huge sanitary towel the policewoman had given her in her knickers. She no longer cared if anyone was looking at her and it wasn't really pixilated. A song that she used to sing to her kids was going around her head.

Red is the colour of a pretty pillow box,
Orange is any orange on a tree,
Yellow's the colour of a bag of lemon drops
Green is a piece of seaweed in the sea

She could smell her own sour breath when she covered her head with the blanket. Her armpits stank like the nocturnal animal section in London Zoo. There was a high-pitched ringing in her ear. When she closed her eyes, she saw the teenage boy in the car all curled up, looking up at her like a great big kid caught during a game of hide and seek. She thought of Atal and masturbated under the blue blanket in the hope that she might sleep afterwards. It didn't work.

CLOSING SPEECHES
May 2018

Ebeid's barrister did his best. He was a local barrister, young and good-looking. He seemed to Kate to be the most appealing of the barristers to this Kentish jury. He asked that they not make assumptions about the mother's actions that day "even though helping her son was something most mothers would do". He reminded them that they had to be convinced beyond reasonable doubt that the mother had helped her son get into the boot and that the son did not simply take advantage of the chaos of the day and try the boot of the car his mother travelled in, just like he tried all the boots of the cars that came to the camp.

"Perhaps the son had noticed that the boot was unlocked when he picked up the bag of clothes and food his mother had brought for the Syrian population in the camp. Perhaps he did not tell his mother this, in order to protect her. The prosecution has absolutely no proof that the mother had planned putting her son into the boot from her texts to Ranim, both from the day and the weeks preceding the trip. I ask the jury, how can you know, beyond reasonable doubt, that the mother knew what her son was going to do, when there is no evidence to suggest it. No eyewitnesses, no CCTV, no texts, no overheard conversation – nothing."

Jitendra got up. They had gone through the closing speech notes in the cupboard room. She cleared her throat and straightened her gown.

"Ladies and gentlemen, ask yourselves this: why on earth would Kate Mancini do what she's accused of? Why would she? She's in her fifties. She's spent her whole life working hard, building her career, doing the work she loves. That's who she is. And look at the facts. She doesn't know Ebeid's son. There is no link between them at all. Yet the prosecution asks you to believe that, out of nowhere, she agreed to smuggle people across borders, to help people she doesn't even know, and - extraordinary as it sounds - to bring the press along to see it happen. Does that make any sense to you? It doesn't to me."

Jitendra went on. "Kate Mancini isn't a criminal. She isn't reckless. She isn't connected to Ebeid or her son in any way. What does make sense is this: she went on a work trip, doing her job, and she got caught up in something dreadful. Maybe she was careless. Maybe she left a door open. Maybe someone took advantage. That could have happened to anyone. And yet - here she is. In the Crown Court. On trial. For the very first time in her life. You've heard her evidence. She's told you, she had nothing to do with this. And she's not just standing alone with her word. She's supported by the most independent evidence there is - the telephone records. That evidence backs her up. That's why I say to you, as clearly as I can: Kate Mancini is not guilty.

"Now, I know that immigration and Calais are controversial topics. People have strong views, particularly perhaps, in Kent. But those views aren't what this case is about. Whatever you think about those wider issues, they cannot affect your verdict here. When you came into this court, you swore an oath or made a solemn promise. You promised to decide this case only on the evidence. And the law is clear: you cannot convict unless you are sure – sure - of guilt. Suspicion is not enough. Guesswork is not enough. So, I ask you; are you sure? Sure, that Kate Mancini is guilty? Or do the facts point to other, reasonable explanations? I suggest that when you look carefully and fairly at the evidence, you cannot possibly be sure. And remember this: you must judge each defendant separately. Your verdicts may be different for each person. And Kate Mancini is in a very different position. She has no connection at all with Ebeid or her son.

"Finally, let me thank you. You've been here for two weeks, taken from your homes, your families, your work. You've sat through endless phone records, and yes - that map which may well be the worst map in the history of court cases."

For God's sake, Kate thought. A map as communal scapegoat.

"You've given your time and your attention, and that matters. But now the responsibility is yours. And it's a serious one. You promised to judge only on the evidence. And when you ask yourselves whether you are sure, beyond doubt, that Kate Mancini knew what was happening, the answer is clear.

"You cannot be sure. Because she is not guilty."

Kate had thought the ending was too courtroom drama when Jitendra had read it to her in the box room. But it worked. The jury looked serious and thoughtful.

Jitendra turned to look at her. Kate nodded her thanks.

Ranim's barrister then jumped up eager to give his summary. Why would Ramin risk her own family, who were settled and thriving in the UK, a daughter at Oxford for an acquaintance she barely knew. Ranim was a pillar of society who headed her own charity for Syrians in London. It was out of character, and she just wouldn't do it. Ranim loved this country and was grateful for the lives she and her family lived here. Then right at the very end he threw it in.

"We don't know about the others who are involved in this case though. It could be possible that in the last five minutes, when Kate, Ebeid and the photographer were standing and waiting outside the Mother and Baby bus waiting for the interview to finish they didn't make a hasty plan to put the boy in the boot? Ebeid says that she does not speak English, but we do not know how much English the boy speaks. It is possible that Kate was overcome with pity for the boy and right at the last minute decided to help him. If Kate did not feel a great deal of sympathy for those in the Calais Jungle, she would not have been arranging to visit people there in the first place. The phone records prove that my client was not good friends with either Kate or Ebeid, and we have now understood that my client was in fact on the bus during the last interview. Kate Mancini was not on that bus. Kate Mancini was outside with Ebeid and her son."

Jitendra's face had a slightly green hue as she ushered Kate to the box room after the court had been adjourned. Kate had seen her in court going up to Ranim's young barrister and having an angry exchange. Jitendra hadn't let her speak to her family first but had grabbed her a bit too tightly by the arm. She threw off her wig without removing the curvy grips, so they scattered on the floor. Jitendra didn't seem to notice.

"That was completely unethical of Ranim's barrister. Fucking inexperienced idiot. I told you that on the first day we agreed not to mention certain things. Do you remember me telling you? Like why Ranim didn't tell you clearly that Ebeid had a son in the camp when she had asked if her friend could come. Like why no one in your whole team told you that Ebeid had a son in there? Also, you asked me not to say that Ebeid had been alone in your car with her son after you had set off into the camp, which I was keen to do. So, we could have done it, but you didn't want to, for some fucking reason. I mean that's obviously how he got in. The mum could have found out the boot door didn't lock and told him or just wedged something in there, so it didn't close properly. I mean, what mother wouldn't have done that, if it was his last chance to get to the UK and the rest of his family. I would have done that. Wouldn't you?"

"But I still don't know if the mum was involved. I don't think there is any proof. And their prosecution case was that we had all been planning together for weeks, isn't it? And that completely fell apart. That has no evidence."

Jitendra looked at her as if she were stupid. "I don't think you understand the seriousness of what that lawyer has just done. Throwing it in there as the last thing the jury hears about the case is not good. It is not good at all. We don't have a chance to refute it. If their summing up had come before ours, I could have rebutted it and spoken about the confusion about why you were kept in the dark about her son being there and also about Ebeid's lack of English. Maybe the jury will work out that the photographer would have heard that conversation and would have been all too happy to tell the court that he had heard that as he is the main prosecution witness. I doubt it though. Juries are never as smart as that. Fuck. There's a real tide of hatred towards migrants and refugees starting to brew up and the judge wants to make an example of you."

Jitendra looked close to tears. She looked Kate in the eyes. "As you know the verdict will probably come in tomorrow. I must tell you Kate and I'm afraid that you have to tell your family that because of what

Ranim's barrister just did and the judge taking against you, I don't think this is going to go your way."

Jitendra continued. "The judge has said to us that you will go straight from the court to prison if you are found guilty as he wants to give the sentence on the same day. Apparently, he is going on a sailing holiday to Greece and wants it all sown up this afternoon."

What? What was Jitendra saying? She couldn't take it in.

"I'm afraid I am going to have to suggest that you pack a prison bag tonight and take it to court tomorrow. It may well be possible that he would sentence you to longer than the seven years we originally thought."

"How much longer?"

"Some of my colleagues have said ten years, because you are the driver. But you would probably serve half of that." Kate thought she heard herself let out a groan. Five years.

"And they are considering making trafficking a life sentence."

"What? I can't go home first. I thought that is what usually happens. I thought you got your sentencing later."

All she had with her were three navy dresses.

"I have to say this judge is a total cunt."

Kate had never heard Jitendra say that word before.

"It usually happens when someone is sentenced with murder or terrorism, but trafficking is considered a serious crime. The judge wouldn't want to seem lenient on the driver with someone stuffed in the back of her boot."

Kate lay with her eyes closed on the earth of a raised flower bed beneath some Japanese maple shrubs in the courtyard with her arms crossed over her chest. She didn't care if she had to go into court with the earth and leaves all over her back and in her hair. Her appearance didn't matter anymore. It wouldn't affect the outcome. Jim lay next to her, also with his eyes closed. She thought they probably looked like a stone couple on a medieval tomb. She could feel from where their shoulders were barely touching that he was trembling. Was it possible that he was more nervous than her? She had got used to her heart banging in her chest and the constant whizzing in her ears.

He whispered something to her, "I want to go into the court and get them to send me to prison. I deserve it. You don't. You are a good person and I'm not. It should have been me standing in that witness box."

Oh God, what the fuck was he going on about? He seemed to have completely lost it, and he's only been in court for two days.

"Thanks Jimmy, but it doesn't really work like that. I appreciate it though. And you don't deserve it."

"I do."

He took her hand, but as both their hands were so trembling and sweaty, they both decided at the same time to let go.

Twenty or so of her family and friends were around them, some sitting on the brick wall, standing around and others were on the bench. The jury had been out for two and a half hours, and they were all murmuring and chatting around her. She was thankful that they were not addressing any of their conversation directly to her as she felt she couldn't speak. Charlie and Billie were close to her and kept leaning towards her and touching her head, or arm or leg. Sometimes Charlie would lean down and kiss her forehead.

Her mother and Billie had rushed to Marks and Spencer to buy knickers, bras and tracksuits and she and Bille had put together a prison bag from her three navy blue dresses and her one pair of jeans and a jersey while her son had paced the beach hut saying what a total stupid arsehole Ranim's lawyer was. They also created a sponge bag with toiletries, just like Kate used to do for her kids when they were going on a school trip. Did they even allow you your own toiletries in prison? She decided not to mention it.

Kate had come out of the court cupboard room to the anxious faces of her family. She told them that Jitendra had said that Ranim's lawyer's summing up was extremely damaging, particularly as it was the last thing that the jury would hear.

Charlie and Billie and her mother burst into tears.

"I thought it was going so well. I mean, from the start when the photographer was so discredited. I thought it was all going to be OK. I thought you'd just get a rap on your knuckles," Kate's mother said.

"Why did Ranim's barrister do it?" Billie asked.

"I suppose he wanted to set Ranim apart from us. Jitendra said that they had agreed not to mention certain things and Ranim's barrister broke that pact. I mean, it's only a gentleman's agreement, I suppose," Kate said.

"And we all know that gentlemen don't keep their agreements," said her mother.

They all somehow managed a laugh.

That night, Billie, Charlie, and Kate lay on duvets on the floor of the hut, her mother on the sofa, not even bothering to get into bed.

"Knowing you, you'll be OK in there. You'll become a prison campaigner, for sure," Billie said.

"I just feel that if it really is your last night of freedom, you should be eating the most delicious meal ever, or dancing or swimming in the moonlit sea or doing something amazing, Mum," Charlie said.

"I'm not hungry and I'd rather just lie here with you a lot, if that's OK."

Kate's mother stopped crying for a bit to sing a couple of protest songs in her warbling voice but no one else joined in. Billie and Kate played the South American song that had uplifted them each of the seven days they had driven into the court a couple of times.

"I bet you wish you had never gone to Calais that day, Mum" Charlie said.

"I don't think like that Charlie, I really don't."

"I'm jolly angry with the mother and son," her mother said.

"I'm not," Kate said. "I would have done the same for Billie and Charlie in a heartbeat. No question. The rest of the family had escaped Assad and it probably seemed a small step to try and get her son back with his family."

"I love you so much Mum," Billie said and buried her head into Kate's hair. Kate carried on staring at the wooden ceiling while her mother and children slept.

Charlie came running around the corner. "Mum, Mum, they want us back in. They're going to read the verdict."

Right, this was it. Kate's friends dusted the earth and leaves from her back, and she held her son's and daughter's hands as they walked back into the courtroom. Ranim and Ebeid were already sitting in the defendant's area staring ahead. She joined them, sitting in between them as she had for the past eight days. Ebeid was praying under her breath and rocking backwards and forwards. The jury walked back into the room. Were they being deliberately slow to sit down? In the eight days they seemed to have formed allegiances with each other and so like school children people wanted to sit next to those they liked and there was some shuffling around. The jury had chosen the young red-headed woman to be the foreperson. She stood up and turned towards the Judge.

"Have you reached your verdicts?"

"Yes, we have Your Honour."

Was the Judge deliberately pausing for drama like in a reality TV show?

"How do you find Ebeid Farid?"

"Guilty."

Ebeid screamed and sobbed into her headscarf. Kate tried to reach out to touch her by stretching her right arm, but she was too far away. Shit. Wasn't the case against them that they were all in this together. Did that mean that they would all be sent down?

"How do you find Ranim Dawoud?"

"Not guilty."

Oh my God. What did that mean for her?

The Judge lent forward his microphone.

"And how do you find Kate Mancini?"

"Guilty, Your Honour."

There were cries of horror from the gallery. Kate looked up and saw her children leaning over the railing screaming and wailing.

"Noooo, Mum. No. Mummy. Please, this can't be right." Billie screamed.

She saw Jim, standing up above her mother, his arms flailing around, shouting at her.

"Take me to prison instead." And Charlie turned his tear-streaked face to look at him in confusion.

Kate felt herself mouthing to her children and her mother that it would be alright, but no sound came out. She saw herself in water, swimming in the sea, with someone who was guiding her and calmly pointing downwards to something he felt she must see. Then she made it out, with dabbled water against its shell, a beautiful turtle, grazing from some coral.

THE TURTLE

Paulus and his father had already made their catch and so felt relaxed enough, finishing an hour or so before they had expected. His father thought they could pull their boat up at the beach on Kanawa island there and have their lunch and look at the Westerners from the three boats that were moored by the pier. Paulus thought that perhaps his father wanted to look at the women but could not say so because he thought Paulus might say something to his mother. They lay on the warm sand to eat the Ubi Nuabosi Paulus' mother had packed for them and his father fell asleep on his back.

Paulus decided to go swimming off the long jetty just with the mask, snorkel and flippers they always took on fishing trips.

He was swimming and turning around in the water to look at the shafts of light through the beautiful blue water and the walls of many tiny fish - silvery fish. Paulus was just thinking that it would be good if someone else was seeing this miracle of beauty alongside him when a swimming woman banged into him under water, their glass masks almost crashing into each other. They both quickly stood up out of the water which came to their chests and pushed their masks onto the top of their heads.

She said something to him which seemed to be an apology. Paulus smiled at her and was rewarded with a warm smile back. She was not nervous of him. Paulus gestured for her to follow him in the water by pointing downwards. She nodded enthusiastically.

She surprised Paulus by being able to keep up with him in the water. If Paulus went down almost to the bottom, she came with him so that he could point out each beautiful fish and coral he saw. He saw her eyes grow wide with amazement beneath her mask at how many colours there were in the sea that day. The sea was showing off for them both, surrounding them with colour and light. Paulus was proud of his ocean.

They were swimming side by side in harmony when a turtle appeared swimming below them casually feeding from the coral. He took her hand, and they stayed as still as they could, nodding their heads at each other under water and then both looking down at it. The turtle was as cool and calm as anything. It was a rare one, a hawksbill, with black broken patterns on its head and flippers, one of those his father and he knew had been made scarce by the prawn trailers. He wished she knew how to tell her what she had seen, but she seemed to understand how special it was. After that he guided her back to the beach to join her western friends on the boat. She nodded her head and touched him on his arm while the water fell down her body from her hair. He nodded back and she took her mask, snorkel and flippers off and walked down the beach back to the pier. She turned to wave and smile at him.

Paulus joined his father who was still asleep and let the sun dry his body. When he woke up, he didn't tell his father about his swim with the woman and seeing the turtle. He just kept it to himself. It made him feel happy. He wondered if she would tell anyone about meeting him and the turtle or even think about him and the turtle again.